THE
TRINITY
GAMBIT

THE TRINITY GAMBIT

BY
WILLIAM SPEIR

Progressive
RISING PHOENIX PRESS ®

Acknowledgments

I want to thank all of my loyal readers, without whom I would not enjoy the creative process of writing.

Thanks to Amanda Thrasher and Jannifer Powelson at Progressive Rising Phoenix Press for believing in me and my books.

Special thanks go to my editorial team (Ray Flynt and Jim Newman) for their patience and their valuable contributions, suggestions, technical details, and corrections.

Deepest gratitude goes to my wife of 22 years, Lee Anne, for giving me the freedom to pursue my passion. She is the love of my life. I am also grateful for my family, without whom there would be no words worth writing.

It is to all of my family and friends who have faithfully and selflessly put on the uniform to defend this great country that this book is gratefully dedicated.

THE OPENING

"The chess-board is the world; the pieces are the phenomena of the universe; the rules of the game are what we call the laws of Nature. The player on the other side is hidden from us. We know... to our cost, that he never overlooks a mistake, or makes the smallest allowance for ignorance."

— **Thomas Henry Huxley**

CHAPTER 1

————•————

Washington, DC
October 2027

Kate Davidsen exited the Yellow Line Metro and pushed her way through the crowd to the escalators that led to the Pentagon's security checkpoint at the Metro Concourse entrance on the southeast side of the Defense Department's sprawling headquarters. It was a beautiful autumn day in the nation's capital, but Kate was too preoccupied to notice. Her mind was focused on the meeting that started in 15 minutes.

Kate was classified as a CIA Operations Language Officer, but she worked closely with both the Directorate of Analysis and the Directorate of Operations. In her role, she interacted with CIA operatives in the field and with foreign assets gathering and providing information, and she provided the in-depth analysis of the information to her superiors. When she wasn't traveling all over the world to meet with her contacts, she had an office at CIA headquarters in northern Virginia. Today, though, she was beginning a new assignment at the Pentagon.

I don't know if I should feel annoyed or flattered. It's a high visibility assignment, but my normal work is important—especially now that the world is going all to hell.

Kate stood in line, waiting for her turn to pass through one of the dozen security gates, which had replaced the old turnstiles. She had her lanyard in her hands, with her CIA access card hanging in the back and her new Pentagon access card hanging in the front. When it was her turn at the gate, she pressed the Pentagon card on the scanner, entered her code on the keypad, saw the green light appear and the gate swing open, and walked through quickly. *Less than 10 minutes.*

She put the lanyard around her neck, pulling her ponytail up and over the lanyard so it would sit flat on her collar, and followed Corridor 10 to the D-Ring. She reached the D-Ring's elevator bank and jumped inside the car closest to her just as the door was closing. The car was crowded, but Kate was a slender, athletically built young woman, and she easily squeezed herself away from the door so it would close. She glanced at the control panel and noted that the button for the third floor had already been pushed.

The elevator stopped on the second floor, and Kate moved out of the way so most of the car's occupants could exit. As the doors closed again, she glanced at her watch. *Six minutes.*

Standing in front of the polished metal door of the elevator, she glanced at the six people left in the elevator car. Four wore Air Force uniforms, and one other person was dressed as a civilian like she was. Her eyes lingered on him for only a moment, so he wouldn't notice her sizing him up. He was tall with the physique of a runner, but without the hardness that comes from running marathons or participating in Iron Man competitions. His sandy hair complimented his tanned skin, and his hazel eyes were fixed on the center of the elevator door, as if he were willing the doors to open so he could get to where he was going.

The elevator stopped on the third floor, and Kate and the other civilian exited. Kate double-checked the room number for her meeting and turned right to head for Wedge 3 between Corridors 8 and 7.

"Excuse me." A man's voice interrupted her thoughts about how to get to the conference room. She turned.

The sandy-haired man from the elevator looked embarrassed. "I'm sorry to bother you, but I've never been to the Pentagon before. Do you know how to reach this conference room?" He held up a small card with a room number on it.

Kate stared at him for a moment. "That's where I'm heading. It's this way." She gestured in the direction she was going and motioned for him to follow her.

As they followed the D-Ring counter-clockwise toward the north end of the building, the man said, "Thank you. I guess you're with the same task force that I've been assigned to. I'm Steve Barksdale, by the way. NSA."

Kate glanced at him. "Kate Davidsen. CIA."

"Pleased to meet you," Steve said pleasantly.

They walked in silence, crossed Corridor 8, and reached a side hallway on the right blocked by a security door. The sign on the door indicated that their conference room was on the other side of the door. Kate swiped her Pentagon access card across the reader, and an outline of a right hand appeared on the screen. Kate placed her hand on the reader. The screen flashed green, but nothing happened.

Kate looked at Steve. "Try yours."

Steve swiped his card. When the outline of the right hand appeared on the screen, he put his hand on the screen, and the screen flashed green. Kate heard a soft buzz, tried the door, and it opened.

Steve chuckled. "What's so funny? Kate asked.

Steve pointed to the screen where he had placed his hand. In red letters, it read: "All persons standing on the red square must each swipe their card and have their biometrics scanned before entry to this secure facility will be allowed. Do not attempt to allow entry to any individual who has not had their identity and access authorization confirmed."

Kate looked down and saw that she and Steve were both standing on a red square. Then she looked up at Steve. "I guess it helps to read the instructions carefully." She held the door for him, and they both entered the hallway. She heard the door close and the locks engage behind them as they walked down the hall.

They reached the conference room with a minute to spare. The only windows in the room faced the secure hallway. There was a large wooden conference table in the center of the room surrounded by comfortable-looking chairs. Most of the seats were already taken; there were only two seats left open at the table, one on each side, apart from the seat at the head of the table. Kate and Steve separated and quickly grabbed the remaining seats, leaving the seat at the head of the table open.

Kate looked at the other people sitting around the table. In addition to her and Steve, there were three others in civilian clothes—two men and one woman—and five uniformed members representing the Army, Navy, and Air Force branches, along with the Coast Guard and Border Patrol. Kate noted that no one representing the Marines was present. *I guess the Navy has them covered.*

A moment later, a man walked into the conference room and closed the door. He appeared to be in his late-forties or early-fifties, with grey-brown receding hair and a slight limp. The way he carried himself gave the impression of being someone who was all business and no-nonsense. He entered a code into the keypad next to the door, and security blinds lowered to cover the windows. The conference room door's locks engaged, and the keypad glowed red.

A computer-generated voice announced: "SCIF mode engaged; room is secure."

This was not the first time Kate had been in a SCIF, or Sensitive Compartmented Information Facility. Far from it. But the fact that she was in one now—in a biometrically secured hallway inside one of the most secure buildings in the world—

told her that the meeting was more than just a pow-wow between the various intelligence services. This was something far more important.

The man walked to the head of the table. "My name is Gregory Rosemont. I'm the Presidential Special Advisor for Global Intelligence," he said with a southern accent, "and I've been appointed the leader of this Interdepartmental Intelligence Team. I understand that none of you was told what this meeting is about or why you were chosen for this assignment. I'll get to that in a moment. First, everyone introduce yourselves. We're going to be working together for quite a while, so we'd better get to know each other from the start."

Rosemont gestured to the Air Force officer to his right. "Let's start with you."

"Major Anthony Vandyke, Sixteenth Air Force, Air Combat Command."

"Major Vandyke is one of the Air Force's top global intelligence officers," Rosemont added before gesturing to the uniformed officer next to Vandyke.

"Lieutenant Commander Moira Kirkland, Office of Naval Intelligence," the red-haired naval officer said.

"Commander Kirkland is an expert on foreign weapon platforms at the Farragut Technical Analysis Center."

"Captain Sterling Michaels, 902nd Military Intelligence Group."

"Captain Michaels is part of the Army Counterintelligence Center of the Military Intelligence Corps—one of their up-and-coming stars," Rosemont stated.

"Steve Barksdale. NSA."

"Mr. Barksdale is a counterintelligence expert, specializing in the Asian Theatre."

Kate looked at Steve from across the table. *Asian counterintelligence. I wonder what role that's going to play in what we're all doing here.*

7

"Liz Sweeny, Department of Homeland Security," the petite blonde next to Steve said.

"Ms. Sweeny is with the Cybersecurity and Infrastructure Security Agency of the DHS," Rosemont said cryptically.

"Clay McGrath, FBI."

"Special Agent McGrath is not part of the counterterrorism or counterespionage units of the FBI," Rosemont explained. "He's a field agent from the Dallas office. He's here because we need someone on the team who's *not* part of the intelligence community. He's here to provide a fresh perspective and alternative thinking."

Kate saw several heads nodding around the table. *It's good to have an outsider on hand to keep us focused.*

"Lieutenant Commander Ronald Benson, U.S. Coast Guard." Benson was a stern-looking African-American officer who looked like he could deflect an imminent threat with just his stare.

"Commander Benson has been protecting our coastline for most of his life," Rosemont stated. "And his insights into our vulnerabilities are invaluable."

"Mason Petersen, U.S. Border Patrol." Peterson's tanned and weathered appearance was evidence to how much time he spent in the hot sun along the southern border.

"Like Commander Benson, Special Operations Supervisor Petersen has been protecting our borders on land for more than a decade. He, too, can provide valuable insights into our vulnerabilities."

It was Kate's turn next. "Kate Davidsen, CIA."

Rosemont gestured toward Kate. "Ms. Davidsen is an Operations Language Officer, but she works directly with intelligence gathering assets, and she analyzes their data. There's little going on in the world that she doesn't know about or have people in place to inform her about. She's isn't tied to a single geographic territory, so her skills and knowledge are both

8

incredibly valuable to what we're here to do."

And just what ARE we here to do? Kate was more curious than ever.

Rosemont gestured to the last person to be introduced, who looked like he must have played football in college. "Grant Chamberlain, Defense Intelligence Agency."

"Mr. Chamberlain is with the Defense Clandestine Service, working with our spec ops units around the world." Rosemont sat down at the head of the table. "As you can see, we have people in the room who supply intelligence to set policy, we have people who supply intelligence to implement policy, and we have people who must act on intelligence to defend the nation. That covers most of the bases."

Rosemont placed his hand on the table in front of him and pushed aside a panel, revealing a computer tablet. He tapped the screen and the overhead lights dimmed. Projectors along the ceiling illuminated the white panels on the walls around the room. Animated maps appeared showing the very thing that kept Kate from sleeping at nights.

"Our changing reality," Rosemont said as he stood and walked around the room, pointing at each animated map. "Three years ago, the United States was the safety valve keeping all of the world's conflicting forces at bay. Then we elected a fresh slate of federal politicians who had a new agenda, and before we knew it, all of our military forces had been recalled, and the country turned its attention inward. We began fighting among ourselves instead of maintaining the peace around the globe. With no safety valve, regional conflicts broke out in Latin America, the Pacific, and across Europe and Africa. China conquered Australia, almost all of the Asian-Pacific nations, and invaded Russia all the way to the Urals. The Islamic Caliphate swept across Africa, southern and central Europe, and the Middle East. And the cartels and their allies now control almost all of South and Central America. Only The United States, Canada,

Greenland, Iceland, and the Caribbean nations are not yet caught up in one of the regional conflicts."

Turning to face the room, Rosemont asked, "Is there anyone in this room who believes that any of the remaining free countries will remain free for long? Is there anyone in this room who believes that we'll *remain* free for long if we don't do something?"

Everyone at the table shook his or her head.

Rosemont nodded. "The president feels the same way. That's why he authorized this team. Put simply, we're to figure out what's happening around the world, how it happened, who's behind it, and what to do to keep the U.S. and its few remaining allies from getting sucked into it. Simple, right?"

There were chuckles around the room.

Rosemont returned to his seat at the head of the table. His face was serious as he continued. "Full disclosure. There are people in this room who were on both sides of the recent Civil War. That's by design. We've come back together as a single, united people, and if we're to heal the wounds that tore us apart for a second time in our history, we must relearn how to work together. I'm not going to say who was on what side, and I leave it to each of you to decide if you want to reveal that to the others in the room. I consider it a non-issue. If you don't feel that you can work with someone from the other side, stand up now, and I'll dismiss you from the team and replace you with someone else. But if you decide to remain on the team, I don't want to hear later on that you can't do your job because of your co-workers' pasts. Is that understood?"

There were nods around the table.

"Does anyone want out?"

No one stood.

"Good. That subject is closed. Leave it closed, and do your jobs. Now, does anyone have any questions about what we've been tasked to do?"

"Mr. Rosemont?" Captain Michaels raised his hand. "How long is this assignment?"

"Until the president says that we're done," Rosemont replied. "It could be weeks. It could be years. There's no way to know."

"Where will be working?" Special Agent McGrath asked.

Rosemont tapped on the tablet and a floor plan of their section of the Pentagon appeared on the wall behind him. "This conference room is permanently assigned to us, as are the six workrooms across the hall. There are also a few conference rooms at CIA, NSA, and DIA that are available for you to use from time to time, providing that you leave nothing that can be seen by any other person, regardless of their rank or position in your various branches and agencies. Only the president, vice president, and I are allowed to see your work product, unless the president designates others to see it. No one who's not on the approved list can know anything about what you're working on. That includes your superiors. They can threaten your job, they can threaten you with court martial for refusing to obey an order, but you cannot discuss or reveal anything to anyone. If someone is giving you grief about your assignment, let me handle it. No one but the president or I can fire you or have you court martialed while you're on this team."

"Which brings up another point," Rosemont added. "Your spouses and significant others are not read into this assignment, and they won't be. You cannot discuss this with anyone outside this room or the Oval Office, so I hope none of you talk in your sleep."

There were more chuckles around the room.

"Where will you be working?" Steve asked.

Rosemont used his thumb to point over his shoulder. "I'm in the office next door. If I'm not there, a sign on the door will let you know where I am; plus, we're all going to be linked to the same digital calendar and secure drive for our work products.

I'll give you the details and passwords later today."

Rosemont looked at his watch. "All right. That's all for now. I have a briefing at the White House. Spend the rest of this morning getting to know each other better, and I'll meet with each of you individually after lunch to discuss your specific assignments and duties, as well as to assign you to your initial work group. We'll reconvene as a team at 4:00 PM, or 1600 for you in the military, to make certain that everyone understands what everyone else will be doing. Then, tomorrow morning, we hit the ground running."

As Rosemont stood and headed for the conference room door, he added, "By the way, in case you're wondering, everyone in the room has the clearance to know everything about you, your projects, your experiences... everything. So don't try to hide behind operational keyword classification or national security or any other such excuse for keeping secrets. There are *no* secrets in this room or on this team. Understood?"

The members of the team agreed. With that, he deactivated the SCIF and exited the conference room.

The team spent the next three hours sharing personal and professional information about themselves. Kate revealed that, even though she was a natural brunette, both of her parents were Norwegian. She had been raised in Adams County, Pennsylvania, just outside of Gettysburg, where her parents taught at Gettysburg College. She was a runner, a swimmer, and adept in fighting arts—necessary skills when doing field work for the Agency. She had attended Northwestern University in Chicago, spoke and wrote nearly a dozen languages fluently, and had been recruited by the Agency right after graduation twelve years ago.

She learned that Steve was a runner, as she had suspected, and that he was also an expert equestrian and rock climber—two activities that he used to relieve stress. He had been raised in Charlotte, North Carolina, and had attended Vanderbilt

University in Nashville—studying Asian culture—before spending several years in Japan, Taiwan, and other Asian countries as part of various cultural exchange programs. He went to work for the NSA upon his return to the United States, where his time abroad helped him in his counterintelligence assignments.

Just after noon, the group left the conference room and walked back to the Concourse area, where the food court style cafeteria was located. The seating area was crowded almost to capacity, so the team had to separate to find open seating. Kate and Steve found themselves sitting together at a small table against the wall.

As they sat, Kate noticed that Steve was staring at her eyes. "What?" she asked.

Steve looked embarrassed. "I'm sorry, but I couldn't help but notice your eyes in this light."

"What about my eyes?"

"I've never seen blue eyes that were dark toward the middle but light toward the outside. It's almost like the pattern is that of a starburst. It's unusual, that's all."

Kate smiled. "So I've been told. Mom had the same eyes. Dad says that's what made him notice her. Blond, blue-eyed Norwegians are a dime-a-dozen. The eyes set her apart from the crowd."

"Was your father dark skinned and dark haired?" Steve asked between bites of his pasta.

Kate shook her head. "No, blond and blue-eyed like Mom. No one knows why the only part of me that looks like either of my parents is my eyes. Kids who had seen my parents used to accuse me of coloring my hair or being adopted."

Steve laughed. "They accused me of being German, but we're Anglo-Saxons from Lancashire, England. My family moved to the States in the 1600s. I even had an ancestor who was a Confederate General during the first Civil War."

Kate lowered her fork, letting her bite of roasted chicken fall back onto her plate. "Brigadier General William Barksdale of the Mississippi Brigade?"

Steve nodded. "Yes. He was killed at Gettysburg."

"I know," Kate said. "On the second day, between the peach orchard and the wheat field."

Steve's eyes opened wide. "I'm impressed that you know that."

"I grew up next to the battlefield, remember?" Kate explained. "In addition to teaching, Dad was a battlefield tour guide on the weekends. I've walked every inch of that battlefield, seen every monument, read every marker, and even volunteered on weekends and after school to do cleanup and restoration. I've known the name 'Barksdale' my whole life."

They continued talking and eating. When Steve noticed some of the other members of the team leaving the cafeteria, he suggested that they return to the conference room.

When they reached the conference room, only half of the team had returned from lunch. They took their seats just before Rosemont walked in.

Looking around, he said, "Not everyone's back yet. That's all right. I'll start with those of you who are here, and I'll get to the rest later this afternoon." He pointed to Clay McGrath of the FBI. "You first."

Kate was the fourth member of the team called into Rosemont's office. In addition to a large desk and credenza at one end of the room, there was a small conference table in the middle and a sofa at the far end opposite the desk. Rosemont gestured to a chair at the conference table and sat across from her.

"Kate, I personally requested you for this assignment."

Kate was surprised at this. She knew Rosemont's name from numerous security briefings—just as she knew the names of several other members of the team—but she had never been formally introduced to Rosemont or any of the members of the team.

Rosemont continued. "I'm on the distribution list for most of your reports; so are the superiors of several members of the team. Your reports are insightful and often brilliant. You see through the clutter, and you're not afraid to voice your opinions, which are correct an uncanny amount of the time. Plus, you have field experience, and I think the assignment I have for you will require interaction with our people and foreign assets around the world."

Kate nodded. "Thank you. What *is* my assignment?"

"We have members of the team who are going to focus on how America needs to prepare itself for what's happening around the world—most of the team, in fact. But I don't think we can defend ourselves unless we know who the enemy is."

"But we know that, don't we?" Kate asked. "There are three regional conflict theatres: Latin America, the Pacific Rim, and Europe-Middle East-Africa. We know who the aggressors are."

Rosemont made a dismissive gesture. "Yes, yes, yes. But how did three regional conflicts begin almost simultaneously? And why did their starts coincide with the events that led to the recent Civil War? It's too much of a coincidence for my taste. So, what I want from you is to know how these conflicts managed to start at almost the same moment with no warning whatsoever, who's behind each of the conflicts, and which of these aggressors has America on its radar as the next target. In other words, who are we defending ourselves against? One of them? All of them? We need to know."

Kate nodded. *Rosemont's right. You have to know who you're defending yourself against to know how to best defend yourself. Each aggressor has a different strategy, style, and objective. These must be known so the rest of the team can do its job.*

"Who will I be working with?" Kate asked.

"I'm pairing you with Steve Barksdale," Rosemont replied. "Clay McGrath and Grant Chamberlain will be helping you from time to time, but they're floating between teams, so you'll only be able to use them periodically. Steve will be your full-time partner on this."

Rosemont handed Kate a large stack of paper files and computer flash drives. "Here's the latest intel from the three theatres. I have the two of you set up in Conference Room B across the hall. There are secure storage safes in there. You are to keep these and any other work materials in the conference room. Don't remove them for any reason until the end of the project unless you have my permission. And keep all materials locked in the safes when you leave the room. When you want to share information with me, I'll come to you. I don't even want you removing files or papers to walk across the hall without clearing it with me first. Understood?"

"Understood."

Rosemont stood. "Good. Send in your partner, and then lock up these files in your conference room. You can start looking at them in the morning."

Kate shook the outstretched hand and left Rosemont's office. She glanced down at the flash drives and the stack of folders in her arms. *Three theatres, three conflicts, three aggressors... and two people have to identify who, what, how, and why so the rest of the team can do its job? I knew this was going to be a highly visible assignment, but I didn't know it was going to be a nearly impossible one.*

Sounds just like what I do every day.

CHAPTER 2

————————— • —————————

Beijing
December 1991

It was New Year's Eve according to the western calendars, and Liang Hao sat in the back seat of the People's Liberation Army staff car, looking out the window at the sights of Beijing. *What am I doing here? I have done nothing wrong.* The twenty-one year-old chess prodigy and grandmaster had no idea why the PLA wanted to see him, but the summons was clearly one he could not refuse.

The car entered Tian'anmen Square, where two years earlier a massacre had taken place during a clash between the military and activists wanting economic reforms. Liang Hao hadn't been in China at the time, but he wouldn't soon forget the images he saw on western television. *Why any of those protestors thought that they could force the Communist leaders to change is beyond me.*

On the north end of the Square stood the massive entrance to the Forbidden City, once the private domain of the Chinese Emperor. Red banners of the Communist Party lined the top of the south wall, with a huge portrait of Mao Zedong hanging in the center. *The Imperial City has become just another monument to Chairman Mao.*

As the car moved out of the square, Liang Hao couldn't help but notice the sharp contrast of architecture between structures of Imperial China and modern China. *The Middle Kingdom has changed so much over the years. We are still the center of the world, but the world has influenced us, and not always in a good way. At least our architecture still hints of our past—not like eastern European architecture, which looks like soulless, lifeless concrete boxes. No style whatsoever. Our modern buildings may clash with the remnants of the Imperial dynasties, but at least they are still uniquely Chinese.*

The car continued heading west toward one of the more modern parts of the city. In the distance, he saw the headquarters of the Central Military Commission, where the senior military and Communist Party officials directed the largest military force in the world. *Is that where they are taking me?*

Liang Hao grew up in eastern China to ordinary parents, but his gift for chess brought him to the attention of the nation at an early age. Then, at fifteen, he faced the Russian Grandmaster for the World Championship. He not only defeated his much older opponent, he humiliated him by defeating him with the four-move checkmate—also known as 'scholar's mate.' Liang Hao became a household name in China, and his skills as a chess strategist became known and respected throughout the world.

But what was less known was that Liang Hao had predicted the fall of the Soviet Union on his way to the final chess match against the Russian Grandmaster. And he not only predicted *that* it would happen, he accurately predicted *when* it would happen. In fact, it had happened just five days earlier—December 26, 1991.

Several minutes later, the staff car stopped in front of the Central Military Commission building. Two uniformed Army officers were waiting for him. When Liang Hao exited the car, they took up positions on either side of him and escorted him inside. They crossed the massive lobby to the elevators. When

18

they arrived on the fourth floor, they led him down a hallway with guards posted across from every door. They stopped at a door close to the end of the hallway and escorted him inside. They closed the door behind him and locked it, leaving him alone.

The room was quite large. Maps of the world and specific geographic areas covered the walls. Glancing up at the ceiling, Liang Hao noticed several small inverted glass domes that undoubtedly contained cameras. Not knowing what else to do, he sat in one of the chairs surrounding the table in the center of the room—waiting for someone to come and tell him what he was doing there.

Fifteen minutes later, he heard guards shouting orders outside the room. A moment later, the door opened. Several military officers entered the room, along with a few civilians. Liang Hao immediately recognized two of the civilians.

Deng Xiaoping, Paramount Leader of the People's Republic of China since 1978, and Yang Shangkun, President of the People's Republic of China since 1988 and Vice Chairman and Secretary-General of the Central Military Commission, entered the room. Liang Hao leapt to his feet and bowed in a sign of respect for the leaders of the Middle Kingdom.

"Sit down, sit down," Deng Xiaoping said, gesturing for everyone to be seated around the table. He took the chair at the head of the table with Yang Shangkun seated to his right. One of the military officers directed Liang Hao to sit at the opposite end of the table from Deng Xiaoping.

"I imagine that you're confused about why you were summoned here," the Paramount Leader began.

"Yes, sir," Liang Hao acknowledged.

"Is it true that six years ago you predicted the fall of the Soviet Union?"

"Yes, sir."

Deng Xiaoping stared at him intently. "How did you do that?"

Liang Hao cleared his throat. "I was preparing for the final match against my Russian opponent. I knew how he played, but I needed to know how he *thought* if I were going to beat him. So I studied the *man*. I studied his culture, the history of where he had been raised and where he had lived... every aspect that could influence how he might strategize his game, how he might react to moves and countermoves, his blind spots and weaknesses, and anything else that might give me insight into how to beat him. By the time I had finished analyzing my opponent, I also had a clear understanding of the Soviet Union, and in that understanding I saw its demise as clearly as I'm seeing you now."

Deng Xiaoping nodded thoughtfully. "And you mentioned this to your escort on the way to the chess tournament?"

"Yes, sir."

"And now it has happened, just as you predicted and when you predicted it would occur. Curious that you saw so clearly what my military strategists completely missed."

Liang Hao looked nervously around the room at the expressionless faces of the military leaders staring back at him.

"Could you do it again?" Deng Xiaoping's question brought Liang Hao's attention back to the Paramount Leader.

"I am sorry, do what?"

"Could you accurately predict another major political event?"

Liang Hao hesitated for a moment, thinking about the question. "I do not know, sir. With enough information and time, it is entirely possible. Is that why I am here?"

Deng Xiaoping held up his hand, signaling that he was not prepared to answer that question yet. "More to the point, could you define a strategy that would *bring about* a major political event?"

That's why I'm here. Liang Hao stared at the Paramount Leader. "What kind of major political event are you trying to bring about?"

Deng Xiaoping stood and walked over to the map of China on the wall closest to the door. The map also showed the former Soviet Union and the other Asian countries on the mainland.

Pointing to China's northern border, he said, "Since the 1950s, most of our strategic military initiatives have been focused on protecting our border with the Soviets. Dozens of times their army pushed south, attempting to change the agreed-upon border. Their goal: the subjugation of China into the Soviet Union. Each time we forced them back. Whenever we would think the border was secure and begin our own plans for expansion, they would push south, forcing us to react to their aggression."

Deng Xiaoping paused, and Liang Hao thought he heard a faint chuckle. "And now the Soviet Union has fallen," the Paramount Leader continued, "and Russia is in chaos. They are in no position to threaten our border now or for the next several years. We have the largest armed forces in the world, and our principal enemy for the past forty years is no more. We can once again turn our sights toward expansion."

Deng Xiaoping walked over to the map of the world on the adjacent wall. "But as we saw in Korea, and as the Soviets saw in Viet Nam, there are other forces around the world that could oppose our attempts to expand our borders. NATO, Europe, the United States... any or all of them could thwart our plans. We need a strategy to successfully expand *and* neutralize any opposition."

The Paramount Leader walked back to the table and took his seat. "Thoughts?"

Liang Hao turned in his chair to view the two maps again. After several moments, he said, "You need more than a strategy to expand while neutralizing opposition."

"Explain," Deng Xiaoping demanded.

"It is one thing to take. It is another thing to hold. If you want to keep what you have taken, you need a strategy that will not just neutralize potential opposition, you need a strategy that will prevent any future opposition. In other words, you must eliminate the ability for any country to *ever* oppose the expansion of China's borders."

Deng Xiaoping looked around the room at his military leaders. "You see, gentlemen, not one of your so-called experts ever hit on that critical fact. Short-term conquest will win us nothing. This is a long game if we want to keep what we take. And it took a chess prodigy to point that out to us."

Looking across the table, Deng Xiaoping asked, "Liang Hao, can you develop for us the strategy you described?"

"How much expansion are you thinking about?" Liang Hao asked.

Deng Xiaoping smiled. "How much do you think we can achieve?"

The two men locked eyes, as if to see into each other's minds. Finally, Liang Hao nodded. "With enough information and time, I can develop any strategy. Once I understand my opposition, I know how to control my opposition. Once I know how to control them, they are already defeated. All that remains is for them to realize it."

Fourteen have come and gone.

Liang Hao looked around the room, where he had been working for a week already. *They have had fourteen other strategists present their ideas for the Paramount Leaders' expansion initiative, and all of the strategies were rejected. Now they are waiting for me to present my strategy. Only I do not yet have a strategy.*

Liang Hao was frustrated. Whenever he was frustrated, he usually played chess, but his chessboard was hundreds of miles away. Still he couldn't shake that nagging in his head that he needed to play a game of chess. No matter how hard he tried to concentrate on the task he had been given, he couldn't get past the idea that he needed to play chess.

Finally, he gave in and went to the door. He knocked and heard the guard outside unlock it. The guard stuck his head in and asked, "What do you need?"

"A chessboard and a chess set," Liang Hao replied.

The guard stared at him. "A what?"

Liang Hao repeated himself.

"Why do you want that?" the guard demanded.

"I need to clear my head. It helps me think."

The guard nodded; then he closed and relocked the door.

I hope that means 'yes.' Liang Hao hadn't left the headquarters complex of the Central Military Commission since the day he arrived. He slept in a dormitory on the other side of the building, where fresh clothes appeared each morning. Guards brought him food and escorted him to and from the dormitory. Military officers saw to his other needs, including supplies, writing paper, maps, and intelligence reports on every country in the world. *It is amazing how good our intelligence service is. Some of these reports provide analysis of events that just happened yesterday.*

Less than an hour later, the guard reappeared with a cheap chessboard and chess set. He set them down and left without a word.

Liang Hao set up the chess pieces on the board. Then he began to play against himself. He had himself in checkmate in six moves, but as he stared at the board, an idea began to form in his head.

Chess games are broken into three phases: the opening, the middlegame, and the endgame. In the opening, you develop the chess pieces by moving them to more advantageous positions, you control the center of the board, and you protect the king. *The middlegame is when the chess pieces are coordinated to attack the opposition's defenses. The endgame is when the surviving pawns are promoted and the king is in play.*

Liang Hao looked up at the world map. Then it hit him. *This is just a giant chess game.* He looked at the map again. *No, this is not one chess game, it is several separate chess games all tied together.*

He jumped up and ran to the door. He knocked excitedly until the guard unlocked and opened it.

"What now?" the guard asked.

"I need six more chessboards and chess sets. Now!"

The guard just silently closed and relocked the door.

Liang Hao was already staring at the world map again. *Multiple games, multiple phases, one coordinated strategy. This will work.*

"What is he doing?" Yang Shangkun asked.

The Vice Chairman and Secretary-General of the Central Military Commission watched the video monitor displaying images from the ceiling cameras in Liang Hao's workroom. Next to him stood the senior Army office assigned to oversee Liang Hao while he was working on the requested strategy.

"He's playing chess, Secretary-General."

"He's playing five separate games of chess," Yang Shangkun corrected the officer. "Against himself!"

They watched the monitor for a while longer. As Liang Hao finished one game, he would write furiously on the sheets of paper he kept with him at all times. Then he'd stop, move to one of the other chessboards, and begin playing again. This had gone on for days.

"What's he writing?" Yang Shangkun asked.

"No idea, Secretary-General," the officer replied. "He never leaves the papers behind when he leaves the room. He eats with them, sleeps with them... he even takes them with him when he goes to relieve himself."

They continued watching the monitor. "How long do we let him continue?" the officer asked.

Yang Shangkun shrugged. "If this is his process, I don't want it interrupted. But if he's wasting our time, he'll never leave this building alive. I guess we'll just have to wait and see what he presents when he's finished."

"Yes, Secretary-General."

Regular chess would never work like this. Sacrificing pawns while cultivating and developing new pawns, only to sacrifice them at the right time. Slight-of-hand initiatives to keep entire governments from seeing what is really going on. Controlling what the world sees us doing so they will never suspect what we are really doing. Letting others fight our battles, only to betray them at the moment of their victory. And all of this spread out over several decades.

Liang Hao played the strategies over and over in his head, looking for anything that he might have missed. He had spent nearly a month developing an intricate series of coordinated and interdependent strategies that, if successful, would accomplish the one thing that no other country had ever achieved. *Total and absolute control of the world. We are playing for the entire world. And it can be done.*

Ah, but the cost. It will be expensive. More expensive than anything ever conceived of. Time and money. It will not be quick. It will take years to develop some of the pawns, and longer still to groom their replacements once it is time for the pawns to be sacrificed. Moves and countermoves. Three separate gambits and a Brilliancy! I have only attempted a Brilliancy twice in my career—succeeded only once—and now I am adapting it to contain and neutralize a superpower so the other gambits will work.

Liang Hao stared at the ceiling, mentally playing four

25

simultaneous chess matches in his head. *What am I forgetting? If I leave something out, it could all collapse, and China would be destroyed by the global backlash.*

Liang Hao continued playing the games in his mind. Then he sat up straight. *What if the Brilliancy fails? Or what if it succeeds at first, but then is undone?* He added another simultaneous game in his mind and played it out. After a while, he smiled. *That will work.* He began scribbling again on his ever-present stack of papers. Then he sat back and restarted the games again in his mind.

For two days, he played the strategies out in his mind, made notes, and played them again. On the third day, he packed up all of the chess pieces and stacked them on top of the chessboards. Then he sat down at the conference table, pulled out a stack of fresh paper, and began writing... and writing... and writing...

For four days, he did nothing but write. Army officers brought him reams of fresh paper, but it never seemed to be enough. Liang Hao kept writing all day and all night, taking the occasional nap at the conference table, rather than return to the dormitory.

On the morning of the fifth day, Laing Hao asked for a typist. Twenty minutes later, an unfamiliar military officer arrived carrying a portable typewriter in its case.

"I'm the typist you requested," he said.

Liang Hao handed the officer the huge stack of paper he had been working on for nearly five days. "I need all of this typed. Can you read my writing?"

The officer flipped through the pages. "Yes, sir."

"Create one copy, and then I will review it. If there are any changes needed, I will let you know. Once it is final, I will need several copies printed. Until then, no one apart from you is to see either these pages or your typed version for any reason whatsoever. Do you understand?"

"Yes, sir."

Liang Hao stretched and yawned. "Good. I am going back to my room to get some sleep. Have someone send for me if you finish before I return."

Liang slept for the rest of the day and well into the next. After he had bathed and put on fresh clothes, he returned to the workroom, where the typist was still transcribing his notes.

"I'm not finished yet, sir," the officer said when Liang Hao entered the room, "but I have much of it ready for you to review while I'm working on the rest."

Liang Hao sat down and began reviewing the typed pages. For the next two days, Liang Hao reviewed the pages, made corrections, and read the new pages while the officer corrected the previous ones. On the third day, he reviewed the final copy, with the officer sitting across from him in silence. Liang Hao read each page carefully.

Finally, Liang Hao looked up and smiled at the officer. "This is perfect. Thank you. I'll need a copy for every chair in this room, plus ten additional copies."

"They'll be ready this afternoon, sir."

Liang Hao nodded. He walked to the door and knocked. When the guard unlocked and opened the door, Liang Hao said, "Tell them that I am finished."

The next morning at 8:00 AM—February 17, 1992—Deng Xiaoping, Yang Shangkun, and the military officers that Liang Hao had met with forty-eight days earlier filed into the workroom to hear the results of the chess prodigy's work. The officer who had typed Liang Hao's notes and several other aides were also in the room, and the guards scurried to bring chairs for the extra people.

Once everyone was seated, Deng Xiaoping spoke. "We're anxious to hear what you have developed, Liang Hao. I hope it is

27

worth the wait. Your competition provided their reports weeks ago."

Liang Hao stood and bowed to the Paramount Leader of the People's Republic of China. Then he passed out copies of his report to everyone in the room.

Deng Xiaoping was visibly shocked at the size of the report. He picked it up with difficulty and thumbed through the pages. "What is this?" he demanded. "All this just to tell us how to expand our borders to encompass more of Asia?"

Laing Hao finished passing out the copies, and then he stood facing Deng Xiaoping. "Of course not, sir. What I am presenting to you is *not* a strategy for expanding the Middle Kingdom's borders across Asia."

"Then what is it?" Deng Xiaoping slammed his copy onto the table. "What took you a month and a half to deliver to us?"

Liang didn't cower at the Paramount Leader's wrath. Instead, his face looked serene—almost as if he were an otherworldly being bestowing celestial wisdom on the people in the room. "This is a strategy for conquering the world."

CHAPTER 3

Washington, DC • Vancouver • Seattle
October 2027

Kate glanced at her watch. 5:45 PM. It was still the team's first day together, and already the people in the Pentagon conference room looked like they wanted to throw things at their fellow team members. Everyone was talking over everyone else, voices grew louder, and a couple of the team members looked like they needed to either take an extra dose of blood pressure meds or a stiff drink of bourbon. *All I did was ask one simple question.*

She glanced at Rosemont sitting at the head of the table. He scowled as he watched the meeting sink into near-anarchy. Finally, he slammed his palms on the table and roared, "Enough!"

The room immediately quieted down. The people at the table turned to look at Rosemont, startled out of their verbal conflagration by his shout.

"You're all supposed to be professionals—the top of your game—and you're acting like a bunch of children at a daycare! This is unacceptable. If one little question causes a meltdown like this, what will happen when we start tackling the *real* issues we're here to solve?"

Everyone looked at him in embarrassed silence.

Rosemont regained his composure. "Now, Kate, would you please repeat your question? And let's see if we can have a civil discussion on the subject, shall we?"

Kate cleared her throat. "I asked if the president had given us any guidelines regarding a defensive strategy. I want to know if we're to limit that strategy to protecting the United States alone, or if we're to include some or all of our remaining allies in that strategy."

"And why do you want to know that?" Rosemont asked, holding up his hand to prevent anyone else from interjecting.

"Because it changes how Steve and I analyze the current situation," Kate replied. "It won't change how we determine who the enemy is, but it will change how we assess their reaction to *our* actions. If we're only planning to defend our own borders, then we probably only have to worry about one enemy for the time being, and Steve and I will have to figure out which enemy will most likely come after us first. But if we include some or all of our remaining allies in our defensive strategy, the potential enemies will undoubtedly react differently. It could even put us at odds with multiple enemies. For example, if we include the Caribbean, it could put us into conflict with the Latin American Block, but if we include Canada, it could put us into conflict with China, and if we include Greenland or Iceland, it could put us into conflict with the Islamic Caliphate in Europe. I don't want to debate the wisdom of which defensive strategy to choose, but I need to know if there are any existing directives or if Steve and I have to look at every possible combination of scenarios."

Rosemont looked around the table, as if defying anyone to speak. When no one spoke up, he said, "That is a very good question. The simple answer is no. The president has not given us any directive regarding the inclusion or exclusion of our allies. Therefore, we need to look at all potential scenarios where our allies are concerned, so the president can make the most informed decision possible when he chooses what our final defensive strategy will be."

"Is there a way we can include any of our allies as we assess the situation and define strategies?" Vandyke asked. "They might be able to provide intel and situational analyses that we can't get with the information at our disposal."

Rosemont leaned back in his chair. He didn't respond for a minute, and then he responded, "On a case-by-case basis, yes. But you cannot share any of your own intel, analyses, or strategies. There is a different mechanism for sharing that. And you cannot let them know that you're exploring the possibility of any joint operations or strategies. Gather what they're willing to share, ask questions, but reveal and commit nothing. And clear any interaction with foreign contacts through me first. Understood?"

"Yes, sir," Vandyke replied.

The meeting broke up an hour later, and Kate and Steve returned to Conference Room B to collect their personal items before leaving for the night. Kate heard a buzzing sound and realized that it was her phone, which she had left in her purse on the far table since it would be useless in a SCIF. She retrieved the phone and checked the screen. One voicemail.

She accessed her voicemail box and listened to the message. Then, without a word, she left the conference room and headed for Rosemont's office, leaving a bewildered Steve behind.

Rosemont was still in his office when Kate walked in. "Do you have a minute?" she asked.

Rosemont nodded and gestured for her to sit in one of the chairs on the other side of his desk. "What's up?"

"I just got this voicemail from one of my contacts in the Canadian government. He and I have worked together a number of times in the past, but… well, just listen." She hit the speaker button on her phone and played Rosemont the message.

> *Kate, it's Iain. I'm back in Vancouver. I'd like to get*
> *together with you for old time's sake. Can you come*
> *here? We'll fire up the Barracuda.*

"What did he mean about 'the Barracuda'?" Rosemont asked when Kate retrieved her phone from the desk.

"It's a code we established a long time ago. It means he's being watched, and he can't come here. The 'fire up' part means the matter is extremely urgent. If he left Ottawa and returned to Vancouver, it means that the Canadian capital isn't safe for him anymore."

"How high in the Canadian government is he?"

"He's currently on Prime Minister Agutter's staff," Kate replied. "But I've known him since he was just an intelligence analyst."

Rosemont nodded. "What do you want to do?"

"Catch the first flight to Vancouver."

"Okay. Go, but be careful. If he's being watched, it could be dicey for you if you're caught with him." Rosemont opened his desk drawer, pulled out a business card, and handed it to her. "Here's the number of our travel services coordinators. They'll make the arrangements. You have a government credit card?"

Kate nodded.

"Good. Do what you need to do, and get back quickly."

"And if I need an extraction?"

Rosemont smiled. "I thought you were an expert in the fighting arts."

Kate shrugged. "Even Bruce Lee got taken down in the end."

Rosemont laughed. "I'll have someone available to help you if you get in to trouble."

"Thank you." Kate left Rosemont's office and walked

back to the conference room, texting Iain that she was coming and asking where they should meet.

A moment later, Rosemont saw Steve walking past his office door, heading out for the evening.

"Steve, come here," Rosemont shouted.

Steve returned and stood in Rosemont's doorway.

"Come in and shut the door."

Steve complied and sat down in the chair Kate had just vacated.

Rosemont filled Steve in on what was happening. "I want you to go to Vancouver and keep an eye on your partner. Don't approach her, and don't let her know you're there until after she finishes meeting with her contact." Rosemont handed Steve the business card of their travel services coordinators. "Make certain that you're not on the same flight out there."

"Yes, sir."

There were no available flights from DC to Vancouver that night, so the next morning Kate caught a 7:00 AM flight out of Ronald Reagan Washington National Airport that stopped in Chicago and San Francisco. When she landed in Vancouver just before 5:00 PM, there was a text from Iain giving the name of a downtown club and a time for the meeting. She acknowledged the time and place, forwarded the information to Rosemont, and headed for the rental car counters.

Once she had her car, she drove to her hotel near the downtown nightclub district and the club where she was meeting Iain. Thursday nights in Vancouver were when most of the thirty-something crowd went out to party or unwind, and she and Iain would look like just another couple out for a good time.

After she checked in and took the elevator up to her room, she looked at the clock and saw that she had just enough time to get a bite to eat, change clothes, and head for the club where Iain was to be waiting.

After a quick sandwich from the deli on the first floor, she changed into an outfit more appropriate for clubbing. She wore a russet faux-suede asymmetrical mini-dress with a single strap over her left shoulder, and brown over-the-knee low-heeled suede boots. She thought about letting her hair down, but she decided to keep it in a ponytail.

She surveyed the hotel room one more time. *I better not leave anything here in case I have to make a quick getaway out of the city.* She packed the clothes she had worn on her flight, put on a light jacket against the autumn chill, grabbed her purse and overnight bag, and left her room.

She arrived at the club with twenty minutes to spare. Even though there were still parking spaces available on the street near the entrance, she parked on a side street. *First rule of spycraft. Don't park in the open, and don't let them see you approach from where your getaway car is.*

Leaving her overnight bag in the trunk, she grabbed her purse, put the strap over her shoulder, and walked around the block to approach the entrance of the club from the opposite direction from the place where her car was parked. She paid the cover charge and walked inside. Music blared from the bandstand on the opposite side of the dance floor. Drunk revelers were already dancing. *We definitely won't be overheard in here.*

She saw someone waving to her left and recognized Iain. She made her way through the crowd toward his table, having to push through several men whose hands tried to grope her ass. She'd had enough when a third man put his hands on her. He found himself sprawled on the floor when Kate mule kicked him with the heel of her right boot.

"Nice kick," Iain said when she reached the table.

"What a prick," Kate muttered. "I thought you Canadians were more polite than that."

"Only when we're sober," Iain replied. "Something to drink?"

"Ginger ale only. I'm working."

"Right." Iain ordered her a ginger ale when the next server walked past the table.

After the server delivered her drink to the table, Kate scooted her chair closer to Iain. "What's up?"

"All hell is breaking loose!"

"I figured that," Kate said sarcastically. "I need specifics."

Iain looked around nervously. "The British Prime Minister contacted Prime Minister Agutter last week. He's officially requesting sanctuary for the Royal Family, parliament, the Royal Navy fleet, the Royal Air Force squadrons, and as many others as can be evacuated from Britain before it falls. He also wants to move Britain's treasury and strategic weapons arsenal over here to keep it out of the hands of the Caliphate."

Kate was surprised that she hadn't heard this already from her contacts in Whitehall. "Is Britain that close to being overrun?"

Iain nodded. "It's amazing they've lasted this long."

"What about the Royal Army?"

"They're going to cover the retreat and evacuation, then they're going to redeploy to Scotland before being ferried over to Norway where the remnants of the European armed forces have gathered for a last stand against the Caliphate."

Kate took a sip of her drink. "What's Prime Minister Agutter going to do?"

"He was all set to allow them in, and that's when all hell broke loose."

"Explain."

"The Chinese ambassador found out—don't ask me how—that the PM was going to grant the British sanctuary. He was furious and demanded that the PM not allow the British to come here… or else."

"Or else what?"

"He wasn't specific, but a military reprisal was

mentioned."

Kate stared at him in shock. *Chinese military forces on North American soil? That would change the balance of power here forever.* "What did your PM decide to do?"

Iain looked bleak. "What could he do? China's our biggest trading partner. Most of our medium and heavy manufacturing was outsourced to China years ago. Our economy would collapse if they retaliated in any way. The PM has decided to deny the British request."

"That would violate the Commonwealth treaty, wouldn't it?"

"Yes, but who'd be left to enforce that treaty. Britain will be lost inside of a month, Australia's already lost, and none of the other Commonwealth countries are in any position to complain one way or another."

Kate took another sip of her drink. She stared at Iain's face. "That's not all, is it?"

Iain shook his head. "China also told the PM that if Canada does anything other than what China tells it to do, China will retaliate to the fullest extent. That's a direct quote—'fullest extent.' The PM is drafting a statement of capitulation like the one your former president was drafting when your recent Civil War broke out. He's going to surrender Canada to the Chinese, and you know what that means. China will send over 'administrators' to oversee the Canadian government's actions and to dismantle our military, since we'd become a protectorate of China."

"And by 'administrators,' you mean military units."

Iain nodded. "Several of the provincial lieutenant governors found out and are threatening to secede from Canada. British Columbia is planning a referendum to vote on secession and make a formal request to the United States to become a U.S. Territory until it can be granted full statehood."

Kate's eyes went wide. *Having British Columbia as part of*

the U.S. will give us a single coastline from southern California to northern Alaska for the first time. That would definitely affect how we structure our defensive strategy. It would also give us a unified bulwark against Chinese aggression. "Would any of the other provinces follow BC's play and request to become part of the United States?"

"I wouldn't be surprised if Quebec made the same request. I don't know about the others. Everybody's waiting to see if the PM will actually capitulate, and then if he does, they'll wait to see who fights it first."

"Is that why you left Ottawa and came back here?"

"No," Iain replied. "Ottawa is crawling with Chinese agents. They're everywhere, trying to find who's part of the opposition to their plans and eliminate them. I argued with the PM for hours over his decision, and the next thing I knew, I was being followed. They even followed me here, although that's not surprising. All of British Columbia's political leaders are being followed, and assassinations have already begun."

"Who's being assassinated?" Kate was sure she already knew the answer.

"Anyone supporting the secession," Iain replied. "Four members of the provincial cabinet have already been killed."

Iain looked around and froze. "Shit!"

Kate followed his gaze and saw three Asian-looking men sitting across the dance floor. Iain leaned close to Kate. "Listen, I don't have much time. We have—or had actually—a source in Beijing. He was killed two days ago, but he managed to get a message out. It was only a couple of words: 'Brilliancy' and 'Trinity Gambit.'"

Kate shook her head. "Any idea what they mean?"

"Not a clue. I know that Brilliancy is a chess term, as is gambit, but no one in the cryptography unit has ever heard of a 'Trinity Gambit.' We're stumped, but our contact gave his life to get those words to us, so they must be pretty important to someone over there."

Iain glanced across the dance floor and looked like he was about to panic. "I've got to get out of here. You should go, too." He put his hand on Kate's arm. "Tell your government that BC wants to become part of the United States, and tell them that they might want to offer sanctuary to the British. It can't hurt to have their Air Force, Naval Fleet, and strategic weapons added to your own capabilities. Canada as we know it is done for. The only thing that remains is to see who wants to become part of the U.S. and who just wants to leave Canada. One thing's for sure, China wants a foothold on this continent, and we have to stop that at all costs."

"Even if it means the total collapse of your economy?" Kate asked, finishing her drink and getting to her feet.

"Better to have our economy collapse than to become the slaves of Chinese Communists."

Kate nodded. She pulled on her jacket and looked around. Iain had disappeared. She glanced across the dance floor and saw the three Asians looking around for where Iain went. Then she saw them look at her. *Great. Now they're going to follow me to find out where Iain went.* She headed for the front entrance.

Just as she reached the door, she felt a hand on her shoulder. She reacted instinctively, grabbed the wrist of whoever touched her, and twisted around, forcing the person to his knees. She was about to kick him when she heard him say, "Kate, it's me."

Kate looked down and recognized Steve, wincing from the pain she was causing in his wrist. "Steve? Jesus, I almost broke your arm!" She released him. "What the hell are you doing here? Following me?"

Steve stood and rubbed his wrist. "Yes, but only because Rosemont sent me."

This annoyed Kate, even though Rosemont told her that he'd have someone available for an extraction if she needed one.

I wanted someone on standby in case something happened, not a watchdog. "How did you know where I was?"

Steve held up his phone. "He sent me a text and told me when and where you were meeting your contact. I just got here about ten minutes ago. He also told me that I'm your backup in case you need someone to handle an extraction."

Kate looked back and saw the three Asians heading for them. *Shit!* She grabbed Steve's hand and led him toward the street. "Well… good, because I'm going to need some backup in a few moments."

They exited the club. "Do you have a car?" Kate asked.

"No, I took a cab from the airport," Steve replied.

Kate looked around. The street was crowded, leaving her little room to fight if she needed to. She decided to head for her rental car. "Follow me. I have a car a couple of blocks from here."

They walked quickly down the block, but as they reached the cross street, four Asian men stepped out and blocked their path.

"Excuse us," Steve said, trying to push past them. The Asian men pushed back.

"Not until we talk to you," one of the Asians said.

Kate began to back up, but when she turned around, the three Asians from the club had caught up to them. "Where is the man you were with in the club?" one of them demanded.

Kate glanced over at Steve and winked. Without warning, she did a spinning kick that caught one of the club Asians in his lower jaw, sending him flying. At the same time, Steve performed a similar kick on the first Asian who spoke to them. The fight was on.

Steve and Kate weren't armed. The Asians were, but fortunately it was only with knives. Steve grabbed the wrist of the tall knife-wielding Asian in front of him and slammed the knife into the chest of the heavy-set one next to him. Grabbing the heavy-set one's knife, Steve plunged it into the tall one's neck. The two Asians fell, leaving Steve with a knife in both hands. He turned toward the man he had kicked, who had gotten back to his feet and was trying to attack Kate's exposed back. Steve brought down both knives onto the man—one sank deep into his shoulder and the other into his chest. He fell backward, hit the ground, and didn't move. Steve faced the fourth Asian, who wasted no time in attacking Steve.

Steve was an adept knife fighter, but his opponent was even better. If Steve hadn't had two knives, he would have been killed almost immediately. But the second blade gave him one advantage: his opponent had to defend against multiple attacks at the same time. Steve almost had his opponent at one point, but the man stepped back to regroup. He didn't see the knife leave Steve's hand, but he felt it when it slammed into his chest. He looked down, saw the knife sticking out of him, and sank to his knees—dead before he reached the ground.

Steve spun around to help Kate, and he saw her standing over the bodies of the three Asians that she had been fighting. She looked at her jacket, which had several rips in it from where their knives connected. "Son of a bitch! Look at what they did to my jacket!" She kicked the men on the ground in front of her.

Steve grabbed her and pulled her back. "Kate, it's just a jacket."

Kate stared at him, and then she nodded.

Steve heard shouting coming from the other end of the block and recognized the language as Mandarin. "We need to get out of here now."

They ran as Kate led him to her car. Steve looked around several times to make certain that they weren't being followed, but he never saw anyone.

"I didn't know that the NSA trained its people in Fairbairn-Sykes knife fighting," Kate commented as they ran.

"They don't," Steve responded. "I picked it up when I was

traveling in Asia before I joined the NSA. I've kept up with it over the years, but I never thought I have to use it in Canada of all places. Who trained you? The CIA?"

"No," Kate answered breathlessly. "I already knew it. Learned it when I studied martial arts in college. This was the first time I ever used it for real, though."

When they reached the car, Kate slid behind the wheel and started the car. "Where to?"

"Just drive," Steve said. "We'll figure it out as we go."

Kate did a quick U-turn and headed away from the club district. "I have a hotel room paid for through the night, but from what my contact told me, it might not be safe to stay here. You? Where's your luggage?"

"I didn't bring any, and I didn't get a hotel room."

Kate glanced over at Steve. "You were just planning to wear the same clothes for a couple of days?"

"I didn't know what to expect when I got here," Steve explained. "What if I couldn't get back to my luggage? What if I had to carry it with me and it got in the way of helping you if you needed it? I can always buy a new shirt at a gift shop and shower in the locker room of a gym."

"Where were you going to stay tonight?"

"I figured I'd get a room near the airport and fly out in the morning unless you needed an extraction."

"What was your plan if I did?" Kate asked.

"Take BC-99 S to I-5 and drive to Seattle tonight. Easy enough to catch a flight back to DC from there."

Kate thought about that for a moment and then glanced down at the clock. 10:30 PM. "We can be in Seattle before 2:00 AM. Why don't you call the travel coordinators and see if you can get us a room near the airport there and a flight to Washington in the morning?"

"Sure thing."

Kate drove toward BC-99 S. When she reached the

onramp, she headed south toward the U.S. border.

In spite of her original annoyance, she was glad that Steve had been there to have her back. *Handsome and a good fighter.* "Sorry about your arm earlier."

Steve chucked, "I should know better than to sneak up on someone from the CIA. I'm just glad I got there in time."

"So how did you get here?" she asked while Steve was on hold waiting for the travel coordinators.

"I caught a flight out of Reagan that changed in Denver and LAX. It was supposed to land just before 6:00 PM, but we were late leaving Los Angeles. I took a cab straight to the club. I wanted to let you know that I was coming before you saw me, but I didn't want to interrupt your meeting."

"Well, I'm glad you were there," Kate said. "Three I could manage. Maybe four. But not seven."

"Do you think they got your contact?" Steve asked.

"I don't know," Kate admitted. "I'll try to reach him tomorrow, but he may have gone underground until he can get out of the country."

One of the travel coordinators came on the line, and Kate drove south while Steve let the coordinator know that their plans had changed. "She's cancelling our return flights from Vancouver," Steve reported.

A moment later, Steve said, "She can get us into the airport hotel in Seattle, but there's only one room available. Is that a problem?"

Kate smiled in the dark. "Not for me. You?"

"Nope."

Steve relayed the information to the coordinator. After a pause, he said to Kate, "There'll be no issues dropping off the rental car. There's a 7:00 AM non-stop flight to DC, and there's another one that leaves at 12:20 PM. Do you have a preference?"

"I want to get back to DC before it gets too late, but if we take the 7:00 AM flight we might as well skip the hotel room, go straight to the gate, and sleep there. I think I'd rather take the noon flight. When does it get to DC?"

"8:30 PM."

"Let's do that one," Kate suggested.

Steve relayed Kate's request to the travel coordinator. A moment later, he said, "She booked the flight."

"Then it sounds like we're all set," Kate acknowledged. "We'll be in Seattle in less than three hours, depending on the backup at the border crossing."

The travel coordinator sent the confirmation to Steve's phone. He checked the details, confirmed they were correct, and then put his phone in his pocket. "What did you learn at your meeting?"

Kate relayed everything that Iain had said.

"I can't believe that China would be so openly aggressive. They must have plans for Canada if they're willing to threaten military action for helping the British."

"It sounds like they have plans for Britain, too," Kate commented. As she said the words, a thought came to her that she was missing something terribly important.

"Why would China care about Britain, unless it's to punish them for Hong Kong?" Steve was referring to the way England had seized Hong Kong from China and controlled it until the late 1990s.

"You'd think they'd be over that by now," Kate commented.

"The Chinese?" Steve snorted. "They have the longest memories on earth. They could take centuries to plan their revenge against someone."

Kate had the feeling again that she was missing something important, but she was tired. *It'll come to me after I've had some sleep.*

The border crossing took only a few minutes. Their credentials allowed them through without having to answer any questions or have their car searched.

Once they were on I-5 heading south, Steve kept the conversation going so Kate wouldn't get sleepy. "Are you married?" he asked at one point.

"That was direct," Kate commented, finding it funny that he'd ask. "No, not married. Never married. You?"

"Almost once, but the job... She couldn't handle all the things that I couldn't tell her."

"I know," Kate responded. "It makes relationships hard. Too many secrets. Too much risk. It forces us to close ourselves off from the people around us."

They talked the whole way to Seattle. Steve offered to drive a couple of times, but Kate politely declined. She loved driving and didn't like being a passenger. By the time they arrived at the airport hotel and returned the rental car, Kate had her second wind and wasn't tired at all.

When they got to the room, she said, "I don't think I thanked you for being there and helping me tonight."

Steve flashed her a smile. "You're welcome. I wish I had been able to watch you fight. Given the pile of moaning bodies I saw at your feet when it was over, I'll bet you were impressive!"

"Ditto," Kate responded. Then she remembered something that her mentor at the Agency told her once. *"Never miss an opportunity to connect with someone, even if it's just for a moment, because those opportunities are few and far between in this business."* She made a quick decision. She walked up to him, pressed herself gently against him, and looked into his eyes. "I'd like to show you how grateful I am."

Steve looked down at her. "Are you sure about that. We work together. What if it causes a problem later?"

"Later will take care of itself," she purred.

He surrendered, pulling her close. When their lips touched, it was electric. They held the embrace, unwilling to let go of each other.

Kate was the first to pull away, but before he could object, she pushed him back to one of the chairs against the wall. She unbuttoned his shirt and then pushed him into the seat. She put her left foot next to him, unknotted the tie behind the knee, and slowly removed her left boot. Then she did the same with her right boot.

Steve could barely take his eyes off her lean, toned legs, but when she knelt in front of him, it wasn't her legs he was thinking about anymore. She undid his belt and pulled off his pants. His boxers came off next. Then she stood, unzipped her dress, and facing away from him, let it slide off onto the floor. Her thong was the last to join the pile of clothes on the floor. Then she turned and faced him again.

In the low light of the room, Steve was captivated by her physique. His eyes took in every inch of her body until she knelt in front of him again. He felt a shiver run through him when her hand clutched the part of him that was already swelling from arousal. As his head arched back, he felt the swelling enveloped in a warm and wet embrace. As her head rose and fell, he began to tremble slightly.

After several moments of the most delightful sensations, Kate stopped. He opened his eyes and saw her stand and turn around. Then she sat on his lap, rubbing herself against him— gently at first, and then with greater intensity. Just when he thought he couldn't take anymore, she shifted, and he found himself deep inside of her.

She moved up and down—slowly at first and then faster. She moaned several times, each time louder that the one before. There were no words, only sounds—the language of the body, not the mind. She arched her back and cried out. Faster and faster she impaled herself on him until he finally released. It seemed like it would never end. When he was finally spent, they were both bathed in sweat. She leaned back and wrapped his arms around her abdomen.

He nuzzled her neck with a feeling of deep satisfaction. A few minutes later, Kate leaned forward and looked back at him. "I don't know about you, but I need a shower."

She got up and headed for the bathroom.

"Why not?" Steve said softly. He got up and followed her.

The next morning, they both dressed and went downstairs to get breakfast and check out of the hotel room. Steve was wearing the same clothes he had worn the night before, but he promised Kate that he'd buy a new shirt at one of the airport gift shops. Kate had changed into a simple t-shirt and jeans. Her ponytail bounced and swayed as she walked across the hotel lobby.

Neither mentioned anything about what they had shared the night before—there was no reason to say anything. It was a thing of the moment, and in their business, you took those moments as they presented themselves. Besides, they were professionals, and they had a critical job to do.

"I keep feeling like I'm missing something," Kate said as they walked from the hotel lobby to the main airport terminal to check-in for their flight. "There's something that's just on the edge of my consciousness about China having plans for Britain, but I can't put my finger on it. And there's something you said on the drive down that seems like a clue I should recognize, but I just can't figure it out."

"What did I say?" Steve asked.

"You said something about the Chinese having long memories and plotting their revenge for centuries."

"What about it?"

"That's just it. I don't know. But I know what I'm going to do when we get back to DC."

"What?" Steve asked.

"I'm heading for the Pentagon and going through the intelligence report again. The answer's in there somewhere, and I can't rest until I find it."

Steve nodded and showed his Pentagon credentials at the airport's security checkpoint. He and Kate were waved though with a salute.

"Want some help?" he asked. "We're supposed to be working on this together. If you're going to be reviewing the intel, I should be there to review it with you."

"It could take all weekend," Kate pointed out. "Don't you have anything better to do on a Friday night?"

"Not when it comes to national security," Steve said.

"Thanks." Kate smiled. *It'll be good to have some help. Maybe we can find the piece that will help me understand what's swirling around in my mind.*

The two headed for their gate and boarded their flight back to Washington.

CHAPTER 4

Beijing
February 1992–March 1993

Deng Xiaoping, Yang Shangkun, and the military officers in the room listened spellbound as Liang Hao presented his strategy for conquering the world. As Liang Hao continued his presentation, he became more animated, moving from map to map along the walls as he explained the Brilliancy and the Trinity Gambit, as he had named it.

"A Brilliancy is a combination of strategies designed to overwhelm an enemy and force them to withdraw from the game. I have identified a linchpin in the strategy for global conquest. The Brilliancy will be directed at this nation. Once this nation has been neutralized, the Trinity Gambit can move toward its endgame. It is called Trinity because there will be three separate strategies in play—all independent from each other, but all integrated and coordinated as part of a central strategy with a single goal in mind."

"And which nation is this linchpin?" Deng Xiaoping.

Liang Hao pointed to the map on the wall next to him. "This one."

"And how long do you think it will take to neutralize that nation?" Yang Shangkun asked.

"Thirty-four years, give or take a year."

"What?!"

Liang Hao nodded. "And that takes into account programs already in place there started by the Soviet Union decades ago. The entire strategy will take approximately thirty-eight years. Keep in mind that this is an incredibly complex strategy with tens of thousands of moving parts, dependencies, and players. It will take that long to groom the pawns, groom their successors who will take over when the first pawns are sacrificed, and so on. There are government officials to corrupt, global organizations to subvert, economic engines to infiltrate, educational institutions to repurpose, wars to start, criminal organizations to bolster, terrorism to fund and nurture, plagues to develop and unleash… It cannot be done any sooner, and it may even take longer if some of the countries we will be targeting do not react exactly as expected."

"Haven't you taken their reactions into account?" Deng Xiaoping asked.

"Yes, sir. But there are always variables to be considered. No strategy is completely foolproof. I have identified three possible ways the linchpin could reassert itself as a superpower before the Trinity Gambit has concluded."

"And what if that happens? What if they reassert themselves because your initial strategy failed?" Yang Shangkun inquired.

Liang Hao smiled. "I have a contingency strategy that will keep the linchpin boxed in and unable to offer any threat. Yes, it means we will have to deal with the linchpin later and differently than desired, but easily still."

Liang Hao gave the attendees a chance to peruse the document he had passed out.

For the next two hours, the attendees read Liang Hao's proposal. Several of the military leaders held their heads in their hands in disbelief and bewilderment as they read parts of the strategy. Yang Shangkun even left the table and paced in the corner several times, as the full implication of the strategies began to sink in.

Deng Xiaoping finally broke the silence. "Just how much is this going to cost us?"

"Everything we have and more," Liang Hao said solemnly. "My estimates are at the end of the document, along with my assumptions regarding profits from the business ventures that will be set up along the way, other ways to recoup expenses, inflation, recessions, and so on."

Everyone at the table flipped to the back of the document.

Suddenly, Deng Xiaoping rose to his feet. "Are you insane?" he demanded.

"No, sir," Liang Hao answered carefully. "The world is China's destiny. If we want the world, this is what it will cost. But once we have the world, we will also have the world's wealth at our disposal."

"This is more than eight times our current treasury!" Deng Xiaoping stated.

"If you will look at the next page, sir," Liang Hao responded, "you will see the estimated unmined gold deposits just within our borders. We have enough gold to fund the entire strategy and then some. We just have to mine it and refine it. And if we target gold producing and other wealth producing nations early on, we will be able to tap into that wealth to handle contingencies. Plus our economy will grow to be the largest and strongest in the world within thirty years, repaying us for much of our initial investments."

"What are these business ventures you mentioned?" Yang Shangkun asked.

"Casinos would be one," Liang Hao replied. "If we control the world's gambling, we control wealth in every nation on the globe. Manufacturing, electronics, space exploration would be some of the others that we will let the world see."

One of the generals stood. "I have a question. If I read all of this correctly, your strategy is to have other people conquer lands that we want for ourselves. Why is that? Why not use our own army?"

"Why use our armed forces when we can use someone else's?" Liang Hao asked. "We use pawns to fight battles for us, and then in their moment of triumph, we betray them and take for ourselves what they have just won. Their forces will be exhausted and in no position to oppose us, and we save hundreds of thousands of Chinese lives—lives that will be needed to hold onto the world once we conquer it. If we fight those battles ourselves, we will be too exhausted to hold onto what we have won. We cannot risk that. Besides, we do not want the world to know that we are involved until it is too late to stop us."

"Explain that," the general requested.

"We cannot risk the world learning that we are behind what will happen. If that occurs, they will unite against us. That is why we will use pawns to do much of the work for us. Each of the opening and middlegame moves and countermoves must appear to be the 'Pawns' Game,' and not have any connection to China. The world must never discover that we are the true adversary sitting across the chessboard until the endgame is nearly concluded."

Another general stood. "It looks like most of your strategy is designed to destabilize the world, set allies against each other, and bolster groups that will further distract and splinter continents, nations, even communities. Is that your intent?"

Liang Hao nodded. "It is harder to defeat a strong enemy. To weaken an enemy effectively, it must be weakened from within, not just from without. Every nation that we need to fall must find itself besieged on all fronts—internal and external—if we are going to take it and hold it. That is why we will use pawns as the destabilizers. When it is time, we sacrifice them. That way, they cannot be used to destabilize *us* in the future."

"I am concerned about your plans for Islam," Deng Xiaoping stated. "We do not tolerate Islamic thinking, even though we have one of the largest Islamic populations in the world. Our official policy is one of repression. How can you think to unleash Islamic extremism on the world as part of your strategy?"

"Because they are just another pawn, sir," Liang Hao explained. "And who would believe that we would fund and promote Islamic extremism abroad when we repress it here? It gives us deniability should anyone begin to suspect that we are behind the rise of Islamic terrorism and aggression. And once we are done with them, we crush them as we take from them what was rightfully ours all along."

"That is a dangerous game, Liang Hao," Yang Shangkun noted. "What if you find you cannot control them once they are unleashed."

"If you are after the world, you cannot play it safe, General-Secretary. And besides, if we are the sole source of funding for the Islamic forces that are unleashed, once we withdraw that funding, they will wither and die. It is the same for the criminal organizations in Central and South America. Once we are ready to sacrifice them, we simply remove their funding and watch them wither before our eyes. Then we walk in and take what is ours from their lifeless hands."

"And what about this section of bio-warfare?" one of the Air Force generals asked. "How do we know that it will not destroy us at the same time?"

"We want the world to think that it did," Liang Hao said. "But we will not unleash anything until we already have the cure on hand to protect us from any potential outbreaks. Some Chinese pawns will have to be sacrificed to keep up appearances, but not enough to place any part of the overall strategy in jeopardy."

"We have sacrificed Chinese pawns before," Yang

Shangkun remarked.

There were laughs around the table.

Liang Hao walked back to his chair and addressed the attendees. "Gentlemen, this strategy is all about moves and countermoves. We make a series of moves, watch how the oppositions' reactions counter those moves, make our own countermoves to their countermoves, and so on until the opposition is finally defeated. Much of this can be planned in advance, and those plans are in the document on the table in front of you. Some must be identified and executed in the moment. You will need to select a team of people whose sole responsibility is to determine when the time has arrived to make a move, assess the countermove, and plan for our response. The strategy must be constantly reevaluated and modified based on unanticipated variables or unforeseen countermoves. This team will be directing millions of people, trillions of yuan, and overseeing the largest military buildup in the history of the world. It will be as if thousands of chess matches are all being played at the same time—each one looking like a stand-alone game when they are all actually part of the same game."

"What do you mean by unanticipated variables?" one of the admirals asked.

"A volcano destroys an island, and twenty countries send aid and workers to help the survivors just as we are about to move against that island," Liang Hao answered. "Suddenly we cannot make our move with all of those foreign observers present. It could also be floods, landslides, typhoons, earthquakes, tsunami, and the like. Acts of nature mostly, but it could also be unexpected civil unrest or civil unity brought about by unexpected events."

The meeting went on for several more hours as the attendees pressed Liang Hao for more details about his plan. Lunch was brought in at one point so the meeting could continue. As it grew later in the day, Deng Xiaoping stood. "This has been most enlightening, Liang Hao. We must now deliberate about your impressive strategy. You have certainly given us more than we anticipated. We will return once we have made our decision."

Deng Xiaoping left the room, followed by Yang Shangkun and the military leaders. Finally, only the typist remained in the room with Liang Hao.

"May I ask what you think of the plan?" Liang Hao asked.

"It is not my place," the typist replied.

"And if it were?"

The typist was silent for a moment. Then he drew in his breath and said, "I have never seen anything like it. To take a problem as big as the world and distill it into a series of steps to crush all opposition and then conquer it all is as staggering as it is sublime. You have inspired me into believing that it can actually be done, and I hope I may serve with you as the strategy is implemented."

"Serve with me?"

The typist nodded. "Surely they would put you in charge of overseeing the strategy. Military and Party leaders come and go. This strategy will require a single hand to guide it. Who better than you?"

Liang Hao shook his head. "No. I am a chess player. That is what I do."

"No, sir. You are not just a chess player. You are a genius, and you have invented a new game—a game that pits you against the world. Who else could play that game if not you?"

Liang Hao sat down. Looking up at the typist, he asked, "Do you think they will let me play that game?"

The typist shrugged. "Only if they want the game to be played at all."

It was three days before Liang Hao was summoned back to the room he had spent so much time in while crafting his strategy.

Only Deng Xiaoping, Yang Shangkun, and the senior Generals and Admirals were there when he arrived.

"Sit down, Liang Hao," Deng Xiaoping said when Liang Hao entered the room.

Liang Hao took his seat across the table from the Paramount Leader of China.

"As you can imagine, your strategy left us with much to discuss," Deng Xiaoping began. "Is it what's best for China? Can we afford it? Can we implement it? Is it the best way to achieve the result? These and many other questions had to be answered before any decisions could be reached."

Deng Xiaoping stared at Laing Hao for several moments. Then Deng Xiaoping gestured to Yang Shangkun.

"Your country needs you to stop playing chess professionally," the Secretary-General stated abruptly.

"Why, Secretary-General?" Liang Hao inquired.

"Because you are needed here to direct your strategy and win the world."

Liang Hao was stunned. *They are going to do it! China is going to be the master of the world, and they want me to make it happen. How can I refuse?* The thought of never playing competitive chess again didn't bother him at all. He was going to be the grandmaster of grandmasters in a new game with the world itself as the prize.

Liang Hao rose and bowed. "The honor is to serve."

"You will work out of this building," Yang Shangkun continued. "An entire floor will be placed at your disposal. You will need a staff. How many will you need to get the strategy ready to implement and how long will you need."

Liang Hao had been thinking about this for more than a day in anticipation that the leaders of China might ask him this question. "Twenty to begin with, but that number will increase to fifty by the end of the first year. I will also need access to intelligence officers, military officers, bankers, industrialists...

representatives from every facet of China's financial, industrial, technological, diplomatic, intelligence, military, and government segments. They must be trustworthy to a fault, open minded, and focused on what it takes to make things happen—practical, not theoretical."

"Why trustworthy?" Yang Shangkun asked.

"Because if any nation gets wind of this, they could rally the world against us, and it would be game over."

There were nods around the table.

"You will be given a residence nearby, with a staff and a driver. You will have around-the-clock security. No one may know where you are, what you're doing, or why you no longer attend chess tournaments. Does that pose any problems for you?"

"No, General-Secretary. I am ready to do as you wish."

"Very good, Liang Hao, very good," Deng Xiaoping said. "Of course, it goes without saying what will happen to you if this strategy should fail."

Laing Hao swallowed hard and nodded. Everyone in China knew the price for failure.

For the next year, Liang Hao and his staff took the original strategy and began breaking it down into individual plans, timelines, dependencies, link points where the plans needed to come together, and resource lists. The amount of money that would be flowing out of China was staggering, but Liang Hao was confident in the strategy's ability to replenish much of that wealth in the future.

In early March of 1993, Liang Hao, the Chief Strategist of the Brilliancy and Trinity Gambit, gave the orders to make the opening moves of the strategy to conquer the world. China's agents began moving into position around the globe to carry out their instructions.

Now we play the game.

CHAPTER 5

Washington DC
October 2027

The plane from Seattle landed at Reagan National Airport just before 9:00 PM. Kate and Steve disembarked and headed for the main terminal.

"Do you have a car here?" Kate asked.

"No, I took a cab," Steve replied. "You?"

"Same."

"Do you still want to go straight to the Pentagon?"

"Definitely," Kate responded. "I slept on the plane, and now my brain's on overdrive. If I don't do something to process all of the information so I can make sense of it, I'll go nuts before Monday."

Steve pointed at the sign for Ground Transportation on their right. "Then let's grab a cab and get on over there."

They reached the taxi stand outside the main terminal and took the first cab in line. The vehicle pulled away and headed for the Pentagon. The five-minute ride was whisper quiet, thanks to the electric engine and the separated passenger compartment. With Washington being a capital city, most taxis had adopted security configurations so passengers could speak freely without the driver being able to overhear their conversation.

They got out at the River Entrance on the north side of the building and entered the security area. Even though it was late on a Friday evening, there were people working all throughout the building—some in uniform, and some in civilian clothes. Once past the security gates, they rode the crowded elevator up to the third floor and hurried to their secure workspace.

Kate looked down the hallway once the security system had allowed them inside. All of the offices and conference rooms were dark. They were alone. Motion sensors activated the hall lights and the break room lights as they walked toward Conference Room B, but everything else remained dark.

Once inside their workroom, Steve asked, "Want me to get us some water?" The break room at the end of the hall—which doubled as their office supply storage closet—had bottled water and other beverages, as well as a variety of snacks.

Even though they had eaten on the plane, Kate knew that hunger was no recipe for good work. "Yes. And snacks. Lots of snacks."

Steve smiled. "Coming up."

He left the conference room and was gone for a few minutes. When he returned, he carried a printer paper box lid with several bottles of water, bags of popcorn and chips, candy bars, protein and meal bars, and fresh fruit to keep them fed throughout the night.

Kate grabbed a water; then she walked over to the safes to retrieve the latest intelligence reports. Not knowing which folders and flash drives she needed, she pulled them all out and dumped them on the table. Several of the folders skidded across the table and nearly fell off the edge next to Steve.

"You really *are* frustrated," Steve commented as he pushed the folders near him back into a pile.

Kate just reached for a folder and began reading.

Five hours later, Kate was even more frustrated. Finally, she slammed down the folder she had just been reading about Mexico and groaned loudly.

"What's up?" Steve asked, looking up from the intel he was reading on Russia.

"This isn't working." Kate stood and began walking around the room. For the first time, she noticed that there were floor to ceiling whiteboard panels on every wall in the room. She smiled.

"Where are the whiteboard markers?"

Steve pointed toward the break room. "End of the hall with the rest of the office supplies."

Kate exited the conference room and walked down the hall to the break room. She found several dozen unopened sets of magnetic whiteboard markers and erasers on the office supply shelves in the far corner. She grabbed two, stared at the remaining sets for a moment, and then grabbed a third. On her way out, she stopped at the refrigerator and grabbed two more apples before walking back to the conference room.

She put the fruit with the other snacks. Then she put the markers on the table, opened one of the sets, and grabbed three different colors. She walked up to one of the whiteboard panels and touched the side of a marker to it. The marker stuck. She walked around the room and touched the other two markers to panels on adjacent walls. Then she grabbed another unopened set of markers, grabbed all of them, and stuck them to the whiteboard panel on the fourth wall.

Steve watched as she went back to the first panel, grabbed the marker, and wrote "Europe-Middle East-Africa" at the top before reattaching the marker to the wall. On the panel on the next wall, she wrote "Asia-Pacific & Russia." On the panel on the third wall, she wrote "Latin American Block." Then she walked to the wall with the complete set of markers and wrote "North America-Caribbean-North Atlantic."

Steve watched her look around the room. "Wanna let me

know what's going on?"

Kate was about to answer when she saw that there was another smaller whiteboard on the wall across from the door. She grabbed one of the unused markers from the first set and walked over to it. She stared at the blank pane for a moment, and then she wrote "Handbasket" at the top. She attached the marker to the panel and turned to face Steve.

"Handbasket?" he asked.

Kate smiled. "As in 'the world's going to hell in a…'"

"Got it."

Kate gestured around the room. "My dad used to say to me, 'Katie, the world's going to hell in a handbasket. It's up to you to find a way to break the cycle and solve this problem instead of just making it worse like so many people have done.' That's one of the reasons I joined the Agency."

Pointing to the folders on the table, she continued. "There's too much data here. We need to organize it. When I'm stuck, I create timelines so I can visually see what has happened. That way I can look for patterns more easily. If we can create timelines—working backwards from today to the point where the world really started going to hell in a handbasket—we might be able to spot commonalities or common triggers that will help us understand why the rest of the world is embroiled in three regional wars, what triggered them, and what it means to the United States."

"You mean which one will suck us in?" Steve asked, getting to his feet.

Kate nodded. "Or which of the three aggressors will turn their attention toward us next."

"Okay. How do you want to do this?"

Kate slid a box of markers across the table to Steve. "Let's go around the room and list all of the events and their dates that we can think of. Then we'll work together and sort them into a timeline. If you think of something that doesn't make sense or you think it needs to be dug into deeper, write that on the "Handbasket" panel. Keep everything on the large panels the same color. If you write something on the Handbasket panel that links to another panel, use the other panel's color so we can see the linkage."

Steve nodded, and the two of them went to work.

After a couple of hours, all of the whiteboard panels were filled with notes. Kate looked at each panel and nodded in satisfaction. "This helps. It's starting to make sense."

Steve stood next to her. "It does, and I already see a common trigger."

"Which one?"

Steve walked over to the North America-Caribbean-North Atlantic panel and circled the notation about the U.S. military forces being recalled from their duty stations round the world. He then put an asterisk on the three other large panels next to the notations "Aggression Began."

"All three of the regional wars began at almost the same time, and they all started as soon as the United States withdrew from the rest of the world."

Kate nodded. "That can't be a coincidence, can it?"

"I don't think so." Steve pulled up a chair in front of the North America-Caribbean-North Atlantic panel and sat down. "Let's start here. I'm curious about several of the notes you wrote. You've got things listed that go all the way back to the early 90s."

Kate pulled over a chair and sat next to Steve. "I wanted to put things into context. I don't believe that the U.S. pulling away from the rest of the world was an accident. If that's the case, then we have to look at the events that led to the changes in U.S. domestic, foreign, and military policy."

"Show me," Steve said.

Kate stood. "Okay. Let's look at what happened in the late 1980s and early 1990s. We had Reagan and Bush Senior as presidents. The Soviet Union collapsed, the Cold War ended, Gulf War I was fought and won, and America regained the pride it lost during the Carter and Nixon administrations. Then out of nowhere, Governor Clinton won the nomination of his party for president when there were others who were considered the odds-on favorites. And he was elected over a president that oversaw two of the most monumental events in recent history. Clinton then proceeded to undo all the good that Reagan and Bush Senior had done. He muddled our foreign policy so badly that none of our allies knew what they could depend on us to do, he attempted to give China Most Favored Nation status, and he failed to extradite Osama bin Laden—or UBL as the Agency's Alex Station designated him—after the country that captured him literally tried to give him to us several times. For eight years, the U.S. slid backwards."

Kate then pointed to other notations on the panel. "Then Bush Junior was elected president, and 9-11 happened, orchestrated by UBL. We began to see terrorists everywhere, and draconian laws were passed that gave the government unprecedented—and arguably unconstitutional—powers to pry and spy on private citizens. The country was united for a while, but it was united out of fear. As the fear began to dissipate, so did the unity, and by the end of Bush Junior's tenure, the country was beginning to show deep cracks all around. In fact, his two elections were also the first time that voter fraud on a massive scale was uncovered and then covered back up."

Steve chuckled. "My father used to joke that he was furious about *his* father starting to vote for one party, because he had only voted for the other party while he was still alive."

Kate nodded. "The cemetery vote, as we called it—one hundred and seventy percent voter turnout in some Florida counties, with all votes going to the party that those counties had never voted for before. Clearly someone was attempting to manipulate our elections to a particular end."

"And then Obama was elected," Steve noted.

"Correct," Kate said, pointing to her notations near the middle of the panel. "From out of nowhere, a freshman senator from Illinois, who had never held any real job that anyone could determine, defeated the old guard and won the nomination for president. Allegations about him having multiple Social Security numbers and multiple names, attending university as a foreign-national student, and not being a legal U.S. citizen were swept under the rug, and anyone making the allegations was ridiculed publically. And once elected, the classes and races became so polarized that the country nearly flew apart at the seams, and the country experienced one of the worst economic collapses in history. It was also the first major push toward socialism that the country had ever openly witnessed."

"It's amazing that we fought three wars and the cold war for over 60 years to stop the spread of totalitarian socialism—Nazism, Sovietism, and Maoism—only to suddenly embrace it here at home as soon as the Soviet Union collapsed."

"And that was just the first time we embraced it, as it turns out," Kate point out.

She continued. "And then Trump was elected on a campaign to undo Obama's damage and secure our borders, which had become little more than revolving doors under the Obama administration. Then a new Trade War and Cold War began to emerge. And what happened next? A plague got released worldwide—one of the Covid strains. Which number was it?"

"Covid-19," Steve replied.

"Right. Number 19. The first one was SARS, right?"

"I think so," Steve replied.

"So in the middle of a Trade War with China, we had a pandemic that started in China by a strain of Covid that was created in China. Economies around the world collapsed, businesses closed permanently because there was no money coming in, and people were so scared that they stayed at home for months out of fear. And just as that situation began to improve, a case of police brutality in one city triggered riots, looting, burnings, and police executions all over the country. Cities even began defunding their own police forces to give in to the rioters as a way to appease them into ending the violence. For the next several years, every time the country was about to return to normal, something else happened to drive wedges between us, keeping races, classes, and geographies separated and fighting each other."

"And then President Munger got elected," Steve said.

"Right. In 2024, another candidate who came out of nowhere. His entire platform was about peace, healing, and unity. No one knew who he was, his background seemed unimpressive, and he refused to debate his opponents during the campaign. He claimed that he wasn't running to compare himself to others but to restore the peace and harmony of the nation. He was like an aging hippy, but the country bought it hook, line, and sinker. He didn't even hold fundraisers, and no one looked too deeply at who was funding his campaign. The general election was a farce with over 50 million more votes cast than there were living registered voters. Munger got elected in a landslide."

"And that's when things turned upside down," Steve remarked.

"That's putting it mildly. His first day in office in 2025, he signed two executive orders. The first one was to muzzle the press. They protested loudly—after all, they had been instrumental in helping to divide the country and causing people to lose faith in all of its institutions. But Munger told the nation that he couldn't afford the press causing people to lose confidence in his programs to bring the country back together. He told America that the way the press presented information was too divisive and would stand in the way of the progress he was making. Then suddenly the press stopped complaining and went silent, like obedient dogs. And nobody thought twice about it. He banned all kinds of public assemblies that he claimed were the kinds of rallies that ended in lawlessness and rioting, but the way he worded the executive order also banned peaceful assemblies. Again, no one complained."

"And that's when he signed the executive order to recall all of our armed forces."

Kate gestured to the panels around the walls. "And that's when everything else started, beginning with the United Nations disbanding. Turkey, Syria, and Iran formed a new Islamic Caliphate, the Middle East rose in support, and their combined forces overran Israel in days. Then they swept across Africa, uniting all of the Islamic regimes and forces there. Once Africa had fallen under the Caliphate's control, all of the Islamic immigrants in Europe rose up and started fighting. That's when NATO and the European Union collapsed. By the way, that's something else to add to the Handbasket wall. Why did the EU begin overruling the sovereign rights of its member nations and force them to accept Islamic refugees into their country unchecked? That policy allowed tens of thousands of insurgents to be positioned all over Europe, waiting for the moment to strike. No wonder countries began withdrawing from the EU over the past decade. Anyway, thanks to that terrible policy, by the time the Caliphate's forces reached southern Europe, they met little resistance. Now the British are hanging on by a thread, and the remnants of Europe's armed forces have fled to Norway, Sweden, and Finland as the last stand against the darkness."

"And that's one of the things *I* added on the Handbasket panel," Steve said.

"What?"

Steve stood up and walked over to the Asia-Pacific & Russia panel. "Chechnya."

"What about it?" Kate asked.

"It's the only part of Russia that's primarily Islamic,"

Steve explained. "It's close to the Turkish border. In fact, only Georgia stands between it and Turkey in that strip of land between the Caspian and Black seas. But the Caliphate forces have ignored them. The Caliphate never crossed the Russian border to help what should have been considered its greatest ally in Russia and a stepping-stone in the conquest of western Russia. In fact, the Caliphate hasn't crossed the Russian border anywhere. Just look at the Scandinavian Peninsula. Yes, the Øresund Bridge between Denmark and Sweden was destroyed, but there's a land route to reach Finland, Sweden, and Norway that the Caliphate hasn't used. Why? Because they'd have to cross the Russian border to go from Baltic Republic of Estonia to Finland by land, and for some reason they won't do that, even though the Russians moved their Baltic fleet to Murmansk. The Caliphate forces haven't even moved north out of Poland into Belarus or the Republics of Lithuania or Latvia yet."

Kate looked at Steve's notation on the Handbasket panel. "Well, China has already taken all of eastern Russia. Perhaps they told the Caliphate to stay out."

"But why would the Caliphate listen to China? China has been repressing its Islamic population for decades. If anything, you'd think the Caliphate would want to rip China a new one at the first opportunity."

Kate frowned; she knew that Steve had a valid point. "Let's come back to that. I think we need to look deeper into the whole Russia situation."

Steve nodded and took his seat again.

Kate walked over to the Latin American Block panel. "This is the one that has me the most confused," she remarked.

"Me, too."

Kate continued. "Mexico, Venezuela, and Columbia banded together, and with the funding of the cartels, and the help of several corrupt government and military leaders, they swept across Central and South America, bringing all of the Latin

American Block countries under one rule—currently, the President of Mexico. But why? What was their end game? It makes no sense. The cartels aren't getting any richer, the economic condition of those countries hasn't improved, the people are no better off, they've made no aggressive moves toward our southern border or the Caribbean... What was the point?"

"It's almost like they were acting on someone else's behalf," Steve commented.

Kate turned and stared at him. "Say that again."

"It's like Mexico, Venezuela, Columbia, and the cartels were acting on behalf of someone else. Someone who wanted chaos in the western hemisphere. Someone who wanted the U.S. distracted here so we wouldn't focus on what was happening somewhere else."

Kate thought about this for several minutes. "Sleight of hand," she finally suggested.

"You mean like what a magician does?"

Kate nodded. She saw it clearly for the first time. "We became a totalitarian socialist nation and recalled all of our forces from around the world. The president suspended the First Amendment, but when he signed the executive order to suspend the Second Amendment and disarm all civilians, a resistance movement started. Then it was revealed that President Munger intended to capitulate to China, becoming a protectorate of the Chinese to keep us out of the wars that were starting around the world. When his plan was exposed, the military mutinied, the resistance formalized into a huge fighting force, and the fastest Civil War in North American history took place to overthrow the Munger presidency. The state legislatures called for an 'Article V Convention' to amend the Constitution and redefine the limits of the executive, legislative, and judicial branches of the government, and to reaffirm the unalterable rights of all U.S. citizens. Then new elections were held, and that's when

President MacKendrick was elected. America was ready to retake its place as a superpower, but Central and South America were embroiled in a conflict that we'd surely have to deal with first before looking to help the rest of the world."

"And then the Chinese threaten Canada into capitulating like Munger was about to do, which would have the U.S. sandwiched between a Chinese protectorate to our north and the Latin American situation to our south." Steve walked around the room to the Handbasket panel. "If you wanted to keep the U.S. out of your business, what better way to accomplish it?"

"Meaning that everything—all of this—is really the design of one source?" Kate asked.

"Why not?" Steve asked.

Kate sat down. Her mind was racing, and in the middle of it, she remembered something that Iain had said to her in Vancouver. "Trinity."

"What?" Steve looked confused.

"Trinity! Remember when I told you that Iain had a contact in China that managed to get three words out before he was killed? The words were 'Brilliancy' and 'Trinity Gambit.'" Kate gestured around the room. "What if we're looking at the Trinity Gambit right here?"

"The three regional wars?" Steve asked. He looked around the room slowly. "Could be... But what about 'Brilliancy?'"

Kate moved toward the conference table and slid aside one of the panels that concealed a computer tablet. "Iain said that it's a chess term." She tapped the tablet screen and looked at the definition of Brilliancy. "A Brilliancy is a combination of strategies designed to overwhelm an opponent and force them to withdraw from the game."

Steve stared at the North America-Caribbean-North Atlantic panel. "Could *we* be the Brilliancy? Could the U.S. becoming a totalitarian socialist nation and withdrawing our armed forces be the decisive defeat needed for the Trinity

Gambit to launch around the world?"

"My God," Kate exclaimed. "We've been played from the very start." She walked over to the North America-Caribbean-North Atlantic panel. "Everything that has happened for the past thirty-plus years has been part of someone else's game. We're all just pawns…" She looked up at Steve. "Chess. Everything keeps pointing to a chess game."

"Multiple chess games," Steve noted. "Our real enemy is a chess master, and we didn't even know the game had started."

"No telling how far the game has gone if we've been caught up in one for thirty years, if not longer."

Steve tapped his marker on the Asia-Pacific & Russia panel. "We still haven't figured out how China fits into all of this."

Kate walked over to the panel and stood next to Steve. "China indeed. Before anyone knew that they were on the move, they regained the one thing they've wanted for nearly 80 years: Taiwan. Then they invaded Japan, something they had tried to conquer several times ever since the Mongol Empire ruled China. Next, North and South Korea, Viet Nam, Cambodia, Laos, and Thailand fell. China overran all of the Asian countries on the mainland in less than six months. Then they took the Philippines, Malaysia, and Indonesia. And then they shocked everyone and invaded Australia! New Zealand fell next. What I don't understand is after they took Nepal, they took India. India has a huge Islamic population. Why didn't the Caliphate insist on taking India when it had the chance?"

"That's another anomaly between the Caliphate and China that we've identified," Steve said. He wrote that on the Handbasket panel.

"You're the expert on China," Kate said when Steve rejoined her. "Was there any intel that said China was about to invade Russia?"

"Not a word," Steve replied. "Although we all should have

guessed it. The Soviet Union had been pushing against China's northern border for decades. It only makes sense that they'd retaliate someday. But moving against Vladivostok, Petropavlovsk-Kamchatskiy, Magadan, and Sovetskaya Gavan to seize Russia's Pacific deep-water fleet was not just unexpected, it was genius. It more than tripled the size of China's Navy and gave them access to dozens of attack and missile submarines, along with Russia's entire surface fleet and strategic weapons in the Pacific. It changed the balance of power in the Pacific forever. And then they pushed west all the way to the Urals before the Russians regrouped and began mounting an effective defense using the mountains…"

Steve turned and saw Kate over at the Handbasket panel, writing furiously. "What are you doing?"

"I finally figured it out," was all she would say.

Steve walked over to see what she was writing. He watched for several minutes until she looked up at him with a look of triumph on her face.

"What?" Steve asked.

"Remember when I told you that something I said and something you said in Vancouver was stuck in my mind, but I couldn't figure it out?"

"Vaguely."

"I figured it out. I said that China had plans for Britain and Canada. You said that China would be willing to its plot revenge for centuries. The Chinese obviously had plans for the U.S. if President Munger was about to capitulate to them. The Islamic Caliphate has resisted going up against the Chinese for no apparent reason. The chess game that the U.S. has been caught up in has been going on for decades. What's the one thing that all of these have in common?"

"China," Steve replied.

"Exactly!"

"So you're saying that China planned all of this," Steve

gestured around the room, "and manipulating the U.S. into withdrawing its forces allowed three regional wars to begin?"

"Not begin," Kate corrected him. "They had already been set in motion. Perhaps years earlier. But everything was waiting for the U.S. to withdraw its forces and turn its attention on itself so the actual fighting could start without our interference. Now who do we know that could plan something so intricate, so meticulous, so far reaching?"

"China." Steve looked impressed. "But it's only a theory, not fact."

"A theory that fits the facts almost perfectly," Kate countered. "How did Israel fall so quickly? We weren't there to protect them. How did Taiwan and Japan fall? We weren't there to protect them. How did NATO fall so quickly? We weren't there to protect them. How did Latin America fall so quickly? We weren't there to protect them! It all fits! Our military forces around the world had been keeping everything in check, and as soon as we removed them, three aggressors rose up and practically conquered the rest of the world. And look at where things stand now in the U.S. We have a huge undocumented Islamic population, so we're at risk from them if we make a move to liberate Europe. We have a huge undocumented Hispanic population, so we're at risk from *them* if we make a move against Central and or South America. And should we make any moves in the Pacific... well, remember: China owns most of our debt, they control most of our manufacturing and hi-tech industries, they have massive real estate and bank holdings across the country, and there's a huge Chinese population here in the U.S. and in Canada. Hell, our recent Civil War is probably the only thing that kept the rest of the world from going up in flames already, and now Canada is being threatened to hold us in check."

"So you don't believe that the recent Civil War was part of China's plan?"

Kate shook her head. "Why would it be? One moment, we've become a socialist nation and are about to surrender to China without them having to fire a shot at us, and the next moment we've overthrown our socialist government and are reestablishing ourselves as a world power. If that was part of their plan, it's a pretty stupid one, don't you think? And it could explain why they're behind the Latin American crisis and what's happening in Canada right now—their response to us going off plan."

"That could be true," Steve conceded. "And by the way, 'hold us in check' is another chess term."

"Chess, chess, chess..." Kate stopped. Her eyes widened. "How long would you estimate that China might have been planning all of this?"

"Assuming that China is behind it all?" Steve closed his eyes for a minute. "If you're right that this all started in the early 90s—let's say about the same time that the Soviet Union fell—then they've been working on it for about thirty-six years."

"Typical of the Chinese?" Kate asked.

Steve nodded.

"And it feels like multiple chess games are being played on a world stage, right? You said so yourself."

Steve nodded again.

"And the use of chess terms and chess moves would imply that someone well familiar with the game of chess could be behind the overall strategy that China is following, right?"

Steve stared at her. Then he went over to the exposed tablet in the conference table. "I'm going to see if any Chinese chess grandmasters disappeared around thirty-six years ago."

"Why disappeared?" Kate asked, sitting next to him at the table.

"Because you don't devise a strategy like this and then hand it off to someone else while you go play in chess tournaments. The strategy would need constant monitoring and

72

adjusting—moves and countermoves. The Chinese would make him stay with the strategy until the games were finally won. He would have dropped out of sight around that time; the Chinese would want to keep him safe and away from the public eye."

Not finding what he was looking for, Steve expanded his search. Then he found an article about a chess tournament in Berlin from May 1992. The headline read, "Chinese Chess Grandmaster Liang Hao Misses First Tournament Since Defeating Russian Opponent Seven Years Ago."

"Look at this." Steve moved over to give Kate room to see the tablet.

Kate leaned over and read the article. "Liang Hao," she said to herself. "China's youngest grandmaster at the time he missed the tournament. He defeated the Russian grandmaster years earlier in just four moves! Sounds like someone the Chinese would use to create their strategy, don't you think?"

"Possibly," Steve admitted. Pointing to the Handbasket panel, he added, "We still have some anomalies to work through before we can state with any certainty that we're on the right track."

Kate nodded and glanced at her watch. "It's 6:30 AM, and we've been up all night. Why don't we go to the cafeteria and get some breakfast. Then we can come back up here, work through the unanswered questions, match the timeline we've created against the intel we've been receiving, and then decide if we feel that this is the right direction. If we do, we'll break for the day, come back tomorrow, and spend the day documenting our brief to deliver to the rest of the team on Monday. Otherwise, we'll call it a weekend and start fresh on Monday. Deal?"

Steve nodded. "Deal."

Kate gathered the folders and flash drives, and she locked them in the safe. Then she and Steve left the conference room.

CHAPTER 6

Beijing • Bogota • Kandahar • Khartoum •
Macau • Maastricht • Wuhan
1993-2026

Kandahar, 1993

The intermediary—a native of Bangladesh who had been a Chinese operative for years—entered the house on the outskirts of Kandahar, Afghanistan where seven leaders of the Taliban waited for him. The meeting had taken months to set up, since the various Taliban leaders, who had been the leaders of the mujahideen—freedom fighters against the Soviet occupation of Afghanistan—distrusted each other as much as they hated the Soviets. They had come together against their common enemy, but in the absence of that enemy, old hatreds flared and threatened the war-torn country with a new and terrible civil war.

The intermediary bowed as a sign of respect. "As-salam alaykom," he said. *Peace be upon you.*

The leaders responded, "Wa Alykom As-salam." *Unto you be peace.* He was directed to sit and passed a cup of a steaming liquid that smelled of peppered tea.

"You asked to see us," the leader seated in the middle said after a moment.

"I did," the intermediary acknowledged. "I've come to

help you."

"Did you know we needed help?" one of the leaders asked his fellow leaders. The leaders chucked.

"I don't see that we need any help," the first leader stated flatly.

The intermediary opened his satchel and withdrew seven flat gold ingots with no markings on them—untraceable. He tossed them on the pillows in front of the leaders. "Are you quite certain about that?"

The first leader's hand flew for the Charay Khyber knife tucked in his sash. "You attempt to buy us?" he shouted. "I will gut you like a goat."

The intermediary remained calm. "Not at all. Forgive me if it appears that way. This is not a bribe. This is funding. A gift from a friend."

"Explain!" The first leader kept his hand on the hilt of his Charay knife.

"The Soviets all but destroyed your country," the intermediary said smoothly. "Now the people are trying to learn how to lead themselves again. All of you were once united against the common enemy, but now you've splintered into warring factions just as you were before the Soviet occupation. But your destiny is to rule, not fight among yourselves. While you squabble, the people of Afghanistan are selecting others to lead them. Others! After all that you did to free them from the Soviets! Where's the gratitude for your sacrifice? Where's the respect? No, this must not be. You should rule this land, but you need money to rebuild and transform your armies into a united fighting force that can take and hold this country... and then expand your borders as your power and influence grows throughout the region. You need to recruit more fighters, train them, supply them, feed them, clothe them, and lead them. This takes money—more money than Afghanistan has left, after the Soviets stripped it bare. This," the intermediary gestured toward the gold on the floor, "is a sample of what I can provide. Gold, weapons, training… you could be the envy of the world, and I want to help make that happen."

The first leader relaxed his grip on the Charay knife's hilt. "And what's in it for you?"

The intermediary smiled. "Unity in the region under powerful and stable leadership. Plus, there are natural resources owned by your neighbors in the region that we'd like exclusive access to… or at least access to at a price well below market value. For these and other considerations that we'll discuss later, we're prepared to provide all of the funding you need for as long as you need it to take what is rightfully yours. Everyone needs generous friends. Don't you?"

The intermediary reached into his satchel and produced seven more ingots. He tossed them next to the others. The sound of the ingots clinking against each other made a distinctive sound that echoed softly throughout the room.

"And who is it who is being so generous with us?" one of the other leaders asked.

"That doesn't really matter, does it?" The intermediary upended his satchel, dumping even more gold ingots on the floor in front of them.

"No," the first leader stated, removing his hand from his knife.

The leaders looked at each other and began to laugh—not mockingly, but as people let in on an inside joke. Then they reached for the gold in the floor in front of them.

Khartoum, 1993

The Filipino businessman in the employ of the Chinese was escorted into the dimly lit room in the back of the Hookah Lounge in the heart of the Sudanese capital city of Khartoum. His blindfold was removed, and he was forced into a chair with its back to the door. He blinked several times to clear his vision, and then he saw the tall man sitting across from him.

"Are you bin Laden?" the businessman asked.

"Yes," came the curt reply.

"Do you know why I'm here?"

Bin Laden shifted in his seat. "I'm told that your associates have supplied arms and funding to the Taliban, and that now you wish to do the same for me."

"That is correct," the Filipino confirmed. "We have a common goal and a common enemy. You have the network of operatives needed to carry out operations well-beyond this region, and we have the financial resources and weapons to support your activities."

"And why should I allow *you* to help *me*?"

"Because we'll help you do things that others have only dreamed about. Operations that will bring nations to their knees and elevate you to the spiritual and military head of the next Caliphate."

"Why do *you* care about that?" bin Laden demanded.

"Because we have a common goal and a common enemy. So far, your efforts against that enemy have been to attack their presence here in this region. What if I told you that we'd help you attack them on their own soil—drive a knife right through their heart?"

"It has been tried," bin Laden said dismissively.

"Not by us," the Filipino stated.

Bin Laden was curious. "What do you have in mind?"

The Filipino pulled out a folded set of papers from his jacket pocket and slid them across the table. Bin Laden picked them up, unfolded them, and read. After several minutes, he stared at the Filipino.

"You're quite serious about this?"

The Filipino nodded.

Bin Laden's expression showed the difficulty he was

having controlling his rage. "A second attack on the same target that we failed to damage a few months ago, but this one designed to succeed so devastatingly that the enemy might never recover? Are you trying to mock me? Do you think our failure was just a joke?"

"Not at all. Your recent attempt will lull them into a false belief that the target is indestructible. You will show them that it is not. If this new attack is coupled by a number of other attacks at the same time, then it is entirely possible that the enemy won't recover from it."

Bin Laden leaned back in his chair. "Tell me more."

An hour later, the Filipino drove through the streets of Khartoum toward the airport. When he reached the airport, he went to a payphone and placed a call to a secure line. "Four-two-three-three."

"Connecting," said the voice on the other end.

Another voice came on the line a moment later. "Report."

"Meeting successful."

"Good. Are you heading for your next meeting?"

"Yes. But tell me again why I should meet with two organizations that are essentially the same. We have al-Qaeda onboard…"

"Because al-Qaeda will eventually be defeated for what it is going to do, and we need someone to pick up the torch when they fall."

"I understand."

The line went dead. The Filipino hung up the receiver and headed for his departure gate.

Beijing, 1993

Liang Hao met with several bankers, industrialists, and members of the diplomatic corps to set the next phase of the strategy in motion.

"We're going to take over two former Soviet Union initiatives and re-task them for our own purposes," Liang Hao announced.

"Which initiatives?" one of the diplomatic corps members asked.

"Beginning with Stalin, but continued by Khrushchev, Brezhnev, and Andropov, the Soviets infiltrated the West's educational institutions with the objective to train the future generations to embrace world socialism, distrust capitalism, and work to bring socialism to the Western world—focusing primarily on college-level journalism, business, and economics studies, but also infiltrating the primary education levels. It worked very well in Europe, but it gained a significant foothold in America during and after the Viet Nam conflict. Since there is no longer a Soviet Union to support that initiative, we are going to step in and use it for ourselves. We need to increase socialism's acceptance in the West if our strategy is to succeed."

"And the second initiative?" the diplomatic corps member asked.

"It builds off the first one," Liang Hao replied. "Control of the media. Even Stalin knew that whoever controls information controls the minds of a nation. American news outlets are overextended financially. They are worried about something called *ratings*, and they've embraced a ridiculous concept they call *infotainment*, trying to turn news into entertainment to bolster their viewership. We are going to invest in these news outlets until we control them. Then *we* control what people know and what they think... about any and everything."

"An excellent plan," the diplomatic corps member said.

"Next, we are going to set up a number of large companies around the world," Liang Hao stated. "They will be... what is the American word... *conglomerates* that will have dozens of subsidiaries. Those subsidiaries will also have a number of subsidiaries. These will include investment banking, manufacturing, high-tech, real estate, stock brokerages, media outlets, and other companies that will advance the strategy."

"Won't we need to buy or build manufacturing facilities where these conglomerates are located?" one of the industrialists asked.

Liang Hao just smiled. "Why would we do that? These companies will only exist on paper. None of it will be real. Oh, they will produce financial reports, they will pay their taxes, but they will not actually *do* anything. They are our way of infiltrating the West and seizing control of their economies."

Liang Hao tossed a set of dossiers onto the table. "For instance, one of the conglomerates will be set up in Northern California. There is a politician who is in the U.S. House of Representatives, and that is her district. She is broke, and her husband has had a steady string of failed businesses throughout his career. She cannot pay off her campaign debt, and the people she borrowed money from are closing in around her. We are going to make her husband a director of one of the conglomerate's subsidiaries, and we will also hire him as a consultant to one of the other subsidiaries."

"What will he be consulting about?" the industrialist asked.

"Nothing," Liang Hao replied.

"So we're going to pay him consulting fees for doing nothing?" one of the bankers asked.

"Correct."

"What about his directorship?" the industrialist asked.

"He will not do a thing there either," Liang Hao stated. "We cannot be seen bribing public officials, but we can hire their spouses or other family members. What we will pay this politician's husband will pay off her debts and allow her to live a lavish lifestyle. We will fund her future campaigns through the subsidiaries for a while. Then, when she needs us the most, we will stop funding her campaigns and start funding one of her competitors. That is when we will tell her the price for our continued support. If she agrees, we will stop funding her competitor and restart funding her campaigns. From that moment on, we will own her vote, and we will own her."

"All the way to the White House?" another banker asked.

Liang Hao shook his head. "She is too corrupt already for that, and she will be even more corrupt by the time we are finished with her. There are other positions in the U.S. government where she can serve our needs without her being the face of our initiatives."

The banker frowned. "If she's so corrupt, how do we keep her under control? How can we ensure that she's not taking our money with no intention of giving us what we need?"

A member of the diplomatic corps spoke up. "We can plant a spy in her staff," he suggested. "Or we can put an agent of ours close to her in a position to hear her conversations—especially when she thinks her conversations are private."

"What kind of position would allow us to listen in on her private conversations?" the banker asked.

The member of the diplomatic corps smiled. "We typically use chauffeurs. He could plant listening devices in the car and monitor her phone calls. And if he becomes a trusted member of her staff, he could also plant listening devices in her home and office."

The banker nodded approvingly.

"What if we find out she's cheating us?" the industrialist asked.

Liang Hao chuckled. "Then we fold the conglomerate that has been paying her husband and financing her campaigns, and we make public all of her corrupt acts. It will destroy her, and it will serve as a warning to the others."

There were nods around the room.

Liang Hao went through a list of American politicians that they would be investing in, including governors, senators, and congressional representatives.

"We will also be investing in organizations that will help keep America divided," Liang Hao stated. "NAACP, ACLU, Black Panthers, white supremacists, neo Nazis, anti-government militias, secessionists… if they can create division and enrage others, we will fund them."

"What will the investment banks do?" one of the bankers asked.

"Target struggling companies in industries that we want to control," Liang Hao replied. "We purchase their debt, and then we take control of them. After that, we start moving their manufacturing and product development here to China. Then we buy their competitors, merge them together, and move *their* manufacturing and product development here as well. Before anyone knows what we have done, we own the economic engine of the entire nation, in addition to the supply line for consumer goods that are in high demand."

"Will this be limited to the United States?" one of the members of the diplomatic corps asked.

"Oh, no," Liang Hao assured him. "This will be going on in every geographic region that we ultimately want to control. We will sow hate and fear while making them totally dependent on us. We will purchase their national debt until no country would dare to defy us out of fear of us cutting them off from our funding. But remember, this must all be done through legitimate-looking companies. These conglomerates must be a spider's web of subsidiaries, holding companies, and international corporations that completely shield us as the source behind it all. We must be invisible, and we must avoid giving anyone a reason to dig deeper into what these fictitious company are really doing."

The representative from Malaysia in the employ of the Chinese sat down in his hotel room with the delegates from Belgium, France, Italy, Luxembourg, the Netherlands, and West Germany.

"Ladies and Gentlemen, I've been reviewing your treaty for the re-envisioning of a European Union that goes beyond simply an economic block to counter the United States and Japan. I find it absolutely fascinating. Could you tell me if it has sufficient support for ratification?"

"Why do you want to know?" The delegate from Italy asked.

"Because I see it as a blueprint for something that might work to bring peace and prosperity across Asia," the Malaysian replied. "We have been exploited for generations, we've been pawns in the wars of others, and we are unable to stand on our own without help. Who should we turn to? China? They've been part of the problem all along. Perhaps if we were to turn to each other, we could stand united for the first time in our histories. Your treaty is a beacon of hope for other regions around the world who desperately need such unity. That is why I want to know. If you succeed, then perhaps we can replicate your success ourselves."

The French delegate spoke up. "It has support, but not enough for ratification. We have little funding with which to get our message out to those we need to reach and convince. Besides, people are afraid of a unified Europe. They remember all too well the last time Europe was under a single government."

"Until we can move past the memories of Nazism," the West German delegate interjected, "there is little hope of building the unity that we envision."

"What do you need to help convince the people of the positive intentions you are proposing?"

"Funding," the delegate from the Netherlands stated. "We

must advertise, inform, educate. We cannot do this without funding, and our governments have little funding to invest in this venture."

The Malaysian nodded. "What if we could provide you with funding?"

"Why would you do that?" the delegate from Luxembourg inquired. "You're not part of Europe."

"No," the Malaysian admitted, "but we have a vested interest in your success. If you succeed, we might succeed in doing the same. If you fail, none of the countries in my region will take a unifying initiative seriously. They'll point to your failure as proof that it will never work for us. We need your success if we're to convince our own people that unity is the answer."

"How much funding do you propose?" the Italian delegate asked.

The Malaysian quoted a number.

"You're serious?" the French delegate asked.

The Malaysian nodded.

"And what do you get from this?" the West German delegate asked.

"A chance to save my own people. And hopefully closer relations between our Union—if we succeed in creating one—and your Union. Of course, I'd need access to some of your inner workings if I'm going to replicate it for Asia—nothing confidential, of course, but just enough so that we may learn from any mistakes you make along the way."

"That seems reasonable," the delegate from Belgium stated. The others nodded in agreement.

Macau, 1993

The banker from Beijing entered the building where the owners of the Macau gambling houses waited for him. Representatives from the Singapore gambling houses were there as well.

"Good evening, gentlemen," the banker said as he sat down across from the others in the room. "Shall we get right to the point?"

Before they could answer, he pulled out a stack of financial reports and contracts from his briefcase and put them on the table in front of him. "How long to do you expect to remain in business if you keep losing money like this?"

The others in the room were shocked. Before they could protest, the banker continued. "Don't even bother trying to lie to me. Your combined losses are in the tens of billions, while casinos in America and Europe are making more money than ever. Attendance at your gambling houses is off forty-five percent, and there's no indication that it's coming back anytime soon. Macao is no longer the gambling destination of the world, and Singapore is no better off. If it weren't for Singapore's sex trade, no one would go there at all. Those are the facts. You know it. I know it. The question is this: do you want my help or not?"

"What kind of help?" one of the owners from Macao asked.

"Unlimited funding for starters," the banker began. "and complete coverage of your outstanding debts."

"In return for what?" the owner from Macao demanded.

The banker leaned forward. "We own you. But you'll continue to run things on our behalf. We'll form a syndicate to run gambling here, and another syndicate to run gambling in Singapore. We'll put up the investment money to update your casinos, build hotels and resorts, and modernize every aspect of your operations. And then, through you, we'll invest in casinos and resorts around the world. For instance, there are three in the United States that we're interested in: two in southern Connecticut and one in Oklahoma. These are small Indian casinos now, but we see potential in them. And with enough money, we can have laws changed that will allow casinos all across the United States, breaking organized crime's control of Las Vegas and Atlantic City gambling once and for all. Then you'll partner with the Las Vegas casinos and resorts to bring their brands here. We'll invest in their operations and help them expand, and then, through you, we'll control gambling across the globe. You'll be the face of the first global gambling syndicate, and no one will ever know that we're the bank and the *true* owners."

The banker looked around the room. "Oh come on, gentlemen. It's an easy choice. Go bankrupt and close your doors forever, or sit on top of the largest gambling enterprise ever imagined... with all of the wealth and power that goes along with that. Do we have a deal? Or shall I call in your markers, which I just happen to have with me."

He opened his briefcase again and withdrew several stacks of paper tied in neat bundles. Each sheet had a stamp on it from the various gambling houses in Macao and Singapore.

"You have the contracts with you?" the owner from Macao asked.

The banker reached for the stack of contracts on the table and slid them across to the casino owners. "Of course."

The contracts were passed out, and the casino owners read through them. After several minutes, the Macao owner motioned to his aide, who handed the owner the jade *yin jian*—the company chop used to stamp official seals on a document. The owner signed his name on the contact and put the chop of his gambling house next to his signature. The others did the same. The banker collected the contracts, reviewed the signatures and chops, and then put the contacts in his briefcase.

Then he bent down and picked up the markers. He walked over to the fireplace on the far wall and tossed them in the fire.

"A pleasure doing business with you, gentlemen," he said, heading for the door. "My representatives will get in touch with you this week to set up the syndicate and begin the modernization and expansion of your businesses."

Bogota, 1995

It wasn't often that the heads of the Columbian cartels met together, but this was no ordinary occasion. A banker from China wanted to meet with them, and it was foolish to ignore a banker.

They selected a church as a neutral site—not an easy task since there were few neutral sites left in Columbia thanks to the constant infighting between the cartels, not to mention the government raids—aided by the United States military as part of their "War on Drugs."

The cartel heads were already assembled when they were notified that the banker had arrived. Chairs had been placed in a circle around the small chapel—each one with a side table next to it. This was to keep any of the attendees from reaching for a weapon unseen.

The banker entered the chapel and sat in the empty seat across from the windows. A large crucifix was mounted on the wall behind the chair. "Good morning, gentlemen," he said as he made himself comfortable.

"Your meeting, your agenda," the cartel head hosting the meeting stated.

The banker nodded his head. "I have a business proposition for you, and I'd like you to consider it very carefully."

The host gestured for the banker to continue.

"My employers feel that you have been underutilizing your resources, and your infighting is preventing you from realizing a critical economic reality: there is more money to be had by working together than there is by competing against each other. I'm here to propose several new business ventures that leverage your existing capabilities in new and profitable ways. But these ventures will only work if you stop fighting among yourselves and work together—with us—as partners. And not just us. We have partnerships with similar businesses as your own in other parts of the world that you'll be able to tap into—not as competitors, but as partners sharing resources, markets, risks, and rewards. We will provide your banking and investment needs, and you will use your capabilities to bring about certain... shall we say *strategic initiatives* of ours to a successful conclusion."

"How would that work?" the host inquired. "Competition has been a part of our business since it began."

"To what end?" the banker asked. "You cultivate new pipelines and markets, competition moves in, your business suffers while you deal with the competition, and you either lose your investment or you have to rebuild with whatever you have that survives. Each of you has your own product manufacturing, your own transportation and distribution networks, and your own security forces. Does the world need fourteen sources for cocaine? Does it need thirty sources for heroin? What if there were one group responsible for sourcing the products you sell, and multiple groups for getting that product to separate and individual markets? And what if those groups getting that product to market also handled other products? There are businesses around the world that need your services: human traffickers, terrorists, spies, thieves... the list is endless. You have developed tremendous capabilities, but you only bring in a fraction of what you could because you use them for a single purpose. How much money could you make by using them for multiple purposes? How much money could you keep if you weren't spending it on killing off the competition and then having to replace your own losses? How much money could you keep if, instead of each of you having to bribe public officials, your banker handled that on your behalf, allowing you to keep your money while we ensured that public officials were only bribed once and not by each of you individually—making them lots of money at your expense and cheating all but one of you each time you need something from them?"

"And I suppose that our competition across the globe has already agreed to this?" the host snorted.

"As a matter of fact, yes."

There were shocked looks around the room.

"You mean the opium and hashish producers in the Middle East have already agreed to work as part of a global cartel?" The host sounded skeptical.

"I mean exactly that," the banker said calmly. "As have the Africans, Malaysians, Indonesians, Australians, Thais, and Chinese. All we need is for you to agree, and the drug trade will be controlled globally for the first time, and each of you will have access to new markets and incalculable wealth as you branch into new ventures with our help."

"And what do you want in return?" the host asked.

"As I mentioned before, there are some strategic initiatives we have in mind for the Americas that we'll need help with in the future, but those won't start until after we get the new businesses set up and running profitably. You'll get your money first, and then you'll help us with our ventures. That seems fair, don't you think?"

"Why do I get the feeling you have designs for our part of the world," the host said shrewdly.

"Because you are a very perceptive individual," the banker said. "But you can only profit from it, I assure you."

The meeting went on for several hours and the banker outlined several of the future initiatives he had planned, as well as details about how the cartels would be restructured. In the end, the leaders of the cartels agreed to the banker's proposals.

As the banker sat on his jet heading back to China, he placed a call to a secure line from the phone onboard the plane.

"Four-two-three-three."

"Connecting," said the voice on the other end.

Another voice came on the line a moment later. "Report."

"Meeting successful. The cartels have agreed to our proposals. The wire transfers need to be made immediately, and then we can begin working with them to restructure their businesses."

"Good work. Are you heading back?"

"Yes. There's much to prepare before we meet with them again. It almost seems a shame what we're going to do with them in the end."

"They are just pawns. Vital, yes, but disposable. And when we're done with them, they'll never know what our true goal was until it is too late. That is one advantage to having them keep *their* wealth in *our* banks. When we are ready to cut them off, they will have nowhere to go to replace their losses, and they will be able to offer no resistance to our… shall we call it *hostile takeover?*"

The banker chuckled. "Indeed."

"What about the other business?"

"We will have absolute control over the Panama Canal," the banker replied. "They were happy to promise that in return for what they think they're getting from us."

"Excellent. I will see you when you get here." The call ended.

The banker put the receiver down and looked out the window at the Pacific Ocean far below him. *So many pawns. How does he keep them all straight?*

Wuhan, 1998

Two senior officers of the Chinese People's Liberation Army walked into the Chinese bio-warfare laboratory in Wuhan and were escorted to the director's office.

The director, who had only learned that they were coming a few minutes earlier, jumped to his feet as they entered the room.

"Gentlemen, welcome to our facility. May I get you refreshments? How may I be of service?"

"No refreshments," the senior officer stated, taking a seat across form the director's desk. "This is official business, and we're in a hurry."

"Of course," the director said, settling back into his chair. He waited for the officer to speak.

"We need a plague," the officer began. "Actually we need several over the next twenty years or so."

"I beg your pardon?" The director did not expect this.

The officer filled in the director on what was needed and how it would be released to create panic and destabilize economies around the world.

"You can't be serious. Germ warfare has been banned by nearly every nation! We'd be bombed out of existence if we were caught releasing plagues in other countries."

"Not if we released them here first," the officer said evenly. "Then it would just look like an accident. Poor containment protocols here at your laboratory, which led to people across the region being infected and also infecting persons who were then traveling to other countries. We'd have deniability, and since no plague will be released until we have already developed the cure, *our* losses would be minimal. Everyone else's losses would be considerably more, since it would never be revealed that we had the cure all along."

"And I suppose I'd be blamed for it all," the director accused the officers.

"Only if it came to that." When the officer saw the director blanch, he added, "Oh, come on, Director. You direct the operations of a facility that makes diseases as part of a bio-warfare program that officially doesn't exist. What did you expect?"

"Not this." The director put his head in his hands.

The officer took a paper out of his notebook and handed it to the director. "Pay particular attention to the signature at the bottom."

The director read the document. After a few minutes, he looked up and nodded. "It shall be done."

The two officers stood. "You have three years to have the first one and its cure ready. You know the price for failure."

"Of course." Everyone in China knew the price for failure.

The officers left the director's office and drove back to Beijing.

Beijing, 2000

Liang Hao met with the bankers, industrialists, and members of the diplomatic corps to review the status of the strategy and to prepare for the next phases. Representatives of the military were also in attendance.

"The U.S. and European automobile manufacturers have moved many of their parts manufacturing facilities to China already," one of the industrialists reported. "None of the Japanese companies will even talk to us, but that was expected. We now control most of the personal computing fabrication in the world, but the branded companies still won't send us the processor chips or anything else on the banned list. Those get installed once the computers reach the countries where they'll be sold."

One of the diplomats spoke up. "We're still working on getting Most Favored Nation status by the United States. That will remove all technology bans and give us access to their newest and most sensitive technology. It will also allow us to start fabricating computer chips and processors, and with the intelligence gathering firmware built into the chips themselves, no secrets will be safe from us."

Liang Hao nodded.

"We control gambling on all continents, including Russia," one of the bankers reported. "Profits have exceeded our expectation, and gambling addictions have increased tenfold."

"We control at least thirty percent of the government officials in Europe, North America, Central America, and South America," the next banker added. "In some places we control over fifty percent. And we control most of the Election Supervisors in the United States. We own the American electoral process, and we can use it at any time."

"The global drug trade is now ours as well," the first banker continued. "As a result of restructuring their businesses, human trafficking profits are up two hundred percent, and the pipeline for smuggling insurgents into the Unites States, Canada, Australia, and across Europe is at full capacity."

"What about the media and news outlets?" Liang Hao asked.

"We control all but one in the United States," a third banker reported, "most of the ones in Canada, and several in Europe. State-run outlets are harder to infiltrate, but efforts are continuing. In the outlets that we don't control outright, we still have a number of reporters, editors, commentators, and producers under our control, so we're able to spin most news stories however we want, whenever we want."

"Excellent," Liang Hao stated. Turning to the military officers, he asked, "How goes the military expansion?"

"On schedule," the senior military officer replied. "We are on target to launch our blue-water naval vessels, and the Army is at three million active soldiers, not counting reserves."

"And where do we stand on our plague?" Liang Hao asked.

"It will be ready on time," the senior military officer assured the room. "Early testing looks quite positive. They're just refining the cure so that we can control any outbreak here in China."

One of the diplomats interjected. "The European Union is doing exactly what we want them to do. Their interference in their member nations' sovereign rights is creating friction, as are the proposed immigration reforms. All will be in place when we need it to be."

"Are our Islamic pawns ready to do their part?" Liang Hao asked.

"Yes, Chief Strategist," another one of the bankers reported. "The principal initiative is still on for next year. The planning is completed, and they've already started moving their people into position."

Liang Hao nodded and leaned back in his chair, feeling satisfied. *Moves and countermoves. So far, the enemies and the pawns both are behaving as expected. Will they continue walking into the traps I have set for them?*

Beijing, 2001

"Chief Strategist, the attacks have begun!"

It was September 11, 2001, and reports were coming in from the United States regarding al-Qaeda's devastating attacks around the country.

"What has happened so far?" Liang Hao asked.

"Both of the World Trade Towers in New York were hit, and the Pentagon in Washington was hit."

"Is that all?" Laing Hao's elation quickly changed to frustration. "What about the Sears Tower? What about the U.S. Capitol or the White House? What about the eight other targets that were supposed to be hit?"

"There's no word on them," the military liaison reported. "The plane heading for the Capitol was brought down in Pennsylvania by the passengers. There are reports that they heard about what the other three planes had done and didn't want to die as tools of a terrorist plot. We're also getting reports that President Bush ordered all air flights grounded, and he sent up the Air Force to shoot down any plane that didn't comply. It looks like none of the other targets will be hit after all."

"What is the condition of the New York targets?" Liang Hao asked.

"I'm checking on that," the military liaison replied. After a minute he said, "Both towers have collapsed. They estimate the death toll to be over five thousand."

Liang Hao nodded. *It is not what we wanted, but it is enough. The Americans will be outraged, and they will demand the heads of the people responsible.*

"Are the media outlets ready to start releasing *our* version of events after the initial hysteria wears off?"

"Yes, Chief Strategist," one of the bankers replied.

Liang Hao nodded. Turning to the other bankers, he said, "Cut off funding for al-Qaeda and shift that funding to the group we have been grooming to replace them. Once America commits forces against al-Qaeda and anyone giving them assistance, we will need someone new that the Americans do not know about to continue the fight."

"Yes, Chief Strategist," the bankers replied.

Beijing, 2008

"Chief Strategist, we own the next American election," the banker reported. "And their financial markets are poised for collapse. The candidate you selected is turning his political party upside down, and he's ready to do his part once elected."

"And the other politicians of his party?" Liang Hao asked.

"Also ready to do their part," the banker replied. "They'll tear the country apart with their socialist programs and race/class baiting initiatives. No matter who wins the next election,

America will never fully recover."

"Have we identified the candidate that we will use to finally bring the U.S. under our control?"

"Not yet, Chief Strategist. It can't be one of the current party leaders, so we're beginning to cultivate outsiders so they'll be ready when needed."

"Remember, we are targeting the 2024 election," Liang Hao reminded the bankers. "The current pawns will all have been sacrificed by then, and the new pawns must be ready to step in at that time."

"They'll be ready," the bankers assured him.

Beijing, 2026

Liang Hao was ushered into the meeting room where Xi Jinping and the senior military leaders were waiting for him. Xi Jinping was the Paramount Leader of China, General-Secretary of the Communist Party, Chairman of the Central Military Commission, *and* President of the People's Republic of China, and he had held these positions for more than thirteen years.

When Liang Hao approached the table, he saw that there was no chair waiting for him. *I am not here to meet, I am here to explain what went wrong with our strategy in North America.*

"Explain your failure regarding the United States," Xi Jinping demanded before Liang Hao reached the end of the table across from him. "For more than thirty years, we've supported a strategy that was supposed to bring the Unites States under our control. And on the eve of that happening, their military mutinied, the people rose up, and the socialist government that you worked for years—and spent billions of our gold—to achieve was overthrown in less than a month!"

"There was no failure, Paramount Leader," Laing Hao replied calmly. "The strategy took into account that the United States might overthrow the socialist government that we put in place and attempt to reassert itself in world events. That is why the contingency strategy was developed to keep the U.S. penned in until we have finished with the eastern hemisphere. Then, we will take control of Canada and Central and South America, leaving the U.S. with no choice but to capitulate. It will just be later than originally planned, but well within the overall strategy and timeline that was originally approved."

"And you're convinced that the United States will not interfere with our other strategies around the globe?" Xi Jinping asked darkly.

"No, Paramount Leader. I am not convinced of that at all. What I *am* convinced of is that no interference will result in any negative impact to our strategy. The United States will be too distracted by events happening closer to home, and the strategies related to the rest of the world will be too far along for the U.S. to pose any threat."

"I have your assurance on that?" Xi Jinping insisted.

"Yes, Paramount Leader. Just as your predecessors had."

CHAPTER 7

——— •━ ● ━• ———

Washington, DC
October 2027

Kate and Steve left the cafeteria and returned to their secure conference room just before 7:30 AM on Saturday morning. The cafeteria was crowded for breakfast, and it took longer than expected to get their food and find a place to sit.

"We probably should have brought the food back up here," Steve said as they reached the security door outside their hallway.

"I know," Kate agreed, "but we've been working for the last nine hours straight, and I needed to be somewhere else for a while to clear my head."

They sat at the conference room table and looked around at the notes they had written on all of the whiteboards. "Are you still convinced about China being behind it all?" Steve asked.

"Yes."

"You still want to go through all of the intel and see what we have that either lends itself to your theory or contradicts it?"

"Yes."

"And what about the Handbasket list?"

Kate looked at him. "I hope that something in the intel will help with that. Otherwise, we may need to reach out to our

Agencies or to assets in Russia and Europe for their perspective on the border situation. It's probably too late to look into the EU immigration issue."

"True. But by reach out, do you mean go over there or just communicate with them from here?"

Kate hesitated before answering. Normally she'd advocate traveling, but with the places where she needed to go being active war zones, she didn't think it was a wise suggestion. "Communicate from here for now. It might be hard getting there and back safely, and whatever we learned could die with us."

"Good point. Let's get started."

Kate retrieved the folders and the flash drives from the safes and put them on the table. Then Steve and Kate each picked up a folder and started reading the contents, looking for any linkages to the notes they had written on the panels.

Over the next three hours, they read the intel from countries all around the world. If they found something that confirmed Kate's theory, they wrote the control number next to the notation on the panel (the control number that uniquely identified an official field transmission was the "Ref Number," and the control number that uniquely identified finished intel was the "Product Number"). If they found something that contradicted Kate's theory, they wrote the control number on the Handbasket panel.

When they were done, there were two control numbers on the Handbasket panel from intel that was several months old. The rest of the intel supported the notations on the whiteboard panels around the room.

As they looked around the room, Steve stated, "It's still not proof."

"Short of infiltrating the Chinese government, how do you propose we get proof? We're analysts. We sift through facts, look for linkages, and report that to decision-makers so they can take appropriate action. We're not lawyers, looking for proof beyond a reasonable doubt. Proof is in the rearview mirror in this business."

Steve nodded. "And your theory fits the facts that we have available to us."

"So we report the facts and our theory, and hopefully we'll be given more resources and intel to continue testing the theory until we're positive that it's right or prove that it's wrong. What else can we do?"

"I know one thing I'd like to do before we present this to Rosemont."

"What's that?" Kate asked.

"Run all this past Clay McGrath and Grant Chamberlain. They're supposed to be floating between teams and providing different perspectives on our work. If they think we're on the right track, I say we present it to Rosemont first thing Monday morning."

"Give them a call and see if they can come in today."

"Okay." Steve called both men to see if they were available. As it turned out, both could be at the Pentagon within the hour.

When Clay and Grant arrived, Kate and Steve walked them through what Kate had discovered in Vancouver and what she and Steve had done since arriving at the Pentagon the night before. Then Kate walked them through the timeline and her theory, and Steve presented the intel that supported her theory.

Once everything had been presented, Kate asked, "So what do you think?"

Clay and Grant both got up and walked around the room, looking at the whiteboard panels. When Grant got to the one labeled Handbasket, he laughed and pointed it out to Clay. Then they continued walking around.

After about twenty minutes, Clay looked at Kate and Steve. "A Chinese chess grandmaster, multiple global concurrent chess games thirty-plus years in the making, the events leading up to the recent Civil War, the Caliphate, the cartels, and China's explosive expansion… all part of a single master plan? It's staggering. It's terrifying. I don't want to believe a word of it, but my mind is already thinking about how it's the only explanation that addresses everything that's been happening. I pray that you're wrong, because if you're right then it means that we've been played for fools going back over thirty years."

Clay gestured to the whiteboards around the room. "I think you're right. If this were a case, and I had what you've presented to us this morning, I'd already be going to the U.S. Attorney to prepare indictments and secure warrants."

Kate and Steve thanked him for his comments. Then they looked at Grant.

Grant nodded in agreement. "Some of this dovetails with what the DIA has been working on for the past few months, but we didn't take it so far back, and we completely overlooked the political manipulations. Seeing it presented in this context helps me see some of the things that DIA got wrong. I can't find any flaws in the theory, other than to agree with Clay that it's terrifying to think that we've been a player in someone else's game, manipulated at every step. It's infuriating. But I agree with Kate that the recent Civil War may be the only thing that saved us, and it may be something we can build on to undo at least some of the damage the U.S. allowed to happen when Munger pulled all of our armed forces back home."

'When are you going to present this to the team?" Clay asked.

"Hopefully Monday," Kate replied. "I'll reach out to Rosemont and find out if he wants to see it first or if he wants the entire team to see it together."

"Why don't you call him now?" Grant suggested. "If he can get here before Clay and I leave, we can give him our perspective."

"All right." Kate dialed Rosemont's number, and he

answered immediately.

"Hello, Kate. Are you two back from Vancouver?"

"Yes, and we're at the Pentagon with Clay and Grant. We've uncovered something that we'd like to run past you before we share it with the team, and we'd like to share it with the team Monday morning."

There was a pause on the line. "I'll be there in less than an hour," Rosemont promised. Then he hung up.

Kate put her phone away. "He's on his way."

Rosemont walked into the conference room fifty-five minutes later and sat down at the table. "You two look like hell," he said, looking at Kate and Steve. "Have you slept since Vancouver?"

"Not really," Steve answered. "Just the occasional nap here and there. We're running on fumes right now."

"Okay, show me what you've got before you pass out."

Kate and Steve walked him through the events, timeline, theory, and intel just as they had with Clay and Grant. Clay and Grant then gave Rosemont their assessment of the work that Kate and Steve had done.

Rosemont took quite a while to digest the information. "The information about Canada and the British is of major and immediate concern. I'll try to brief the president about that later today. As for the rest, I'm with Clay. I don't want to believe a word of it, but in the absence of evidence to the contrary, I can't ignore it either. It fits the facts that we know of, so it gives us a starting point. Good work!"

"Thank you," Kate and Steve said in unison.

Rosemont stood and gestured around the room. "You'll need to type all of this up and make it pretty for when you present it to the team Monday morning. You'll also need to create a summary. The president prefers to start with a summary."

"The president?" Kate asked.

"Yes. I'll set it up so you can brief him after you've briefed the team. That way you can include anything that the team has to add. He'll need to see this as soon as possible—especially since I'll have already briefed him about the Canadian and British situation."

Kate nodded and looked over at Steve. "We'll be ready," Steve promised.

"Do you need anything else from Clay or me?" Grant asked.

"No," Kate responded. "Thank you both for coming in and reviewing this with us."

"No worries," Clay said.

Rosemont gestured toward the whiteboards from the doorway. "Don't forget to scrub the boards clean after you've typed it all up." Then he, Grant, and Clay left them alone in the conference room.

When Steve heard them exit through the security door at the end of the hallway, he said, "The president!"

"We're going to have to make all this look *very* pretty," Kate responded. "If we can get it finished today, we'll have all day tomorrow to rest up and be ready for Monday."

"Let's get started!

Kate and Steve finished documenting all timelines, open Handbasket issues, links to the existing intel, and the president's summary just before 10:00 PM that evening. They each had taken naps throughout the day, but both were mentally exhausted. Still, they were satisfied. Steve printed two final copies for them to review, and after making a few minor grammatical changes, both decided that their work was done.

Kate shredded earlier versions of the document while Steve printed fresh copies for the team and for the presidential briefing on Monday. Steve bound the new copies while Kate threw the food and beverage trash into the bins in the breakroom at the far end of the hallway. She grabbed a bottle of whiteboard cleaner from the supply shelves, returned to the conference room, and began wiping the whiteboard panels clean of all of the notes from that weekend.

When Steve returned from the printer area with the fresh copies for Monday morning, the conference room was spotless. "It hardy looks like we've been here at all," he remarked.

"Let's put those documents in the safes with the intel," Kate suggested.

Steve brought over the copies, and Kate placed them in one of the safes before locking it. Looking around, she asked, "So, are we done?"

"We're done," Steve confirmed.

"Then let's get out of here!"

Kate grabbed her overnight bag from the corner of the room, where it had been sitting since they arrived Friday night. As they walked toward the security door, Steve asked, "Where's your car?"

"At home. Yours?"

"Same."

"We'd better call for a car service," Kate suggested. "I don't want to be riding the Metro this late at night. Besides, it's a long walk from the station to my house."

"The Metro doesn't even go near where I live," Steve commented. "There are kiosks for car services at the Concourse and River entrances. We can get cabs or one of the other services from there."

"River entrance is closer," Kate pointed out.

"River entrance it is."

As they rode the elevator to the ground floor, Steve asked, "Which way are you heading?"

"West. You?"

"South."

Kate nodded. *Too bad.* "That must be a hell of a commute

to the NSA, isn't it?"

"It is," Steve confirmed, "But I work odd hours so the traffic isn't too bad. Besides, I travel a lot, and I love my house more than I hate my commute."

The elevator reached the ground floor, and the doors opened. At the same time, they each turned to the other and said, "Hey, do you want to..." They both laughed.

"You first," Steve said.

"No, you," Kate insisted.

"I was just going to ask if you wanted to get a bite to eat or something to drink."

Kate smiled. "I was going to ask you the same question. Did you have a place in mind?"

Steve mentioned one of the eateries nearby. "Seems heavy," Kate commented. "And I'm not into crowds right now. I know a place that's a little further away. The whisky's good, the popcorn is always fresh, and the kitchen makes great sandwiches and omelets."

"Sounds perfect," Steve said, getting hungry. "Where is it?"

"My place."

"Are you sure the kitchen will still be open by the time we get there?" Steve asked coyly.

"If it's not, I'm sure we can think of something."

Kate's two-story colonial was in the McLean-Tysons Corner area of northern Virginia, an area that catered to the DC power base with easy commute to DC and the major airports. It was also close to her office at CIA headquarters. Her street was in a heavily wooded area, and her home was surrounded on all sides by woods and creeks.

The sounds and smells of autumn were all around. Hardwood smoke from her neighbors' chimneys wafted through the clearing where her house sat, and leaves crunched beneath

Steve's feet as he walked to her front porch. The cool breeze rustled as the piles of leaves along the edge of the woods were disturbed and redistributed across her yard and driveway.

Kate unlocked her front door and deactivated her alarm system. Then Steve followed her inside. She didn't bother turning on the lights.

Steve woke the next morning to the smell of bacon cooking. He threw on his clothes and followed the aromas downstairs to the kitchen. Kate, with her hair up and wearing just a long t-shirt, was busy making breakfast when he arrived. He took a seat at the kitchen table, doing his best to stay out of her way.

"Coffee's in the carafe," she said, pointing to the coffee bar to her left. "Juice is in the fridge."

Steve found juice glasses next to the carafe and orange juice in the door of the fridge. He poured himself a glass and then returned to his seat at the table. He looked around at the brick kitchen and admired the layout. Everything was in easy reach, and the appliances were arranged with efficiency of movement in mind.

"Eggs. Scrambled, fried, or omelet-style?"

"How are you making yours?" Steve asked.

"The same way I make yours," Kate replied.

"Scrambled."

"With or without cheese?" Kate asked.

"Without."

"Bacon or sausage?"

"Either one."

"I have both," Kate told him.

"Both."

"Toast. White or wheat?"

"White," he replied, sipping his juice, which was fresh squeezed. "How long have you been up?

"An hour," Kate replied, whisking the eggs in a bowl.

"I didn't hear you get up."

"Quiet as a spy," Kate quipped.

Steve laughed.

Kate poured the eggs into the skillet and then put four pieces of bread into the toaster. "Can you get the butter and honey out of the fridge?"

"Sure." Steve retrieved them from the fridge.

"There's jam, too, if you want it."

"No, butter's fine. Where are the plates?"

"Plates are in the cupboard behind you, and the utensils are in the top drawer. We need forks, knives, and a serving spoon. Oh, and a serving fork."

Steve went over to the cupboard, saw two drawers, and opened the left one. It had placemats and napkins in it. "Do you want placemats and napkins?"

"Yes, thank you."

After Steve had set the table, he sat down and continued watching her cook. Specifically, he couldn't stop staring at her lean, taut legs extending below the t-shirt.

The eggs were done at the same time as the toast. She loaded up a serving platter with the toast, eggs, bacon, and sausage, and placed it in the center of the table. Then she poured herself a mug of coffee and sat across the table from Steve.

"Dig in."

Steve helped himself and then handed the utensils to Kate so she could serve her plate while he buttered his toast. He took a bite of the eggs first. They were delicious. He took a bite of bacon and sausage and found them equally good. "Breakfast is perfect," he complimented.

Kate smiled.

They both ate hungrily. Once the meal was finished, Steve tried to help with the dishes, but Kate ordered him back to his seat. She had the kitchen cleaned in no time. Then she poured herself another cup of coffee and sat down again.

"What kind of coffee is that?" Steve asked. Coffee was hard to come by those days.

"Kona." Hawaiian coffee was terribly expensive, and getting more expensive all the time now that it was the only coffee grown in the United States. Central and South American coffee shipments had stopped more than a year earlier. "I can't afford to drink it too often, but this felt like a special occasion, so I splurged."

Steve held up his juice. "I switched from coffee to juice when the coffee shipments stopped. Had to give up tea at the same time. I hear chicory is making a comeback for die-hard coffee drinkers, just like during the first Civil War."

Kate made a sour face. "Have you ever tried chicory? It's ghastly."

"I know," Steve admitted. "But folks in New Orleans love it."

Steve finished his juice and looked at Kate. "Breakfast was great, last night was wonderful, and we're briefing the president tomorrow. I need to go home and get some rest. Plus I need a shower."

Kate smiled. "I'll call you a cab." She disappeared into another room, and he heard her talking on her phone. A minute later, she returned. "Cab will be here in fifteen minutes."

"Thanks. Can I use your bathroom?"

Kate pointed down the hallway he had used to enter the kitchen. "Halfway down the hallway toward the stairs. It's on the left."

"Thanks!"

When he exited the bathroom several minutes later, Kate was dressed and looked like she was ready to go for a run. Steve sat on the bench by the front door, and Kate began stretching. A few minutes later, a horn sounded outside the house.

"Let's get to the Pentagon early tomorrow morning so we can go through everything one more time before we meet with the team," Kate suggested.

"6:30?" Steve suggested.

"Perfect." She reached up and kissed him on the cheek. "Last night *was* wonderful. We'll have to do it again."

Steve kissed her cheek and opened the front door with a big grin on his face. "Sounds good to me." He stepped outside, got into the waiting cab, and drove off.

The next morning, Steve walked into Conference Room B in the secure hallway of the Pentagon at 6:25 AM, only to find that Kate was already there and going through the documentation.

"You're early," he remarked as he sat down across from her.

"Trains were on time this morning," Kate commented.

They both went through the documentation, but neither found anything that needed to be changed.

"Are you going to leave in the part about Liang Hao?" Steve asked.

Kate nodded. "I think we should for now. It's easier to *confirm* a name than to discover one."

Shortly after 7:00 AM, Rosemont stuck his head into the conference room. "Are you two ready for this morning?"

Both Kate and Steve acknowledged that they were.

"Good. The team will be here at 7:30, and you brief the president at 11:00. I'll be going with you."

"Did you brief him about Canada and the British?" Kate asked.

Rosemont nodded. "He had heard that the British were requesting sanctuary, but he hadn't heard the rest. He met with his Security Council yesterday to discuss what to do about Canada, but I don't know what they decided."

"You're not on the Security Council?" Steve asked.

"No, I chair the Global Intelligence Council," Rosemont replied.

Rosemont left the conference room.

"Might as well take everything and wait in the main conference room," Kate suggested.

Steve grabbed the documents and followed her across the hall.

Over the next twenty minutes, the other members of the team filed into the conference room. Rosemont was the last to enter. He activated the SCIF and sat down.

"Our members from the CIA and NSA, with help from the FBI and DIA members, have developed a frightening analysis of the current situation, triggered by a meeting they had with a contact from the Canadian government in Vancouver last week," Rosemont began. "They're going to present the results of their analysis to you now, and then they're briefing the president at 11:00. Kate and Steve? Go ahead."

Kate and Steve passed out the documents and walked the team through the material. Then Clay and Grant offered their assessment. Kate and Steve opened the meeting for discussion.

The other members of the team were still debating the results of the analysis when Rosemont noticed that it was 10:15. Holding up his hand, Rosemont said, "Okay, I think we've debated this enough for now. Take the documents and read through them carefully, but don't take them out of this area. Kate, Steve, and I have to leave shortly for our meeting at the White House."

Rosemont motioned for Kate and Steve to follow him to his office.

"Thanks for ending that when you did," Kate said. "They seemed determined to reject our analysis."

"Can you blame them?" Rosemont asked. "If you're right, then they're the ones who played right into China's hands. I actually thought the meeting went well. They'll come around eventually—as soon as they can push their bruised egos out of the way."

Changing the subject, he added, "How many copies do you have for the president?"

"Ten," Steve replied.

Rosemont nodded. "That should be enough, if the three of us bring our copies with us."

"Where is the meeting?" Kate asked.

"The Situation Room," Rosemont replied. "I believe you've been in there before."

"Yes," Kate responded, confused. "How did you know?"

"I was in there for a couple of your briefings when Munger was president. You carried yourself well."

"If I had known he was a traitor, I would have shot him," Kate muttered.

"Not your job," Rosemont reminded her. "CIA isn't supposed to operate domestically." Rosemont looked at Steve. "*You* would be the one who should have shot him if you'd known."

Steve perked up. "Is there still time?"

Rosemont laughed. "Unfortunately, there's a long line in front of you for that particular honor." Looking at his watch, he said, "Let's go. My car's waiting at the River entrance."

The ride to the White House took just over twenty minutes, and the three of them reached the Situation Room with a minute to spare. Senior civilian and military officials were already there. Only the president and vice president were missing.

An aide showed Rosemont, Steve, and Kate where to sit, and then he took the documents and passed them around the table. As soon as he finished, President MacKendrick and Vice President Morey walked into the room. The people at the table started to stand, but President MacKendrick motioned for them to remain seated.

Once the president had taken his seat at the head of the table, Rosemont stood.

"Mr. President, I'd like to introduce Kate Davidsen and Steve Barksdale, our representatives from the CIA and NSA. Kate is the reason we know about the Canadian and British situation, and both of them have crafted a... well... a frightening theory regarding the present situation. My team is still reviewing the document that is in front of you on the table, but our representatives from the DIA and FBI support the theory."

The president nodded toward Kate and Steve. "Proceed."

Kate presented the summary of the material first. When Rosemont asked the president if he wanted to review the details, the president nodded.

Kate presented the four timelines that she and Steve had created. Steve reviewed the Handbasket material, which brought chuckles from around the room when he explained the name, and he also shared the intel that linked back to the timelines.

The room was silent when they finished going through the material. After a minute, the president asked, "Do you know who is behind these 'chess games" as you called them?"

Kate glanced at Steve, who nodded to her.

"Yes, Mr. President," Kate said. "We believe it's a Chinese chess grandmaster name Liang Hao, who disappeared from the chess tournament circuit with no explanation about thirty-five years ago, which coincides with when we believe the overall strategy was developed."

"So... you believe this truly is a giant chess game?"

"No, Mr. President," Kate replied. "We believe it's actually four or five giant chess games that are all linked together. The chess game—or games—aimed at the United States is named 'Brilliancy.' The three aimed at the rest of the world are collectively named 'Trinity Gambit.' These are the names that my Canadian contact got from his asset in China."

"And you believe that this began back in the early 1990s, and that virtually everything that has happened since has been driven by these chess strategies?"

"Yes, Mr. President," Kate confirmed. "Sometime around the collapse of the Soviet Union, which would have freed the Chinese military from its principal objective of preventing Soviet incursions along the border."

"And you even believe that they were behind all that happened with my predecessor?"

"Yes, Mr. President. His actions make sense in this context but in almost no other context. The fact that the withdrawal of American armed forces from around the world coincides with the moment that the regional wars began, implying that the regional wars were ready to begin but waiting for something to happen first, leads to no other conclusion. Whoever is behind the wars is also behind the withdrawal of our armed forces from the war zones. President Munger wasn't behind the three wars, so it must be someone that he chose to obey. And look at the countries that fell the fastest: Israel, Taiwan, and Japan, three countries that we've spent decades protecting. It simply cannot be a coincidence, sir."

The president nodded. "Does anyone else have any questions?" The president looked around the table. No one spoke.

Looking at Kate and Steve, the president said, "I'm grateful for the work that you've done. What are your next steps?"

"We'll continue confirming this theory as much as we can," Kate replied. "We need to reach out to any of our surviving assets in the war zones, and we need to consult every surviving intelligence agency contact that managed to infiltrate China before the wars began."

The president nodded. "Do so. But do so quickly. We're caught in a noose, and there isn't much time to free ourselves. Oh, and by the way, there *are* no surviving U.S. intelligence agency contacts who infiltrated China before the wars began. If you want to know what has been going on inside China, you'll need to find a contact from one of the other intelligence services that still exist."

As the people around the table started to close their reports of Kate and Steve's analysis, the president asked, "Before we adjourn, I have just one question for the two of you."

Kate and Steve looked directly at the president.

"Do you actually believe that China is behind all of the things that you've included in your analysis?"

"Yes, Mr. President, I do," Kate confirmed.

"Yes, I do, too, Mr. President," Steve echoed. "I didn't at first, but now I have no doubts."

The president stood. "Thank you both for your assessment and your honesty. I'll take it under advisement."

The president and vice president left the room, followed by the others who attended the briefing.

"That went *very* well," Rosemont whispered to them as they collected their notes and papers.

"It did?" Steve asked. "No one asked a single question."

"They weren't here to ask questions. They were here to assess the two of you. This is the most dangerous time in U.S. history, and the president isn't going to base policy on intelligence analyses that the analysts don't believe in. Now that he knows *you* believe what you presented, he's more likely to take it seriously. Well done!"

THE
MIDDLEGAME

"All warfare is based on deception. Hence, when we are able to attack, we must seem unable; when using our forces, we must appear inactive; when we are near, we must make the enemy believe we are far away; when far away, we must make him believe we are near."

— **Sun Tzu, "The Art of War"**

CHAPTER 8

———— • ————

Washington, DC
October 2027

President MacKendrick met with his cabinet, the Joint Chiefs of Staff, and several other key members of his administration in the Situation Room later that afternoon. The leaders of the various intelligence services were there, including Rosemont. The key topic of discussion was Kate and Steve's theory, which had been officially designated as "Handbasket." The president also wanted an update on Canada; the Security Council had been briefed the day before about what Kate discovered in Vancouver.

"If true," Rosemont said after presenting the material, "the political implications of Handbasket are staggering. But of greater and more immediate concern is the Canadian and British situation. Canada's capitulation will trap us between the Latin American Block to our south and Chinese troops to our north. At the same time, Britain's request for sanctuary presents us with an opportunity... if we're ready to risk angering one of the three aggressors currently at war."

"What opportunity?" the president asked.

"The only countries not directly involved in any conflict at the moment include us, Canada, Greenland, Iceland, and the Caribbean islands," Rosemont replied. "For some reason, the

Latin American Block has left those islands alone, and they stand as a buffer against the Latin American Block moving north via any route other than Mexico. If we want to keep the Latin American Block from having a sea route to our southern border, we're going to have to protect those islands. But that would stretch our Navy thin. If we had access to the British fleet, they could protect the Caribbean islands, leaving our fleet free to protect our Atlantic coast... and to be used for whatever else we may need the fleet for."

"That would work to help secure our southern border," Vice President Morey noted, "but our northern border is still at risk. I understand that Canadian Prime Minister Agutter is addressing parliament a week from tonight. That's probably when he'll present his capitulation decree. If that happens, we'll have to move quickly to defend ourselves on two borders, which we can't do indefinitely."

"What about British Columbia's request to become a U.S. territory?" Secretary of State Chandler asked. "That could give us a barrier against China sending troops into Canada."

"I haven't reached out to Lieutenant Governor Upton yet," the president replied, "but I do think that we should plan for how we might accept their request."

"It could pose a real problem for the Pacific fleets," Secretary of the Navy Charles stated. "That's a lot of coastline to defend against China's new Russian-made blue-water fleet if they decide to send troops over here."

"What about the fleet out at Pearl?" Secretary of the Army Pelham asked, referring to the naval forces stationed at Joint Base Pearl Harbor-Hickam in Hawaii. "It could strengthen your West Coast defensive capabilities considerably."

"Yes, and leave Hawaii completely undefended in case China decides to move against it," Secretary Charles pointed out. "They've already seized almost every other island chain in the central and western Pacific, and it would put their blue-water fleet in striking distance of every West Coast city in North America."

The room erupted with arguments over saving Hawaii or protecting the other states against invasion. After several minutes, the president interrupted the debate.

"I was elected President over *all* of these United States," President MacKendrick stated. "And I don't like the idea of abandoning one of them. But there are larger issues here. We're in a fight for our continued existence. Just like damaged limbs have to be amputated so the body can survive, we may have to sacrifice one state to save the rest of them. We cannot allow China to gain a foothold on the North American continent. Period. If that means accepting British Columbia's request and moving the fleet from Pearl to our West Coast, then that's what we may have to do. We're caught up in a chess game here, people. Hawaii may have to be a pawn that we sacrifice if we're going to survive."

There was stunned silence in the room. Rosemont was the only one nodding in agreement with the president.

"How do we tell the Hawaiians that we're abandoning them?" Secretary Chandler asked.

"We don't," Vice President Morey answered. "If we did, the Chinese would surely find out about it. Just as Churchill had to sacrifice Coventry to the Nazis in order to protect the secret that the British had broken the German Enigma code, so we, too, will have to sacrifice the citizens of Hawaii in silence for the greater good."

"I hate that term, 'greater good,'" the president said softly.

"So do I, Mr. President," the vice president admitted. "But in this case, I'm afraid it's the truth."

"But how would we keep the Chinese from taking advantage of the evacuation of Pearl Harbor?" Secretary of Defense Wolfe asked. "I'm not willing to give up that asset so easily."

"Then we don't," Secretary Charles said. "We destroy the naval base when we redeploy the fleet. We deny the Chinese their prize."

"But what about the harbor itself?" Secretary of the Airforce Hunter inquired. "Buildings can be rebuilt. It's the harbor that they'll want."

No one spoke up. Then Secretary of Commerce Williams cleared his throat. "I have an idea."

"Don't stand on ceremony," the president advised. "Speak up.

"Well, as you know, shipments of oil from all over the world have stopped," Secretary Williams began. "We don't even have enough oil in our own reserves to send to Hawaii as it is, apart from what's needed by the military. The last shipments of petroleum for civilian use sailed over a year ago."

"So what?" Secretary Wolfe demanded.

"So," Secretary Williams continued, glaring for a moment at Wolfe, "the tankers we sent to Hawaii are still docked out there. They're just sitting empty with nowhere to go. What if we sank them in the harbor channel? That's what the Japanese tried to do with our battleships when they attacked Pearl Harbor in 1941."

"The channel has been expanded since then," Admiral Longstreet, the Chief of Naval Operations, reminded him. "It's deeper and wider now."

"And supertankers are larger than World War II battleships," Secretary Charles pointed out. "If we sink several supertankers in the channel, it could take years to clear the channel for use. Pearl Harbor would be of no use to the Chinese, making any invasion of Hawaii simply a move against our national morale, more than a blow to our defensive strategy."

The president nodded slowly. Then he turned to Rosemont. "Mr. Rosemont. Based on your team's work on Handbasket, do you believe that the Chinese will have anticipated the moves that we've been discussing? Namely, granting sanctuary to the British, using their fleet and air forces to protect the Caribbean, making British Columbia a U.S. territory, redeploying all of our Pacific naval forces to our West Coast, and sacrificing Hawaii after we've destroyed Pearl Harbor's military value to the Chinese?"

Rosemont shook his head. "No, Mr. President. I believe that our recent Civil War confounded their strategy, and they're still trying to figure out how to deal with our failure to capitulate. I doubt that any strategy of theirs dealing with North America includes what we've discussed here. My guess is that it stops with Prime Minister Agutter's capitulation decree and an assumption that the Canadians will just be good little sheep and go along with it. They seem more focused on containment, rather than confrontation with the United States. There are too many pieces still in play for them to be ready to take us on directly."

"Are you sure about that?" Vice President Morey asked.

"Not one hundred percent," Rosemont replied. "But within the context of Handbasket, assuming that it's accurate, it seems the most likely."

"And in the absence of deeper intel from China, that may be as certain as we'll ever be," CIA Director Franklin added.

"Agreed," National Security Advisor Thornton stated.

"Mr. President?" General Bellingrath, Chief of Staff of the U.S. Army, spoke up.

"Yes, General."

"Sir, I have a concern regarding British Columbia. If they split from Canada, and we accept them as a territory, we'll need to send in troops to occupy the province immediately to prevent the Canadian armed forces from challenging their secession. And British Columbia has a large contingent of Canadian military forces there already. We could end up in a shooting match with the Canadians. Plus we'd need to secure the Yukon Territory as well. They border both Alaska and British Columbia, and if they remained loyal to Canada, they'd be in a position to jeopardize our defensive strategy."

"And don't forget about the Arctic sea-lanes," Admiral Longstreet added. "China could still invade Canada through the Beaufort Sea, using the new shipping lanes that Russia was opening up in the Arctic. If we don't control the Yukon Territory, we've exposed a back door that could cost us British Columbia *and* Alaska."

The president shifted in his chair. "It sounds like I need to reach out to Lieutenant Governor Upton immediately, tell her what we're thinking, and have her find out what plans the Yukon Territory has should Prime Minister Agutter capitulate next week."

Turning to Secretary Chandler, he said, "Will you set that up? I want both of us there for that meeting. Also set up an urgent meeting with the British Ambassador for the two of us to meet with him later today."

"Yes, Mr. President," Secretary Charles said.

"So we're moving ahead with British Columbia, Britain, and Hawaii?" Secretary Wolfe asked.

"Britain, yes," the president stated. "I need to know about the Yukon Territory and the Canadian military before committing to British Columbia, which will affect what we do about Hawaii. But if the Yukon Territory also wants to become a territory of the United States, and the Canadian military units in those provinces mutiny or can be otherwise contained, then yes, we will move ahead with British Columbia and Hawaii as we've discussed, including scuttling Naval Station Pearl Harbor and Hickam Air Force Base."

President MacKendrick looked around the room. "We need operational plans drawn up for everything we've discussed and any contingencies we need in place should situations change. I want those by the end of the week. Any questions?"

Secretary of State Chandler spoke up. "When will you

brief the leaders of congress? A resolution will need to be passed authorizing you to accept British Columbia's and the Yukon Territory's petitions to become territories of the United States."

"First thing in the morning," the President replied, "at my weekly meeting with the leaders of the House and Senate. Anything else?"

Heads shook around the room.

The president stood. "Very well. I'll notify you about my conversations with the British Ambassador and the Canadian leaders. That's all, ladies and gentlemen."

With that, the President left the Situation Room.

The autumn sunset blazed with oranges and purples as the British Ambassador arrived at the White House an hour later and was escorted into the Oval Office.

There was concern that Chinese operatives in Washington might see the Ambassador arriving, but given the United States' interest in its long-time ally, the meeting could easily be explained away as the president wanting an update on Britain's efforts to remain free of the Caliphate.

The vice president was in the Oval Office with the president and the Secretary of State when the Ambassador was ushered in. They all sat down on the two facing couches in front of the Resolute Desk.

"Mr. Ambassador," the president began, "I'll get right to the point. I understand your government authorized its ambassador to Canada to officially request sanctuary for the Royal Family, the government, the Royal Navy fleet, and the Royal Air Force squadrons."

The ambassador looked shocked, but the President held up his hand. "Don't ask how I know that. And don't ask how I know that it will be refused, if it hasn't been already. China has intervened and threatened Canadian Prime Minister Agutter, and he's scheduled to declare capitulation to China's demands next

Monday, making Canada a Chinese protectorate."

"China?" Sir Harold Dumbarton, Ambassador from the Court of St. James, sputtered. "Why do they care if we retreat to Canada? They have no involvement in what's happening in Europe or over here…"

Sir Harold's eyes went wide. "They don't have involvement… do they?"

"It's being looked into," the president confided. "But it appears that they do."

"Dear God protect us," Sir Harold whispered. "I must inform Prime Minister Halstead immediately."

"We can do that from here, if you'd like," the president offered. "He should also be informed that the United States is extending an offer of sanctuary for your Royal Family, military units, and any other refugees who can be transported here before… well, before the worse happens."

A look of gratitude crossed Sir Harold's face. "That's very generous of you, Mr. President. Yes, I think we should inform the Prime Minister of this together. But what about Canada?"

The president leaned forward, as did the vice president and the Secretary of State. "We're exploring options with some of the provinces and territories that are understandably concerned about Prime Minister Agutter's actions. It's possible that the Canadian government will not survive the announcement of the capitulation decree, or it may be that Canada itself will break apart in protest. It's unclear what the current political and military situation is, but you can image that a Chinese presence on North American soil is something that the United States simply will not allow."

Sir Harold agreed. President MacKendrick revealed some of the options they were looking into regarding how to use the British fleet and the opportunity with British Columbia and the Yukon Territory.

"I'd hate to see Canada splinter apart," Sir Harold said

sadly, "but given the circumstances and the times in which we're living, I honestly see no alternative if North America is to remain free of what's happening across the rest of the globe."

"I'm glad you see it that way, Sir Harold," the president said. "The security of the western hemisphere has always been of paramount importance to us, and now that the Latin American Block is closed to us and threatening our southern border, we must do everything we can to protect North America."

"What about Iceland and Greenland?" Sir Harold inquired.

"We're still developing options regarding those countries, but we feel an obligation to help keep them free from hostile invasion, just as we did during World War II."

The conversation went on for a few more minutes, and then the president stood and escorted the ambassador to the Situation Room so they could initiate a video conference with Prime Minister Halstead.

When the Prime Minister appeared on the video monitor, Sir Harold informed the Prime Minister about the situation in Canada, and the president extended his offer of sanctuary and his desire to use the British armed forces to expand the defensive capabilities of the United States' southern borders.

"How certain are you about the Canadian situation?" the Prime Minister asked.

"Our information comes from a source in the Canadian government, who is now in hiding for his life from Chinese agents," the president replied.

"God in Heaven," the Prime Minister swore. Then he recovered his composure and said, "Thank you for your offer, Mr. President. I'll discuss it with my cabinet first thing in the morning, and I'll give you our answer after that... say, 8:00 AM your time? I'm certain that His Majesty will look favorably upon your offer as well. Until tomorrow morning then?"

"Until tomorrow," the president responded.

The video call ended. "I'll escort you out, Sir Harold," the

Secretary of State offered.

"Thank you," Sir Harold said. "And thank you all for everything. I imagine we'll be talking again tomorrow."

"I look forward to it," the president said warmly. "Good evening, Sir Harold."

"Good evening, Mr. President." Sir Harold followed the Secretary of State out of the Situation Room.

When the Secretary of State returned ten minutes later, the president initiated a video call with the Provincial Lieutenant Governor of British Columbia.

"Good evening, Lieutenant Governor Upton," the president said when Upton's face appeared on the screen.

"Good evening, President MacKendrick," she responded. "To what do I owe the pleasure?"

"I understand that Canada is about to go through some substantial changes," the president said blandly. "Changes that create concerns as well as opportunities, if handled correctly."

"You've heard?" she asked.

The president nodded. "A highly-placed source in the Canadian government got word to someone who passed that along to me."

"Iain Stewart," she said. "He's still in hiding, but he informed me of his conversation with his contact in Washington. Are you calling to tell me that you're going to reject my request?"

"No."

Her face lit up. "You're going to accept then?"

"No."

Her face fell. "I'm confused, Mr. President."

The president relayed his concerns about the Yukon Territory, the Canadian military personnel in British Columbia, and the need to occupy British Columbia with U.S. troops to prevent Canadian forces from attempting to force British

Columbia to remain part of Canada and accept the capitulation. He also voiced his concerns about the potential of China invading from the north.

Upton nodded. "I understand, Mr. President. I... we've been so occupied with our plans that we neglected to take into account what you'd be facing if you accepted our request. If you'll give me a moment, we can address the Yukon Territory issue right now."

"Certainly," the president said.

Upton's face disappeared from the screen. Two minutes later, a split-screen appeared with Upton on the left and another person on the right.

"Mr. President, this is Territorial Premier MacPherson of the Yukon Territory. Premier, this is President MacKendrick of the United States."

MacPherson smiled. "A great pleasure, Mr. President."

"For me as well, Premier MacPherson," the president responded. "It's always a pleasure meeting another leader of Scottish descent."

"I've just been discussing the capitulation problem," Upton said to MacPherson. "The United States is aware of what's going on up here and of British Columbia's intent to depart quickly should what we expect to happen *actually* happen. The president raised concerns about how your territory will respond to Agutter's madness, what that might do to *our* plans given that your territory borders both us and Alaska, and how the Canadian military forces in British Columbia and in the Yukon Territory might respond. Your thoughts?"

MacPherson's mouth fell open. "My God, Upton, are you mad? You're already discussing this with the Americans? What if Agutter finds out? What if the Chinese find out?"

"They're going to find out soon enough," Upton pointed out. "And wouldn't be better if we have the pieces in place ahead of time instead of reacting to Agutter *and* the military *and* the

Americans all at the same time?"

MacPherson looked troubled. "I suppose so, but I wish you had warned me."

"Excuse me, Premier MacPherson," the president interjected, "but *I* initiated this call, not Lieutenant Governor Upton. Your response to Prime Minister Agutter's declaration is only a piece of a much larger puzzle, and I have limited time to prepare for things that are about to happen very quickly. British Columbia has indicated that a request is forthcoming, but I cannot make any decisions on that request unless I know where you and your territory stand in all of this. Your strategic location could determine the viability of any request made by your southern neighbors."

MacPherson nodded slowly. "I understand. Events are happening too quickly, and it's hard to keep up."

"I completely understand," the president responded.

"The good news," Upton interjected, "is that military personnel don't surrender willingly until they've exhausted all other options. The capitulation is a preemptive surrender, bypassing the military altogether. I have it on good authority that most of the military units stationed in British Columbia will mutiny and will re-form themselves into provincial armed forces when we withdraw from Canada. Those who don't will be ejected from the province immediately."

"Your province has already decided to withdraw?" MacPherson asked.

"Yes. The provincial assembly polled its constituents over the weekend, and in spite of the recent assassinations, the members of the assembly and the people they represent are all willing to exit and request that the United States accept us as a new territory. But if I understand correctly, the United States won't agree unless your territory is part of the equation. Your geographic position would expose our flank should Canadian forces attack or China invade via the Arctic sea routes and the

Beaufort Sea."

"We've talked about it up here," MacPherson admitted, "but we've made no decisions. I'm not certain how I could call for a referendum in time to do any good." MacPherson was silent for a few moments. "However, if British Columbia exited Canada, and then annexed the Yukon Territory—unopposed, of course—before making the official request to the United States, I could convince the territory that this was in its best interest and bypass a vote altogether."

"Would your citizens agree to being annexed and then becoming part of the United States without having any say in the matter?" the president asked.

"I believe they'd prefer it to finding themselves suddenly under Chinese rule," MacPherson replied. "And I hear that Quebec might be seceding as well. It shares a border with the United States, and it would extend your Atlantic defenses all the way to the Arctic."

"Only if New Brunswick, Newfoundland, Prince Edward Island, and Nova Scotia secede, too," the president pointed out.

"Good point," MacPherson admitted. "So much land, so much coastline, and not enough people to defend it from outside invasion and internal stupidity."

'Well said," Upton commented.

"Back to the matter at hand," the president began, "I need assurances regarding civilian support and military intentions in your province and territory. I'll have to send in troops the moment we recognize you as U.S. territories, and I need to know what kind of reception we'll have: an invading army or protectors in a common cause."

"How long do we have to get back to you?" Upton asked.

"Wednesday," the president answered. That was two days away. "Thursday morning at the latest. If Agutter announces the capitulation next Monday night, and you both announce your secession right after that, I have to begin sending in troops immediately to defend your borders from military action launched from the other provinces. I have to get our troops staged along your southern border and the Alaskan border days before that without alerting the Chinese as to what we're doing."

"Things are moving too fast," MacPherson muttered glumly.

"It's not our fault," Upton said, "But it is the world we now live in. Mr. President, we'll do our best to meet your deadlines."

"Thank you both," the president said. "We'll talk again either Wednesday night or Thursday morning." Then he ended the call.

"What do you think?" he asked the vice president and the Secretary of State.

"I think we need to start preparing for war," the vice president replied.

CHAPTER 9

London • Ottawa • Pearl Harbor • Victoria •
Washington, DC • Whitehorse
October 2027

Three days after the United States offered sanctuary to the British, King George VII walked through the corridors of Buckingham Palace. *Will this be the last time I ever see this place?* The Royal Family of the United Kingdom was about to evacuate their ancestral home and relocate to the United States until it was safe to return to London. *That day may not come in my lifetime, if at all.*

The king looked at the priceless works of art that adorned the corridors of the palace that once ruled the largest empire in the world. *It's only a matter of time before the insurgents destroy this palace like they've destroyed every museum, church, and monument across Europe.* The king remembered watching images of the Louvre burning out of control when the Caliphate overran Paris—the cultural icons of generations suddenly gone forever. The Caliphate seemed determined to destroy everything of value and significance to the hearts and minds of the now-enslaved Europeans.

The king passed the official portrait of his mother. He paused for a moment to look at her face one more time. He missed his mother, as did the nation that she had selflessly led for more than seventy years—longer than any British monarch in history.

When Queen Elizabeth II had died a few years earlier, Prince Charles chose to be crowned as George after his maternal grandfather—there were still too many bad memories tied to the name Charles, thanks to the Stuarts and their connections to the Catholic Church.

The king continued down the corridor. He was sad about leaving London. *What the Nazis couldn't make my mother and grandfather do by force, we did to ourselves by allowing Islamic immigrants to overrun the kingdom unchecked for too long. We're responsible for destroying our own nation.*

The king was also sad that he'd be traveling with only a few siblings, cousins, nieces, and nephews, but his children and grandchildren would be traveling separately. Parliament wouldn't allow the Sovereign and the heirs to the throne to travel together. His eldest, William, and his family had taken an unscheduled flight that had already departed. The Prime Minister and most of the cabinet were also on that flight, which had an RAF escort to take it safely to America.

The king's youngest, Harry, was the reason that the king has been wearing only black for nearly a year. Harry and his family had been in Kenya when the Caliphate swept across Africa. They had joined a convoy heading for the airport, where planes waited to evacuate them to safety, but the convoy was attacked. There had been no survivors.

King George reached the waiting room where the remnants of his family waited. He heard the shouting of orders in the courtyard outside and knew that the vehicles that would take him and his family to the airport had arrived. He greeted his wife and hugged two of his grandnieces. That was the last thing that he ever did.

Colonel Thomas Hutchinson of the RAF, commander of the

commandeered Airbus A380-800 evacuating Prince William and the senior government officials to the United States, heard the message coming over his headset. "Please repeat last message," he said into the microphone.

The message repeated. He had heard it correctly. "And this is confirmed?"

Hutchinson listened carefully. "Message received and understood."

The military command post onboard the plane was situated in the forward bar of the upper deck. Communications, radar, and other equipment now filled what was supposed to be the poshest club in the air. The Communications Centre on the ground began relaying additional information but was suddenly cut off in mid-sentence. Turning to his communications office, he ordered. "Get them back."

The communications officer made several attempts to reestablish communications with the ground. "I'm sorry, sir," he finally reported. "I cannot raise anyone in or around London."

Hutchinson nodded. "Very well." He stood and walked toward the first-class passenger compartment of the plane's upper deck. He had a duty to perform—one that he dreaded.

There were over six hundred passengers on board the RAF's Royal Flight. In addition to members of the Royal Family and their security detail, the passenger list included government officials—both commons and peers—and their families. Key members of the military and their families were also on board.

He walked back to where Prince William was sitting with his family. *He's now our king and sovereign.* Leaning down, he whispered in William's ear, "Sir, may I have a private word?"

William nodded, stood, and followed the colonel to the rear of the compartment. The Prime Minister and several of the other senior passengers looked on with curious expressions.

When they were alone, the colonel said. "Sir, I have devastating news from London. Buckingham Palace was attacked less than an hour ago. Six Stinger missiles were fired at the palace just as the military vehicles arrived to transport the king and the rest of the Royal Family to their airplanes."

Hutchinson looked into William's eyes and could tell that the prince knew what was coming next. "I'm sorry to report that the king and the other members of the Royal Family there were all killed in the resulting explosions. There were no survivors. This has been confirmed. And now we've lost all contact with London and our ground control installations. I'm afraid that London has fallen to the insurgents."

William bowed his head and covered his eyes with his hand.

"Your Majesty, is there anything I can get for you?"

William shook his head. The use of the term "Your Majesty" was not lost on him. He was now King. Protocols would require him to select the name by which he would be crowned. He glanced over to the Prime Minister, who was watching the colonel and him intently.

"Thank you, Colonel," the new king said. "I wish to be left alone for a few minutes. Please inform the Prime Minister. He will need to know what has happened."

"Yes, Your Majesty."

"Oh," William said as the colonel turned to leave. "Please inform the Prime Minister that I will be known as William V."

"Yes, Your Majesty."

The colonel then informed the Prime Minister and the new queen what had happened. The queen hurried back to be with her husband in his time of grief, while the Prime Minister informed the rest of the passengers.

After several minutes, the king regained his composure and followed his wife back to their seats. The other passengers in the compartment all stood up when he appeared, and in solemn unison said, "God save the King! God save King William!"

The vice president, the Secretary of State, the British Ambassador, and an Air Force honor guard waited at Joint Base Andrews in Prince George's County, Maryland, to welcome their guests from Britain. It was shortly after midday on Thursday, and the base was on high alert because of the impending capitulation by the Canadian Prime Minister and the U.S. response that had been set in motion that morning. Both British Columbia and the Yukon Territory had confirmed that the Canadian military units based in their areas would mutiny as soon as the capitulation decree was read to the nation. This was the final piece of information that the president needed before committing troops to occupy western Canada, which the Lieutenant Governor of British Columbia and the Premier of the Yukon Territory both insisted would be well received by their citizens. Orders had also been issued to begin withdrawing the Pacific fleet from Naval Station Pearl Harbor, to scuttle the naval base and nearby Air Force base, and to block the harbor's channel with supertankers. The U.S. military was on high alert, but it was also trying to proceed in a way that did not provide any warning to the Chinese about what was happening.

The British Ambassador looked somber as he waited for the Royal Flight to land. Word had been sent ahead about the death of King George. The president had planned on being there to personally offer his condolences, but coordinating the Canadian and Pearl Harbor efforts required him to remain in the Situation Room of the White House. The vice president had been dispatched in his place.

Once the plane had rolled to a stop and the stairs placed at the main doorway, the door opened. The Royal Family's security detail exited first, and then King William, followed by his family and the Prime Minister.

When they reached the bottom of the stairs, the British

Ambassador and the U.S. officials stepped forward to greet their guests and offer their condolences over the loss of the king. The vice president offered the president's apologies for not being there in person, and he extended an invitation from the president for the king and his wife to dine at the White House while they were still in Washington. The invitation included Sir Harold and the Prime Minister. Then the guests were escorted to the long line of limousines waiting to take them to either the British embassy or one of several local hotels that had been reserved for the British refugees.

"We've procured a compound in southern Pennsylvania, Your Majesty," Sir Harold said as they walked to the cars. "You'll remain at the embassy for the next two weeks while final preparations are made, and then you'll be escorted to your new home. The members of your government will occupy the adjacent compounds, so the entire British government-in-exile will be in close proximity with each other."

"Thank you, Sir Harold," the king said. "Why Pennsylvania?"

"Apart from the beauty of the area, it's close to Washington, and yet on the other side of the Blue Ridge Mountains, should Washington ever be subjected to nuclear attack."

The king nodded. The guests entered their limousines. The caravan pulled away and headed for Washington. The vice president and Secretary of State returned to the White House.

In the Situation Room that night, the president reviewed the status of the initiative to secure British Columbia and the Yukon Territory. Congress had quickly passed the resolution authorizing the president to accept the petitions from British Columbia and the Yukon Territory. Now there were over fifty thousand soldiers massed in northern Washington State and southwestern Alaska, waiting for orders to cross the border.

Tanks and other armored vehicles were also ready to cross and defend the new Canadian borders. Additional troops had taken positions along the rest of the northern U.S. border with orders to repel any attempt by the Canadian military to cross into the United States. The U.S. Air Force was also prepared to begin patrolling the new northern border with orders to attack any act of aggression or incursion.

The carrier strike groups at Pearl Harbor were preparing to get underway before dawn, and the remaining ships and submarines at Pearl Harbor would be leaving once the explosive charges had been set and the supertankers had arrived to block the channel. All air squadrons would leave and destroy Hickam Air Force Base when the last of the naval vessels left, and most of the Army and Marine units stationed on the island were being transported back to California onboard the ships of the carrier strike groups. The families of the military members were being air lifted out of Hawaii over the next several days—a move that would certainly be witnessed by the Chinese agents on the islands. It had been a difficult decision, but the president didn't think that the military would abandon Hawaii if their families were still there.

Everything appeared to be in readiness. All that remained was the Canadian Prime Minister's announcement.

Rosemont briefed the team on Sunday morning. "If Prime Minister Agutter announces the capitulation tomorrow night, then British Columbia and the Yukon Territory will immediately secede and request to become part of the United States. As soon as the request is received, our forces will move in to secure the new borders. If all goes as planned, the Canadian military units in British Columbia and the Yukon Territory will mutiny and join our forces to defend the new U.S. territory. Rumor has it that other Canadian provinces may request to become part of the United State, but that is unconfirmed. One thing is certain: the

Canadian parliament will not go along with the capitulation, and how the Prime Minister plans to respond to that is anyone's guess. There's no evidence that the Chinese are on their way to take control of Canada yet, but we can't assume that they won't move quickly when they see the country begin to splinter apart. They need a united Canada to keep us boxed in.

"The U.S. military units stationed at Joint Base Pearl Harbor-Hickam have been recalled to the mainland, and the Navy and the Air Force bases are being scuttled before dawn local time this morning. The carrier strike groups left Friday morning before dawn, and the remaining ships are leaving today. All Army, Air Force, and Marine units have been evacuated, and the military families are being airlifted back to California."

Moira Kirkland was shocked at the implication. "Are we abandoning Hawaii?"

Rosemont nodded. "It wasn't an easy decision, but the president realized that one state may have to be sacrificed to defend the others. Hawaii is just too remote to defend, just like the U.S. Pacific territories were when China annexed them, and the military units stationed in Hawaii are needed to defend our new western coastline."

"Is all this because of Handbasket?" Sterling Michaels demanded.

"I was wondering the same thing," Anthony Vandyke sneered. "That damn document is turning the country upside down!"

"The country was already turning upside down," Grant growled. "So was the world. Handbasket is just the first time we've had a way to make sense of it all."

"That's right," Clay agreed. "If it weren't for Kate and Steve, we wouldn't know what Canada is up to, we wouldn't have been able to offer sanctuary to the British, which will bolster our Atlantic defenses considerably, and we wouldn't know that all three wars are interconnected. Without that information, how could we define an overall defensive strategy that even comes close to working? Handbasket is the most valuable intelligence analysis we have, and it will probably be the most pivotal work product this team produces."

The room erupted as the military members of the team shouted their opposition to what Clay had said. Rosemont wasn't having any of it.

"Shut the hell up!"

The room fell silent.

"We are *not* going through this again," Rosemont shouted. "The president has accepted Handbasket as the most plausible explanation for what's going on in the world, as has the cabinet, the Joint Chiefs, and the Intelligence Council. That means it's policy until it can be disproved by hard facts to the contrary. And by the way, Kate and Steve are working diligently to gather more facts and intel to confirm or adjust their analysis, so no one is sitting still on this. But that's *their* job. As for the rest of you, *your* job is to identify what the U.S. needs to do to survive, and for now, Handbasket is the context you're going to use to define your recommendations. So get onboard, or get out!"

Rosemont glared around the room. "Meeting adjourned." Then he deactivated the SCIF and stormed out.

The rest of the team exited the conference room; Kate, Steve, Clay, and Grant stayed. "We need to find all of the surviving intelligence assets in Europe, Russia, and Asia," Kate remarked, "before this tears the team apart."

"Quite a few of them are in Norway and Sweden," Steve noted. "If we can track them down there, they might be able to point us to others in the region who are still alive."

Kate looked troubled. "I know I was against it before, but I wonder if we should go over there."

"As a last resort," Steve suggested. "Let's see who we can reach through our Agencies' communication channels first."

"I think the two of you need to start on that immediately,"

Clay said.

"And we're available to help," Grant added.

Kate smiled at the offer. "Thanks. Where should we start?"

"CIA?" Steve suggested.

The others nodded.

"Okay," Kate said. "Let's take a drive upriver. I hope you all brought your credentials."

Prime Minister Agutter stood in front of the Canadian parliament at 8:00 PM Ottawa time on Monday night. All CBC channels and Radio Canada stations preempted their normal programming to present the Prime Minister's address.

"My fellow Canadians," Agutter began. "We find ourselves living in dangerous times—perhaps the most dangerous in our existence. Wars rage all around us. Your government has worked diligently to keep the nation from being drawn into any one of these conflicts, but now we're forced to admit that this is no longer possible. Because Canada is not prepared to defend itself against any one of the aggressors bringing conflict to the world, we have concluded that there is no choice but to seek an alliance with a nation that will protect us. For the continued safety and security of all Canadians, I have entered into an agreement with China to protect Canada from the wars that are engulfing the world. Our military will be immediately disbanded, and we will become a protectorate of China. Their armed forces will take on the duties of protecting our borders and keeping our citizens safe. This agreement goes into effect at midnight tonight, Ottawa time."

No one heard the rest of his speech. Parliament erupted into shouting and fist-shaking. The Prime Minister pressed a button on his podium, and suddenly the doors to the parliament chamber burst open. The units of the Royal Canadian Mounted Police who protected Ottawa's government buildings—dressed in full riot gear—poured into the chamber to restore order.

Members of parliament were thrown to the floor, handcuffed, and dragged from the chamber—all broadcasted across the nation.

In the Situation Room, the President and his advisors viewed the broadcast in silence. As they watched the Members of parliament being dragged out in handcuffs, an aide informed the president that the video call he was expecting was ready. The president hit a button on the control panel in front of him, and the center screen changed from parliamentary chaos to images of Lieutenant Governor Upton and Premier MacPherson.

"Good evening, Mr. President," the two Canadian leaders said.

"Good evening," the president responded gravely. "We were just watching the broadcast from Ottawa. How are things in your part of Canada tonight?"

"British Columbia has just annexed the Yukon Territory," Upton announced.

"Without opposition," MacPherson interjected.

"And we have officially seceded from Canada," Upton continued. "We formally request to become territories of the United States."

"What about the military units within your borders?" the president asked.

"Most have already mutinied," Upton responded. "I'm still waiting to hear from the rest."

"Is it safe to begin moving troops across the border?" the president asked.

"Yes, Mr. President," Upton confirmed. "We're about to address the citizens of British Columbia and the Yukon Territory to inform them about what's happening. If you can wait thirty minutes before you cross the border, there should be no issues with your immediate occupation of our new territory."

"That would be 5:45 PM Pacific Time, correct?"

"Yes, Mr. President."

"Very well. U.S. forces will occupy your territory beginning at 5:45 PM."

"Thank you, Mr. President," the two Canadian leaders said.

The president was about to end the video call when he added, "Oh, and Lieutenant Governor Upton, Premier MacPherson? Welcome to the United States of America."

Premier MacPherson sat in his office in the capital city of Whitehorse, the only real city in the Yukon Territory. A single television camera was pointed at his desk, and he was surrounded by leaders from the territory's assembly. His broadcast was being sent out to all corners of his territory.

"Good evening," he said when the red light on the camera illuminated. "Most of you should have seen the shameless act of capitulation committed by Canadian Prime Minister Agutter. He has, in effect, surrendered Canada—and all of you—to China. We were given no chance to vote on this. We were not asked if we supported this. It was simply thrust upon us by a politician who exceeded his authority and who clearly no longer thinks of himself as answerable to the people.

"A few minutes ago, I was informed that the Province of British Columbia wanted to annex the Yukon Territory as part of a larger defensive strategy in opposition to Prime Minister Agutter's illegal actions. I have met with the Territory legislature, and we have decided to accept the British Columbia offer unopposed. It is in our best interest. I was then informed that British Columbia intended to secede from Canada and request to be made a territory of the United States of America. This would extend the U.S. western coastline from Baja California to the Arctic for the first time, and create a bulwark to defend us and our neighbors against any invasion attempt from China. We support British Columbia's actions. At 5:45 PM

Pacific Time, forces from the United States will begin moving into British Columbia and the Yukon Territory to secure our borders from retaliation by the Canadian government, and from invasion by the Chinese. The U.S. Navy will be taking up stations along the coastline, and the U.S. Air Force will begin patrolling our airspace. Do not be alarmed by this. This is in no way part of any aggression against us, but it is something that we have requested of the United States for our own protection. And the U.S. troops will be serving alongside the Canadian military units stationed in our Territory and in British Columbia, who have decided to remain at their posts and help defend our borders in opposition to Ottawa's capitulation decree and the threat of Chinese aggression.

"I will provide you with more information as it becomes available. For now, though, I advise you to stay in your homes and avoid any potential interference with U.S. forces. They are our friends and our protectors. Please treat them as such. Good night and God bless."

Lieutenant Governor Upton addressed the people of British Columbia from the Assembly Chamber in Victoria. Many of the Canadian military units that had mutinied were positioned around the assembly building to provide security.

Upton began her address to the Province by denouncing Prime Minister Agutter's actions as illegal and in opposition to the foundation of freedom and democracy that Canada had been built upon. She then announced that the province had annexed unopposed the Yukon Territory as part of its strategy for border defense, and that, immediately after annexing the Yukon Territory, British Columbia formally seceded from Canada. The declaration of secession had been delivered to the Prime Minister's office a few minutes earlier.

"I must tell you now that the assembly, recognizing that we cannot stand on our own against the forces from China and from the other Canadian provinces, has requested to become a territory of the United States of America, and our request has been granted. Beginning at 5:45 PM Pacific Time, U.S. forces will be moving into British Columbia and the Yukon Territory to secure our borders against invasion from Canada or China. This is not the occupation of a conquering army but the protecting of our borders, our cities, and our citizens against potential retaliation from hostile forces. I am in close communication with the Premier of the Yukon Territory and the President of the United States to make this transition as painless and as positive as possible. Our coastline defenses will be handled by the United States Navy, our airspace will be defended by the United States Air Force, and our borders protected by the United States Army, alongside the Canadian military units here in British Columbia who are standing with us against the Prime Minister's illegal actions. These are our friends, these are our defenders, and these are our brothers and sisters.

"It is our sincere hope that the other Provinces and Territories will overthrow Prime Minister Agutter's puppet government and rescind his capitulation declaration, so that we can all work together in peace for the safety and security of North America, but should that not happen, know that we are safe and secure as part of the United States.

"God bless you all, and God bless the United States of America."

Five empty Ultra Large Crude Carrier (ULCC) supertankers were towed into the center of the 1200-feet wide and 59-feet deep channel connecting Pearl Harbor with the Pacific Ocean. Each ship was just over 1,500 feet long, 225 feet wide, and 114 feet tall. The U.S. Navy vessels that remained behind to destroy the naval base were anchored just outside the mouth of the channel—dark hulks against the cloudless night sky.

Once the supertankers were in position, their anchors were

dropped, and demolition crews swarmed aboard to make their final inspections of the explosive charges that would send the ships to be bottom of the channel and implode the structure of the ships so their upper decks wouldn't protrude so high above the water when they sank.

Once the demolition crews had evacuated the supertankers, the tugs turned around and joined the U.S. naval vessels waiting outside the channel.

For several minutes, there was nothing but silence as the island breezes blew across the decks of the waiting vessels. Then faint popping noises were heard coming from the supertankers. The sounds grew louder, and several of the tankers began to list and collide with the adjacent ships. There were additional popping sounds, and the tankers began to sink. Larger explosions could be heard and huge fireballs became visible as the upper decks imploded and the upper structures of the supertankers collapsed.

Faster and faster the supertankers sank as their hulls cracked open and water rushed in. In less than an hour, they had all settled on the bottom of the channel. The wrecked upper structures of the supertankers were visible as they jutted from the water like twisted metal fingers of some perverse undersea creature that was clawing its way to the surface.

"That should block the channel for several months at least," Admiral Freemont said to his bridge crew as the last supertanker reached its final resting place. Freemont was in command of scuttling Joint Base Pearl Harbor-Hickam.

He turned and gave the order to destroy the Navy and Air Force bases. Down a short flight of stairs, which led to the ship's Command and Control Center, a large bank of radio detonators lined the far wall. Sailors began pressing the firing buttons in sequence. Freemont watched as explosion after explosion destroyed what had been the most important U.S. military asset in the Pacific for nearly 90 years. Only the World War II memorials were spared from destruction.

Once the buildings and facilities had been destroyed, he gave the order to get underway. The tugs returned to the local commercial harbor, and the naval vessels followed Freemont's flagship east toward northern California. The glow from the flames of what had once been the Navy and Air Force bases lit up the night sky for miles as the fires burned out of control and consumed everything left behind.

Prime Minister Agutter was arrested the next morning by members of the Canadian military who had mutinied. Several other provinces had requested help from the United States, and the president was actively negotiating with them to create a united North American defense against Chinese aggression. He didn't necessarily want all of the Canadian provinces to become part of the United States, but he wanted them all working together for their mutual protection.

Elements of the British Royal Navy began arriving in Norfolk, Virginia, including their two carrier strike groups and a host of support vessels and submarines—not to mention a full contingent of Royal Marines. Those ships were resupplied and redeployed to the Caribbean. The president had been in discussions with the leaders of the island nations, including Cuba, regarding their mutual protection, and so far, all had agreed that a unified defensive strategy was the only way that any of them would survive.

Plans were drawn up for a summit of representatives from the island nations, and the Canadian provinces and territories, to craft a unified defensive strategy. Iceland and Greenland were invited to attend, and senior members of the U.S. military, Canadian military, and British military forces in the region would also be in attendance.

The meeting was scheduled to take place in two weeks.

CHAPTER 10

Mexico City • Tampa • Washington, DC
November 2027

The first week of November arrived, and Rosemont's team had finally quit squabbling and were focused on developing strategies for the defense of North America. The summit with the Canadian, Caribbean, Iceland, and Greenland representatives was a week away, and the team had its hands full preparing scenarios for the representatives to consider.

"Where is the meeting being held?" Clay asked Rosemont late one afternoon.

"At the Tampa Convention Center. You'll all be attending, by the way. Reservations have already been made."

"A public convention center?" Clay was surprised. "That's an inviting target for someone to shoot at. It's hard to defend, it's in a public area where it'll be easy for someone to get lost in the crowd... It'll be a logistical nightmare for the security personnel."

Rosemont smiled. "We're counting on that."

"I beg your pardon?"

"You're right. It's an inviting target. So inviting that we *want* someone to try something. If we can catch them, we'll have a better idea about whether or not China is actually involved."

"You're going to risk the lives of the representatives from

all those countries and provinces?" Grant asked.

"Of course not," Rosemont replied. "The meeting at the Convention Center is a fake. The real meeting is at MacDill Air Force Base just south of Tampa. The representatives will be flown directly to the base, while fake delegates will land at Tampa airport and be taken to the hotels surrounding the convention center. They'll all be security agents, and every employee at the convention center, and at most of the nearby hotels, will be security or military. If anyone tries anything, we'll know."

"That's a lot to set up in a short time," Clay remarked.

"Yes, that's why we're hoping it'll work," Rosemont said. "We're counting on nobody guessing that we could have set up a sting like this so quickly."

The banker from China was ushered into the office of the President of Mexico. As members of the ruling council for the Latin American Block, the presidents of Venezuela and Columbia were also there.

"Gentlemen, are you aware of what's happening in Tampa next week?" The banker had no time to waste on pleasantries.

"You mean the summit meeting?" the president of Venezuela asked.

"Of course I mean the summit meeting," the banker snapped. "Do I need to remind you that a unified North America could have serious consequences for our mutual plans in this hemisphere? Divided, the countries are all controllable. But united... we cannot allow that. And that damnable Canada. They never do what they're needed to do when it counts. You three need to find a way to keep that meeting from succeeding."

"How?" the president of Mexico asked.

"Figure it out!" The banker was losing his patience. He was tired of dealing with these pawns and longed for the day when it was finally time to sacrifice them.

"We could bomb the conference facility," the president of Columbia suggested. "Killing all those representatives and military personnel at the same time is the best way to keep the meeting from being a success. Plus none of the countries would agree to schedule another meeting after that, and the United States' plan for unity would die in Tampa."

The banker smiled. "Now you're thinking like allies. Good. Make it happen. You know when, and you know where."

"Do you want it done on the first day or the last day?" the president of Mexico asked.

"First day," the banker replied, getting to his feet. "If the summit ends early, we could miss our chance. Set off the bombs one to two hours into the meeting."

"Who do we get to do this?" the president from Venezuela asked.

"The cartels have experts in this sort of thing," the president of Columbia said. "I'll give one of them a call."

The banker nodded curtly and left the President's office.

November in Tampa was like summer in New England and Canada, but the trade winds blew constantly, making the weather very pleasant for the representatives and for the security personnel.

The fake representatives flew into Tampa Airport from Washington, DC, the Canadian provinces, the North Atlantic countries, and the Caribbean islands. They were met by fake State Department personnel and escorted to the hotels surrounding the Convention Center. Meanwhile, the real representatives flew into Air Force bases around the country onboard private jets, transferred to military jets, and were flown directly to MacDill Air Force Base. Base housing had been set aside for them, and even though it lacked the comforts of the downtown hotels, every one of the delegates understood the security concerns.

The government booked the entire Convention Center for the week to ensure that no one entered the building other than the security personnel and fake representatives.

Kate, Steve, Clay, and Grant were in the security command post in the building across the street from the Convention Center. They were all armed and wearing tactical gear. The walls of the command post were covered with video monitors.

High Definition cameras had been placed so that every inch of the Convention Center and the hotel lobbies could be watched 24-7. Facial recognition software ran constantly, looking for faces that weren't on the approved list. The plan was for the system to find faces that didn't belong. Security was ordered to assume that anyone whose face was unfamiliar to the system was a threat. Elevators and stairways were checked several times a day, but so far, nothing suspicious had happened.

Three large floral vans arrived and began unloading centerpieces for the conference tables. The facial recognition system alerted the command post immediately. "Have three security agents escort them to the main ballroom," the security chief said into his headset.

Three military security officers, dressed as Convention Center security, walked outside and talked to the floral deliverers. There were twelve people from the florist in the vans, and after their credentials were examined, they were led into the Convention Center's main ballroom.

One of the security officers walked behind the group delivering the centerpieces. As he entered the building, he sent a silent alarm to the security office. The credentials of the deliverymen were fake.

When the deliverymen reached the main ballroom on the second floor, they placed the centerpieces on the tables around the room. Then three of the deliverymen engaged the security officers in an animated conversation. The security cameras showed the other nine deliverymen slip away and make their way to the first floor room directly below the main ballroom.

Everyone in the command post watched as the floral deliverymen took off their coveralls and removed what looked like several pounds of C-4 molded to look like their chests and stomachs. The C-4 was placed above the ceiling tiles, directly below where the delegates were supposed to be meeting later that morning.

Once the explosives had been placed, the men went back to the delivery vans to wait for the three others still inside who were distracting the security officers. Less than ten minutes later, the last three deliverymen exited the Convention Center, and they all drove away. They had no idea that their delivery vans had been bugged and rigged with tracking devices, and that more than twenty vehicles and four helicopters were pursuing them.

"Send in the bomb squad," the security chief said into his headset.

Five teams of bomb disposal experts entered the Convention Center and made their way to the room below the main ballroom. They removed all of the ceiling tiles and found the bombs easily. They confirmed that each bomb was made of several pounds of C-4 and rigged with a remote triggering device.

Sergeant "Bull" Foley began disarming the first bomb. As he traced the wires between the detonator and the remote trigger, he suddenly stopped. "Don't touch any of the wires," he shouted.

"Why not, Sarge?" one of the other team members asked as he was about to cut the detonator wire.

"The trigger is wired to send an alert to the remote detonator if any of the wires are cut. The bombers will know that we found the bombs."

"What do we do Sarge?" another member of the team asked.

Foley stared at the bomb he was holding. Then he shouted,

"Pull all the C-4 off the bomb. Just leave the detonator, the trigger, and the power source intact and connected. We'll put all of the C-4 in a safety bin and get it out of here. The detonators and triggers can be placed... on a boat. That way only the boat will be destroyed when the bombers set them off."

The team members quickly removed all of the C-4 and placed it in secure containers hidden in rolling laundry bins, so no one watching would notice. The security chief, who was notified about the plan, made arrangements for a boat to be brought to the waterfront side of the Convention Center, and the detonators and triggers were placed in ice bins before being taken to the boat. Nobody watching should have noticed anything unusual about what was going on.

Within an hour, all of the C-4 had been removed, and the detonators and triggers were on a small boat being towed several hundred feet away from the Convention Center's docks.

The team following the bombers saw them turn onto the Courtney Campbell Causeway, heading toward Pinellas County on the other side of Tampa Bay. When they reached the west side of the causeway, they turned south and drove until they were even with the Convention Center. Then they waited.

Both the real and the fake summit meetings began on time. The fake meeting took place in the main ballroom of the Convention Center to maintain appearances, in case the bombers had observers watching. The real meeting was in one of MacDill's underground facilities.

The team following the bombers saw them remove the remote detonator from one of the vans. One of the bombers turned the key. A moment later, a small boat in water off the Convention Center disintegrated as the detonators all exploded. The bombers looked confused as the team moved in to apprehend them.

The bombers were taken to the Federal Building downtown to be interrogated, while the security team at the Convention Center checked out of their hotels, removed the cameras and other surveillance devices, and sanitized everything so that there was no trace they had ever been there.

Kate, Steve, Clay, and Grant drove to the Federal Building to watch the interrogations. At first, none of the bombers would talk. But after they had been fingerprinted and their identities confirmed, the interrogators had better leverage.

The interrogators spent a lot of time with one of the bombers known only as "Ramone."

"Look, Ramone," the interrogator said. "We know who you are, and we know what you've done. Here's the thing, though. Back when you were a cartel thug, planting a bomb would get you five to ten years for attempted murder and attempted destruction of public property. But you're not a cartel thug anymore. You're here representing a foreign power. That makes what you did either an act of state-sponsored terrorism or an act of war. And it's a crime that you committed against more than twenty countries altogether—many of which have the death penalty, and some even still have death-by-torture. That's what's waiting for you. As for your family? Well, since this was an act of war, that gives us the right to bomb your village and all of the surrounding villages into oblivion. Your family will be burned alive by incendiary bombs that we'll drop on them, and it'll be your fault. War is hell, you know. And that's where you're going, along with the people who helped you, your family, and the families of the people who helped you. Or, you can talk to us and answer a few simple questions. You do that, and your family is spared. You tell us something truly valuable, and your life is spared. Now, that's a good deal, isn't it?"

Ramone stared at the interrogator. He fidgeted in his chair, clearly weighing his options. Finally he spat out, "If I talk, my family is dead."

"Who's going to know that you talked?" the interrogator asked. "I'm not going to tell them. *You're* not going to tell them. Your friends in the other rooms will never know. The only people your family has to fear... is *us*."

Ramone stared at the interrogator. His jaw moved back and forth as if he were trying to talk but his jaw was preventing it. After a while, he asked, "What do you want to know?"

"Who sent you?"

"The head of my cartel."

"And who asked your cartel to blow up the summit?"

"The president of Columbia."

"And who asked the president of Columbia to contact the head of your cartel?"

"I don't know."

"Think. Real. Hard," the interrogator growled.

Ramone swallowed hard. "The head of my cartel said something about 'the banker.'"

"What banker?"

"All of the cartels used the same banker. It's been that way for more than thirty years, ever since the cartels became a single syndicate. And now the entire Latin American Block uses the same banker."

"I thought the cartels were independent operations that were constantly fighting among each other," the interrogator said.

Ramone laughed. "That's what we wanted you to think. There's actually only one cartel, and it's global. The individual cartels that you know about are just franchises that operate specific territories. It was the banker who set this up a long time ago, and it works pretty well. You should see what we *really* smuggle across your border. Drugs are chump change compared to what our real business is."

"And you use the Cayman Island banks?"

Ramone snorted, "That's just where we keep our petty cash—what comes from the drug trade. The real money is kept somewhere else."

"Where?"

"I'm not sure. It's not really talked about."

"Guess."

Ramone was quiet for a moment. "I never met the banker, but I did see him once. He's Asian. I think someone said he's Chinese."

Kate, Steve, Clay, and Grant stood in the observation room, watching the interrogation. When they heard Ramone's last comment, Clay looked at Kate. "There's your proof, Kate. Handbasket is correct. China is responsible for what happened in Latin America, and it all started over thirty years ago, just like you said."

"According to him," Grant pointed out.

"Yes, according to him," Clay admitted. "But we have a dozen prisoners, and we can use what Ramone just said to try to get confirmation about this banker."

Over the next twenty-four hours, the other prisoners were interrogated multiple times. Eight finally confirmed that the head of their cartel gave them the order to bomb the summit, five confirmed that it was a request from the president of Columbia, and two confirmed that the banker—a mysterious Asian—was behind the plot.

"That's three now who have referenced an Asian banker," Clay reminded Grant.

Grant nodded. "I believe that constitutes proof that the Latin American part of Handbasket is accurate."

"We need to tell Rosemont," Steve suggested.

Kate looked at her watch. It was approaching noon on the second day of the summit. "He'll be tied up until after seven tonight. Let's get cleaned up, changed, and get some real food in us before we meet with him."

"Any suggestions?" Grant asked.

"I know a one-of-a-kind steakhouse not far from here. Best in the world!"

"Sounds good to me," Clay said.

They weren't able to see Rosemont until after 8:00 PM. They met in one of MacDill's secure conference rooms with the rest of the team.

Clay recapped the sting on the bombers and their subsequent interrogations. He emphasized the revelation about the single global cartel managing the drug trade, the other businesses that the local cartels really did, the involvement of the president of Columbia in the bombing, and the involvement of an Asian banker who set up the global syndicate more than thirty years ago and demanded that the summit be bombed.

"Do we know for certain that he was Chinese?" Rosemont asked.

"No," Clay replied, "But evidently China is part of the global syndicate. Would they be part of something that they weren't running?"

Rosemont frowned. "I don't like using a negative to prove a positive, but you raise a valid point. Why would China join someone else's business venture? It doesn't seem right, does it?"

"So that confirms part of Handbasket, doesn't it?" Clay asked.

Rosemont nodded. "The Latin American part at least. Now we just need to prove the other pieces."

"We're working on it," Kate noted.

"Keep at it," Rosemont said. "Given the direction that the summit is going, we need to know for certain before we can finalize any of the plans."

"It could take a while," Steve interjected.

"You don't have a while. Work fast."

Grant's secure phone chimed, and he excused himself to take the call. When he came back a few minutes later, he asked, "Is anyone here aware that troops from the Latin American Block are moving north through Mexico toward our southern border?"

CHAPTER 11

———————•————————

Murmansk • Oslo • Tampa • Washington, DC
November 2027

The secure conference room at MacDill Air Force Base fell silent, and Rosemont stared at Grant for a moment. "Is this confirmed?"

Grant nodded. "That was my boss at DIA. Satellites picked up the movement several hours ago. At first they thought that soldiers from the Latin American Block were on joint maneuvers, but the number of convoys heading north is staggering, and they're coming from countries other than just Mexico, Venezuela, and Columbia."

"Are they staging somewhere or just heading for the border independently?" Michaels asked.

"Unknown," Grant replied.

"What about supply lines? Vandyke asked.

"Also unknown."

Rosemont frowned. "Well, we need to know. Barksdale, you, Vandyke, Michaels, and Kirkland get with your people and find out what's going on down there."

Turning to the Homeland Security members of the team, Rosemont said, "Sweeny, you, Benson, and Petersen check with your people and find out if DHS is prepared to repel an incursion from Mexico or if troops are going to be sent down there."

"What do you want the rest of us to do?" Clay asked.

"I want you and Kate to keep focusing on Europe, Russia, and Asia. We still need to understand the situation over there, and we need contacts on the ground who can tell us what's going on and how things got where they are. I understand that at least one of the British officers here is from their military intelligence service and worked closely with MI-6 before London fell. Tap into him and see what he knows."

"Right."

Kate and Clay sat in a smaller conference room down the hall, looking through stacks of intel reports. The British intelligence officer was in a meeting, but he promised to stop by later that night.

Kate tossed another folder onto the table in frustration.

"What's wrong?" Clay asked.

"I'm tired of looking at intel reports that are second- and third-hand, and the Agency's assets outside the U.S. haven't been any help in months. I need to be talking to the sources—foreign assets on foreign soil."

"A jet can get you to Norway in about nine or ten hours," Clay noted. "But getting out of there safely could be a challenge now that the UK has fallen. Video conferencing is dicey at best, and cellular communications are virtually nonexistent. Sat-phones are still working, but I don't know how many of the assets you want to talk to over there have them."

Kate had a thought. "Wait a minute. You're with counter intelligence and counter espionage, right?"

Clay nodded.

"So what about foreign agents here in the United States?" Kate continued. "Surely there are agents who are trapped here now that their countries have been overrun. What about what they can tell us? There must be Israeli, Russian, European

159

Union, and Japanese intelligence officers stranded in the U.S.—especially since most of their embassies are closed and the staff either recalled or in exile. Doesn't your group monitor them to find out who their U.S. contacts are and to make sure they don't see things we don't want them to see?"

Clay nodded. "We don't know who all of them are, but we know some of them."

"Has the FBI made any attempt to bring them in now that their employers are out of business, so to speak?"

Clay chuckled. "Not to my knowledge."

"Can you find out?" Kate asked. "Think about what they might know that'll help us. Particularly the Russians. I really need to talk to a Russian."

Clay placed a call to the Deputy Director responsible for domestic counterterrorism and counter espionage. When the Deputy Director finally answered the phone, Clay relayed Kate's request. Kate could tell from Clay's side of the conversation that it was taking a fair bit of convincing to get the Deputy Director to agree to Clay's suggestion.

Five minutes later, Clay ended the call. "He said he'll start rounding up the ones we know about, and he'll promise them amnesty and sanctuary if they'll help us."

Kate's eyes lit up. "Great! What about Chinese agents in the United States?"

"We've had problems identifying them in the past, and their employer is still in business," Clay pointed out. "What about the Chinese agents in Canada?"

"We can ask the Canadians to round them up and turn them over to us. Their presence could be considered that of an insurgent, given how they threatened the Canadian Prime Minister. That gives us more latitude in our interrogation techniques."

"You know who I'd like to get my hands on?" Clay asked.

Kate shook her head.

"That banker running things in the Latin American Block. Can you imagine what *he'd* be able to tell us?"

Kate leaned back for a minute. She knew that there were CIA assets still operating in Latin America, but their intel had been spotty for some time. However, if they all had a single focus—that of identifying and tracking the banker—that intel could lead to an op to catch the banker and sweat him for information.

She picked up her phone and called her CIA superior. When he answered, she relayed the intel they had gathered already about the Asian banker and asked about using the surviving Latin American Block assets to identify, track, and apprehend the banker.

"He's running it up the chain," she said when she ended the call. "He said he'd call me back tomorrow."

Clay looked at Kate for a moment. "You really want to go to Norway, don't you."

"I really want to go to Norway."

Clay nodded. "Let's go ask Rosemont. I can start sweating the foreign assets we round up here and in Canada, and you can talk to the field agents hiding out in Scandinavia. Of course, you'll have to contact them first and make sure they're in a position to meet with you."

"Already in the works," Kate confided. "My boss has been tracking them down for the past week."

Rosemont was in favor of the plan to interrogate foreign operatives in the U.S. and Canada, but he was completely opposed to any member of the team leaving the country for *any* reason. "Do you understand the danger involved in what you're asking?" he demanded.

"Of course," Kate replied evenly. "I've done field work before, as you well know. It's why my analyses are valuable. The intel I use is unfiltered and unedited. If you want to know what's going on, *I* need to talk to the people who actually know. I can't do that from here."

Rosemont just stared at Kate. "You know it'll have to be approved by both the president *and* the Norwegians. And there's a high likelihood that any plane you use to get there will be commandeered before you're ready to fly back. Oh, and don't even think about using a submarine. You'd be gone at least two weeks, and I can't spare you for that long. The best I can do is to give you five days total, and that includes travel time. But first you have to convince me that you'll be able to meet with enough operatives over there to make the trip worthwhile, and you'll have to get the necessary approvals for the trip before I'll authorize it. Are you planning to take anyone with you?"

Kate shook her head. "I can move faster alone. And if the plane is of concern, I can parachute in. Then you'd only have to figure out how to get me out and back home."

"Parachute... into Norway... in November?" Rosemont sounded incredulous.

"So it'll be a bit chilly," Kate retorted.

"Chilly?! You'll freeze your ass off! Ground temperature will be between twenty and thirty degrees, but can you imagine how much colder it will be up in the air when you jump? You're insane!"

"That's why insulated suits were created," Kate reminded him. "Besides, this is one of those things that must be done for God and Country."

Kate spent the next two days contacting every surviving and reachable operative hiding out on the Scandinavian Peninsula. She managed to track down eleven, and eight said that they could be in Norway to meet with her in the next few days. She also met with the British intelligence officer, who promised to locate any surviving contacts in Norway, Sweden, and Finland.

"There are also Russians in Norway," the British officer

reported. "Army, Navy, and intelligence. They're coordinating with the remnants of the European militaries to decide what to do if the Chinese enter the Atlantic or the Caliphate crosses the Russian border. They have some *very* particular opinions about the Chinese, which leads me to believe that they have intel you don't."

Kate felt her pulse quicken. "Will they talk to me?"

"Let me see what I can do," the British officer replied as he got up to leave. "I'll let you know."

Kate went to find Rosemont. It was the last day of the summit, and Kate wanted to get everything arranged before flying back to Washington.

"The Russians, eh?" Rosemont commented when Kate told him about Russians being in Norway. "With intel on the Chinese? That in itself could be worth the trip over there."

"What if they want me to go to Russia to see the intel?" Kate asked.

"Then you go, and we'll find a way to get you home from there," Rosemont stated.

"When I get to Norway, there's a good chance that the remnants of the European militaries and governments will find out I'm there and want to talk to me. Do I have any authority to speak for the United States if they should ask for a meeting?"

Rosemont's eyes opened wide. "You mean more than the usual *quid pro quo* of sharing information?"

Kate nodded.

"What do you anticipate that they'd ask for?"

"Our help," Kate replied.

"To do what?"

"I don't know. Counterattack? Evacuate? I won't know until I get there. And as far as the Russians go, their government, their Atlantic surface and submarine fleets, their Air Force, every tactical and strategic weapons system west of the Urals, and any that they brought over the Urals during their retreat, are spread out across all of their military bases along the western edge of the Kola Peninsula on the Barents Sea, close to Finland. If the Chinese bring their fleet into the Atlantic, the Chinese will have the Russians in a pincher, and then *China* will have all of those Russian assets. If the Russians want to discuss their options, am I allowed to have those conversations with them? I know I can't commit to anything, but can I at least listen to what they want to say?"

Rosemont frowned and closed his eyes. After a couple of minutes, he picked up the phone and dialed the number for the White House's main switchboard. A moment later, he said, "Chief of Staff Voight's office."

After a minute, he said, "Voight? Rosemont here. Listen, a member of my team is flying to Norway in a couple of days, with a possible side-trip to the Murmansk naval facilities. She's worried that the remnants of the European governments and militaries, not to mention the Russians, will want to take advantage of an American being there to discuss their options. Not sure that a member of my team is best suited for that, should it happen. Do you have anyone who can go, who has war zone field experience, knows how to parachute from a plane in frigid weather, and is willing to follow her orders in all circumstances, with the possible exception of negotiating on behalf of the United States? Make no mistake, her mission is of paramount importance, and she'll be absolutely in command, but diplomatic assistance would be useful, should the need arise, and assistance helping her with her assignment would be appreciated even if no diplomatic assistance is required."

Rosemont listened for a few minutes. "Kate Davidsen... Yes, the Handbasket analyst... You do? Excellent. Have him report to Kate when she gets back to Washington... Yes, I'll send you her contact information. Thanks, Voight."

Rosemont ended the call and looked at Kate. "Adam Chester will be going with you. He was a Lieutenant in the

Airborne Rangers before leaving the Army and entering government service. He'll be a good man to have your back while you're over there, and he can speak on the subjects that are above your paygrade."

"Language skills?" Kate asked.

"Not sure. You'll need to ask him. If worse comes to worst, you can translate. I know *you* know all the languages you're likely to encounter over there."

Kate smiled. Her language skills were excellent, and she knew that intelligence operatives were the last people who should be negotiating political or military issues. But she didn't know that Rosemont would authorize someone outside the team to travel with her.

"Finish making your travel arrangements, and keep me posted. Oh, and I hear Clay is making progress with the foreign operatives that the FBI rounded up for him. Good suggestion there."

"Thank you." Kate left Rosemont and went to find a private room where she could finish making her travel plans. Rosemont had secured approval for the op, even though he didn't come right out and say so. Now Kate had to make certain that the trip was successful so he wouldn't regret his decision.

At 3:00 PM, two days later, a military transport jet took off from Joint Base Andrews for Norway. The plan was for Kate and Adam to parachute to a farm east of Oslo just before dawn. Most of the operatives they were meeting with were supposed to be waiting for them there. The plane would turn around and land in Reykjavik, Iceland. There it would refuel and wait until it was time to pick Kate and Adam up and bring them back to the U.S.

Kate had very little time to get to know Adam before they boarded the plane. Within the first five minutes of their first meeting, she could tell that he was a no-nonsense, all-business kind of guy. She did learn that he was married with twin 3-year-old boys—one of the reasons that he left the military—and she knew what his job was at the White House, but apart from that, she knew very little about him. He had the skills needed for the assignment, and he was a pleasant-enough person, but everything else was an enigma. *I wonder which side of the recent Civil War he was on. If he was on the losing side, it may explain why he's so aloof around me.*

Kate and Adam spent most of the flight going through the profiles of the people they'd be meeting with, and working out the details of approaching and meeting with the European leaders and the Russians. Adam spoke some Russian, but he was fluent in French and the Scandinavian languages. Kate was fluent in Russian, Italian, Spanish, French, Arabic, Mandarin, and Japanese. In addition, since Kate's parents were Norwegian, she had been raised speaking the Scandinavian languages like a native.

Kate was anxious about the trip—not about the mission but about seeing Norway again. She had been there many times over the years, but this would be the first time since the wars broke out. She was worried about what the war had done to the villages and the landscape that she loved so much. But she pushed that aside and focused on the job at hand. They had three days on the ground before being picked up and flown home. There was a lot to do and not much time to get it all done.

Twenty minutes before they reached the drop zone, Kate and Adam divided up the equipment they were taking with them: weapons, secure sat-phones, recording devices, and backups for almost everything. Once everything had been packed, they put on their insulated suits, their helmets, and their parachutes. Then they moved into position near the rear ramp of the airplane. As the ramp opened, the sudden rush of cold air cut like a knife. They lowered the visors on their helmets, activating the heads-up display, and braced themselves.

Kate felt the plane slowing down as they waited for the

signal to jump. They were still going much faster than she was used to for a parachute jump, but there was no choice. The jet was all that was available with the range they needed. The pilot slowed down so much that Kate was certain the jet would stall. Then the green light lit, and she and Adam launched themselves off the ramp and into the predawn sky. For a moment, she smelled the jet's exhaust and heard the jet engines power up as the plane moved away.

Rosemont wasn't kidding, she thought as she hit the November air. The insulated suit made conditions barely tolerable. She and Adam picked up speed as they fell. Kate watched the altimeter display on the inside of her visor, and when it read the correct height, she pulled the cord that opened her chute. She looked around and saw Adam's chute nearby. In the distance, she observed the northern lights of the Aurora Borealis stretching across the northern skyline. *I've seen it before, but never from the air.* It was still too dark to see the ground with the naked eye; sunrise at that time of year wouldn't be for several more hours. But the heads-up display showed her the trees and the clearing below, while the altimeter let her know how close to the ground she was.

After a while, she noticed a light flashing on the ground, and she wondered if it was gunfire. Then she realized that the light was a signal letting her and Adam know where they were to land. They were right where they were supposed to be.

The flashing light was coming from the snow-covered clearing just ahead. The display in her visor also showed lights coming from windows of a large building nearby. When her altimeter showed that she was close to the ground, she lit and dropped a flare so the people waiting for them would see her landing zone. She saw a second flare drop and knew it must be Adam's.

Her boots made a crunching sound as she landed in the clearing. Adam landed about fifty feet away from her. As she removed her parachute and began rolling it up, she saw people approaching her from the direction of the building.

"Handbasket," a voice shouted.

Kate lifted her visor and gave the proper response in English. "China doll."

The people moved closer. "Ms. Davidsen? Mr. Chester?" The voice had a British accent.

"Yes."

"Ah, good. You're right on time. We're all here. Shall we go inside and get out of the cold?"

"Thank you." Kate and Adam followed them to the building on the edge of the clearing. The snow wasn't deep, so the walk was easy, in spite of the gear they were carrying.

When they got inside, there were about fifteen men and two women waiting. Several were assets that she had worked with before, some were MI-6, courtesy of the British officer that Kate met with in Tampa, and some were from the remnants of the European intelligence services that she didn't know personally. All of them looked weathered and defeated. She and Adam removed their insulated suits and helmets, and then sat down with the others.

"Normally I'd meet with each of you individually in separate locations," she began as she was handed a small plate of bread, cheese, and dried fruit. "But I appreciate your willingness to help me gather as much information as possible in the limited time we have. You know why we're here. We need to know everything you can tell us about how the Caliphate overran Europe so quickly and easily, how they were equipped and funded, why they haven't crossed into Russia, why they haven't invaded the peninsula yet, and what military assets are currently on the peninsula. I'm also curious if any of you have heard of a connection between the Caliphate and China."

"It's interesting that you mentioned equipment and funding," one of the assets that she knew remarked. "In the early days of the insurgent uprising, we confiscated a number of weapons. They were all brand new and all Chinese made. That's not too unusual. But a few of the cells we raided also had stacks of unmarked gold ingots. When we tested their chemical composition, it matched gold mined in China. Now you're asking about a Chinese connection. Evidence suggests that there *was* Chinese involvement, at least with the cells we raided before the Caliphate got the upper hand and forced us north. And that's strange, since the Chinese have always hated Islam."

"Did any of the rest of you discover anything similar?" Kate asked.

A few nodded their heads.

"Did you ever see any Asians in the company of the Islamic fighters?"

No one nodded.

"There were Asians crawling all over Europe in the months prior to the uprising," another asset reported. "We didn't think twice about it. They'd been buying everything they could get their hands on for decades—everything from automobile and consumer manufacturing companies to high tech and telecom conglomerates. And we didn't really get a chance to spy on the Islamic districts too closely. They weren't our priority until it was too late. We had no warning that the uprisings were about to happen. One day it was a calm and peaceful spring day, and the next... Europe was a war zone with uprisings in over thirty cities. And that was just the first day."

"They were everywhere," one of the MI-6 operatives added. "There were no lines of battle, because the fighting was all around. There was no place to regroup, no strategic positioning, and almost no place to retreat. The destruction and death toll was ghastly. If it moved, they killed it. They make Hitler look like an amateur."

One of the Norwegian operatives spoke up. "We have been wondering about the Russian border ourselves. The Caliphate hasn't crossed it once."

"Not even to reach Chechnya?" Kate asked.

"No, and that's the strangest thing," the Norwegian replied. "You'd think that would be their first target, to liberate Russia's Islamic population. But they ignored it entirely. And they could have overrun this peninsula months ago if they had been willing to breach the Russian border to take us by land, but they didn't. It's fortunate that we ejected all of our Islamic refugees when we left the EU, or we would have had to deal with uprisings like the rest of Europe did. As it is, we kicked out the remaining Islamists as soon as the uprisings began. That's why we're still here."

Kate recapped what she had heard so far. "So there was no warning, the insurgents were using new Chinese weapons and were in possession of Chinese gold, the Chinese were buying businesses left and right before the uprisings began, no one knows why the Caliphate hasn't crossed into Russia, and no one knows why they haven't invaded the peninsula. Is that about right?"

"It's not really a mystery about why they haven't invaded the peninsula," one of the Swedish operatives commented. "They don't have any troop transport ships. The European navies brought most of them here and sunk the rest so they couldn't be used by the insurgents or the Caliphate troops. Short of crossing the Russian border, they can't reach us. And if they tried to cross over in unarmored ships, our shore defenses would blow them out of the water."

"So what are the Caliphate forces doing right now?" Kate asked.

"Destroying everything they come across," the French operative said bitterly. "That's all they do."

"But they haven't finished taking all of Europe," Kate pressed him. "They swept over the whole continent, except for Russia and the peninsula, and they just stopped to destroy everything? How can they occupy Europe if there's nothing left of Europe? If their plan is to destroy, why leave two parts untouched? If their plan is to occupy, why destroy everything? And either way, why aren't they finishing the job? They took Africa, they already had the Middle-East, and now they have two-thirds of Europe, but they're making no moves to take the rest of Europe? Why not? It doesn't make sense. They want the world, but they leave two huge pieces alone because... why?"

No one had an answer for her.

They continued talking for the next several hours; the light of the autumn sun remained low on the horizon, illuminating the room's ceiling as it reflected off the snow outside. Kate recorded the conversations and took notes. By the time they broke for a light lunch, she had pieced together quite a bit about the Chinese involvement in Europe in the months leading to the uprising. She had also stumbled on another interesting fact. The Caliphate seemed to be waiting for something. They had pushed north, and then stopped. It reminded Kate of the way that the Latin American block didn't seem to have a goal in mind for after it had conquered Central and South America. *Another indication that they're just pawns in someone else's game.*

After lunch, Kate approached the MI-6 operatives. "Will I be able to meet with any of the Russians?"

One of the MI-6 operatives nodded. "They'll be here later this afternoon. They're looking forward to meeting you, but I think they're going to want you to go to Murmansk with them. They have something there that they say you'll want to see."

Kate nodded. "Thank you for setting that up. Who will I be meeting with?"

"The officer I met with is named Kostya Petrov. He wears the uniform of a Russian Army colonel, but I believe he's GRU—one of their *very* senior officers."

Kate knew exactly what the GRU was. *Main Directorate.*

Their military intelligence service. I've run into them before.

The group took their seats, and the operative from France raised his hand. "Members of my government who fled here know that you have come to talk to us and gather intel. But they want the chance to talk to you about our situation."

"My government wants the same," the Norwegian operative stated.

"And mine," the other operatives said.

Kate pointed to Adam. "And that's exactly why I brought Mr. Chester with me. While I represent the U.S. intelligence agencies, Mr. Chester represents the U.S. government, and he'll be happy to speak with members of *your* government while I'm meeting with the Russians. But if I have to go to Murmansk, I'll need him to join me in case the Russian government also wants to speak to an official representative of the U.S. government."

The group promised to have representatives of their government come later that afternoon to meet with Adam.

The Norwegian, French, German, Swedish, Finnish, Polish, and other European government officials arrived shortly before the Russian military representatives. Adam met with them in another room so Kate could be alone with the Russians.

When the Russians arrived, they seemed surprised that they were meeting with a female intelligence officer. When Colonel Petrov made the introductions, he expressed his surprise by her near-perfect western Russian accent.

"Davidsen is a Scandinavian name, but are you Russian?" he asked. "Perhaps on your mother's side?"

"Kate shook her head. "Norwegian on both sides."

"Well, you speak our language like a native. I guess that's important for a spy."

Kate smiled and gestured for everyone to be seated.

Colonel Petrov started the conversation. "I understand you're interested in knowing why the Caliphate hasn't crossed into Russia and if there's any Chinese involvement in what's going on—apart from their invasion of our country."

"That's right," Kate confirmed.

"Well, China is behind everything going on in the world," he stated. "The Caliphate, Latin America, everything."

"How do you know?" Kate asked.

Petrov looked smug. "We had an asset in China for many years. He worked in the Central Military Commission headquarters in Beijing... as a typist, until he retired a few years ago. In 1991, he was assigned to type up a strategy developed by a young Chinese chess prodigy... a grandmaster, I think... that was being presented to the leaders of the military and the Communist party. He kept a copy for himself. Over the next year, he typed up the detailed plans for this strategy, and again, he kept copies for himself. The chess prodigy trusted this typist and insisted that he and he alone transcribe all of the notes. By the time the typist retired, he had thousands of pages of detailed operational plans for China's conquest of the world. But he believed that the strategy was a blueprint for the end of the world, rather than a conquest of the world for the glory of China, and he wanted nothing to do with it. He made arrangements to turn over all of his documents to us."

"Did he?" Kate asked.

"Yes. But he was discovered and killed as he was driving back home from the meeting. We got away safely with the papers. We had just begun translating them into Russian when China invaded. We feel that the timing of the invasion was accelerated because of the loss of those documents, and that's probably why they didn't have a firm plan for what to do once they reached the Urals."

"Did you finish translating the documents?" Kate hid her excitement.

"No," Petrov admitted. "We translated part of the original strategy, but there were so many documents... we just didn't have time."

"It's unfortunate," he added ruefully. "By the time we translated the sections regarding the Pacific, Africa, Europe, and South America, it was too late to warn anyone about what was going to happen. It had already started. And we had the Chinese invasion to contend with. We put the documents aside and never looked at them again."

"I could translate them," Kate offered. "I'm fluent in Mandarin."

"It would be good to know what their real plans are and what's supposed to happen next," Petrov remarked. "But it's too big of a task for one person. Would you be willing to stay in Russia for the time it would take to complete the work?"

Kate shook her head. "I have to be back in the States in three days. But if you let me take copies of the documents with me, I can translate them and get the information back to you."

The Russian officers looked at each other. Then Petrov spoke. "We have copies of both the translated and the untranslated documents. We can let you have the copies, but there's... a price."

Kate smiled coyly. "And what would that be."

Petrov leaned forward. "First, you must come to Murmansk to get the copies. I'm not inclined to bring them here. If the other countries ever discovered that we had the entire Chinese playbook for all three regional wars and didn't warn them, those weapons and soldiers gathered out there all around Norway and Sweden could just as easily be turned toward Russia. Second, obviously, no one outside of your superiors must ever know where you got the information. And third, I must have assurances that you will immediately let us know of anything you find that could help us in our war with China."

Kate nodded. "Coming with you to Murmansk to pick up the copies is no problem. And I give you my word: no one will know where the information came from, and I'll let you know if

I find anything that's related to your war with China."

The Russian nodded. "Oh, one other thing. Representatives from my government will want to speak with you while you're in Russia regarding the U.S. response to the crisis. I think they have information and questions they want to pass along to your government."

Kate nodded. "I thought that might be the case. That's why I brought a colleague with me who represents the U.S. government and is authorized to speak with your government officials. I'm just here to meet with the intelligence community."

"Where is this colleague?" the Russian asked.

Kate pointed at the door to her left. "He's in the next room, meeting with representatives of the European governments in exile here. If you can wait until tomorrow, we can both accompany you to Murmansk. In fact, with your government's permission, our plane can pick us up at the airfield there, allowing us to spend more time meeting with your government and reviewing the documents. Would that be acceptable?"

"I think I could convince my government of that."

"Good. How do we get to Murmansk?" Kate asked.

"Jet helicopter," was the reply.

Shortly before noon the next day, three Russian helicopters landed in the clearing—one for passengers, and two as escorts in case the Caliphate tried to shoot at them. Kate, Adam, and Petrov boarded their aircraft and flew east toward Severomorsk Naval Base in the Murmansk fjord. Kate had made arrangements for their plane, which was waiting in Reykjavik, to fly to Russia and pick them up at the airfield nearby.

The flight gave Kate her first chance to see the Norwegian countryside in the daylight. She was grateful that the landscape below her hadn't been ravaged by war, but everywhere she looked, she saw military units and equipment standing out against the snow-covered terrain. The Scandes—Scandinavian

Mountains—to the north were snowcapped and beautiful in the midday sunlight.

When they crossed the border into Finland, she saw less evidence of the European military remnants stationed there. The countryside looked deserted underneath a blanket of white.

They stopped once in Finland to refuel. When they reached the Severomorsk Naval Base, Kate felt a thrill to be standing where few U.S. operatives had ever stood. She looked around the fjord at the naval base and the city beyond. The docks were crowded with ships, and she saw Russian's sole aircraft carrier docked nearby. Everything looked bleak in the low arctic winter sunlight and the snow-covered ground and hillsides in the distance. The smell of rust and fuel was everywhere.

She marveled at how ice-free the water was, until she remembered that was one of the natural features of the area and the principal reason why the Russians put their Atlantic fleet along the fjord. Adam was escorted to the building where the government officials were housed. Kate—grateful to be wearing the insulated suit—was escorted to the intelligence headquarters on the other side of the base.

They led her to one of the lower levels of the building. She had to pass through six security checkpoints to finally reach the vault where the Chinese documents were kept. When the door was opened and she was allowed to enter, she felt a shudder go up her spine.

I'm about to see the truth. Now I'll know if Handbasket was correct. But more than that, now I'll know what the endgame to all of these conflicts really is.

CHAPTER 12

Kate spent the next day inside the vault, reading through the original Chinese documents and the Russian translations. Never once did she congratulate herself for correctly guessing what the Chinese were up to. She was beginning to understand how much deeper and expansive the Chinese strategy really was, and she saw where all of the conflicts to-date were really heading.

She had seen nothing of Adam since their arrival in Russia, but she knew that he was meeting with several members of the Russian government to discuss options.

Toward the end of the second day, Kate had to stop reading the Chinese documents and start boxing them up. There'd be plenty of time to read the documents on the plane and back in Washington, but for now, she needed to get them packed.

The plane would be landing the next morning, and there were hundreds of documents that needed to be sorted and labeled. She wished she could digitize them, but the GRU's Murmansk headquarters didn't have the equipment, and she didn't have the time to scan or photograph thousands of pages. *At least they had paper copies available for me to take back.*

Late that afternoon, just as she finished sealing the last

box, Colonel Petrov entered the Vault. "I see you've finished packing up the documents. I'll have them loaded onto your airplane when it arrives in the morning."

"Thank you," Kate said.

Petrov didn't move, and Kate could tell that something was on his mind. "Is there anything else you needed, Colonel?" she asked.

Petrov looked behind him to make certain that no one could overhear him, and then he sat down next to where Kate had been working. He gestured for her to sit next to him. "May I have a private word with you, Ms. Davidsen?"

"Certainly, Colonel Petrov," Kate replied. "And please call me Kate."

"Kostya," Petrov gave her his first name. "There's an intelligence matter that I feel we need to discuss, even though I don't have permission from my superiors. A *quid pro quo,* if you will, for the service you're doing us by translating these documents. Have you heard of the Transpolar Passage?"

"I think so," Kate admitted. "It is paths cut through the polar ice pack that reduce commercial shipping time between the Atlantic and the Pacific, isn't it?"

Petrov nodded. "For the last two decades, we, and China, have been using these shipping lanes extensively. The first ones were created by the natural breaking apart of the polar ice pack, but later we began sending icebreakers to open new lanes and keep those lanes open. We have icebreakers here to keep the other channels along the Kola Peninsula open for our Navy and for civilian shipping, but the bulk of our icebreakers were docked at Vladivostok when the Chinese invaded. They took the entire fleet. Soon after, their combined icebreaker fleet sailed for the Arctic. We originally thought that they were carving new lanes so their ships could reach the northern coast of Canada and invade North America. Now we realize that we were wrong. They have been opening and widening lanes along our northern coast as a shortcut to reach the Atlantic. We didn't know, because so far they've been working along the coastline controlled by China. But they've been spotted west of the Urals, and there can be no doubt that their goal is to construct a way to get their ships to the Scandinavian Peninsula in secret and days quicker than they could by sending a fleet through the Suez Canal."

"Why not just sink the icebreakers? You have enough submarines."

"And so do the Chinese. *Our* submarines! It could start a shooting war underneath the polar ice cap between subs that can track each other easily; or worse, they could send *our* submarines here to sink the fleet in port. Plus, it might invite a nuclear reprisal from China, and while Russia has employed the 'scorched earth' doctrine before to thwart invaders, like we did with Napoleon and Hitler, we don't want to leave western Russia uninhabitable for the next century. Chernobyl was a harsh lesson that we're still learning from forty-one years later."

"How long before the new lanes are finished?" Kate asked, beginning to understand the implication.

"Given that winter is coming, not before the end of the year. The snow is already falling, and the icebreakers are having to retrace their paths constantly to keep clear what they've already opened. It gives us time, but not much."

"Would they send their entire fleet through the Arctic?"

Petrov shook his head. "Not if they're smart. It's too risky to send their carriers and troopships through the ice pack. If I were them, I'd send a blockade flotilla through the ice pack to keep us trapped while their bombers levelled everything of value. At the same time, I'd send my carriers, troopships, and supply ships through the Suez Canal. They'd arrive shortly after the bombers had done their job and all resistance was decimated. Then invading the Scandinavian Peninsula and western Russia would be an easy matter."

"Is this just speculation on your part, or is any of it based on facts, other than the part about the sea-lanes being created?" Kate asked.

Petrov glared at Kate. She held his gaze until his expression finally softened. Then he grinned. "The intel is real. The Chinese are still using Russian sailors because they don't have enough trained Chinese sailors to man our ships. Several of our sailors are fluent in Chinese, and they overheard what I just shared with you. It wasn't easy for them to get the information to us; it finally reached me about a week ago."

"Did your sailors say anything about the Chinese submarines?"

Petrov shook his head. "No, just the surface fleet. We know their subs are deployed along the Chinese coast and are patrolling around their captured territories. As long as they don't think we know what they're up to, they don't see the need to protect their fleets with *our* submarines."

Kate smiled at the way Petrov kept referring to the captured submarines as "our" submarines. She asked, "What does all this mean to your defense?"

Petrov looked troubled. "If the Chinese reach the Atlantic and destroy our bases here on the Kola Peninsula, and the European forces in Norway and Sweden, they'll land their troops on the Scandinavian Peninsula and move across Finland, attacking western Russia along a wide front. Our forces holding the Urals would be flanked, and Russia would fall."

Lowering his voice, Petrov added. "My superiors believe that this is inevitable. By sometime next year, Russia will no longer exist. Our history, our culture, everything to remind the world that we were once here will be lost forever. I don't want to see that happen."

"Why are you telling me this, Kostya?"

"Because something of Russia needs to survive. Something that the Chinese want badly. Something that will make their victory over us a hollow one. I have spent my life serving my country. I'm not ready to see that service wasted."

"What do you want me to do?"

Petrov tried to smile but failed. "Find a way to save something of Russia. I'm certain that the Scandinavians would say the same. Don't let the Chinese win everything. They are a patient people, but they don't react well when their plans don't work out as expected. Make their plans fail somehow. Soon you'll be the only ones left who can do it."

Kate felt for the man. She had seen hopelessness before, but never like this. She wanted to help him, but she didn't know how. Finally, she said, simply, "I'll try, Kostya. I'll try."

The U.S. Air Force jet landed at the airfield near the Severomorsk Naval Base just after dawn the next morning. The Russian ground crew refueled the plane, while GRU officers carried the Chinese documents on board and then wished Kate and Adam a safe flight home.

Colonel Petrov approached Kate with his hand outstretched. When she took his hand, he pulled her close. "Don't forget your promises, and if possible, try to save something of us. *Dasvidaniya*."

"I will. *Dasvidaniya*, Kostya."

Petrov nodded and let go of her hand. Then he snapped to attention as a sign of respect. Kate nodded, and then she and Adam boarded the plane. As she took her seat, she looked out the window. Petrov saluted the plane before joining the others in the vehicles waiting to drive them back to the naval base.

The plane taxied to the runway, and soon it was airborne.

Kate stared out the window for a while, lost in thought, when she noticed two fighter jets flying beside their plane. She glanced out one of the windows on the opposite side of the plane and saw two more. They were Russian.

She exchanged glances with Adam, who had also noticed

the jets. She stood and strode to the cockpit. "Why are there four Russian fighters flying next to us?"

"There are reports of Chinese aircraft in the area," the pilot replied. "The Russians offered us an escort to Iceland, where a squadron of U.S. Air Force jets will meet us and escort us the rest of the way home."

Kate felt better. As she walked back to her seat, she glanced at the boxes containing the Chinese documents. *Do the Chinese know what's onboard this plane, or are they just trying to intercept any planes flying west across the Atlantic?*

Suddenly, the plane lurched to starboard. She grabbed the seat in front of her to keep from being flung across the cabin. She pulled herself into her own seat and fastened her seatbelt.

"What's happening?" Adam demanded.

"There are Chinese fighters operating in the area. That's why Russian fighters are escorting us to Iceland—"

A sudden explosion rocked the plane. Kate looked out her window and saw that one of the Russian fighters had exploded. The other jet was firing its missiles, and Kate saw a flash of light in the distance as the missile connected with its target.

The plane lurched again, this time to port, and Kate clutched the armrest to keep from getting flung into the aisle. The pilot's voice came over the PA system. "Three Chinese fighters just attacked, and our escorts intercepted them. Two of the Chinese jets were destroyed, and the third is withdrawing. We lost one Russian fighter, and another one is damaged and has returned to base. The other two are continuing to escort us to Iceland."

Kate relaxed slightly, but it was the most nerve-wracking flight she had ever taken.

After they reached Iceland, and the U.S. Air Force took over the escort duty, Kate decided that she needed something to distract her. She changed seats and moved closer to Adam. They spent the next hour catching each other up on their meetings in

Norway and Russia. Adam's meetings with the various European government officials yielded some valuable intel, and Kate was grateful that Rosemont had arranged for him to go with her.

When Kate relayed what she had picked up in Russia, Adam was shocked. "We're carrying a copy of the complete Chinese strategy? No wonder they tried to shoot us down."

"I don't think that the Chinese know what's on the plane, unless they have agents inside the GRU. I think they're just attacking any plane leaving Russian airspace for the west."

Adam nodded. "Have you read it?"

Kate nodded. "Some of it. The Russians had translated a bit of it into Russian, but the rest is in Chinese. I'll need Rosemont to have a team of Chinese translators available when we get back."

Kate suddenly stood up and grabbed her gear bag from the compartment over her original seat. She pulled out her secure sat-phone and sat down. Holding up the phone so Adam could see it, she said, "That reminds me, I need to call him."

As she dialed Rosemont's number, Adam grabbed his sat-phone. "I should contact my superiors, too."

Rosemont answered the phone on the second ring. "Kate?"

"It's me," Kate confirmed. "We're on our way home."

"I hear the Chinese chased you out of Russia."

"How did you... never mind," Kate said. "Yes, they did. We lost one of the Russian escort fighters, and another one was damaged and had to turn around."

"It didn't make it," Rosemont informed her. "The plane exploded about fifteen minutes after it left you."

"I'm sorry about that," Kate said somberly. "They saved our lives."

"So, was it worth the trip?" Rosemont asked. "I haven't heard from you in days, so either you were extremely busy, or you were enjoying the sights."

"Sorry about that," Kate said. "I was in an underground

GRU vault at the Severomorsk Naval Base in Murmansk reading the Chinese strategy and operational plans... in Chinese."

"You *what*?"

Kate caught Rosemont up-to-speed on her meetings with the Europeans and her trip to Russia. When Rosemont heard that she was bringing copies of the Chinese documents and their Russian translations home with her, she heard the elation in his voice.

"That's incredible! Does in confirm Handbasket?"

"It not only confirms every bit of Handbasket, but it reveals what's coming next," Kate told him. "I'm going to need a very large team of Chinese translators who can be trusted completely. It would take me months to translate the documents myself, and we don't have that kind of time. Things are happening too quickly in Europe right now."

Kate shared with Rosemont what Petrov had told her about the Arctic sea routes. "The Russians are convinced that the Chinese will bring their fleets into the Atlantic in the New Year. When that happens, everything left of Europe will be lost forever. The GRU colonel working with me made an unusual request before I left. He asked me to find a way to make the Chinese victory a hollow one by denying them something that they prize highly. Then he asked me to try to save something of Russia so it wouldn't disappear entirely."

"Sounds like a Russian," Rosemont said. "What did you tell him?"

"That I'd try," Kate replied. "What else could I do?"

"Nothing. Anyway, great job, Kate. I'll see you when you get back, and I'll have an army of translators waiting for you."

Rosemont ended the call. Kate glanced over at Adam, who was still on the phone. She looked out the window. China sending its fleets into the Atlantic consumed her thoughts. She felt a need to prevent the destruction of all that was left of Europe, but she knew that the U.S. was still too fragile to take on the Chinese directly. *If only there were a way to help that didn't put us in direct conflict with the Chinese... some way that would help with our defense while denying the Chinese something that they want.* She looked over at the boxes. *We have their playbook. We have their plans. There must be something in there that we can use.*

As they flew, an idea began forming in her mind.

As the plane continued toward the U.S. coastline, Kate couldn't shake a thought that was nagging her. She got up, went over to the boxes given to her by the GRU, and started going through some of the documents. When she picked up a document dealing with the Latin American Block, she decided to read it. *If troops are massing along the border, it might be nice to know if that was part of the original plan or just a response to our alliance with the Caribbean nations.*

Kate couldn't believe what she was reading. It described in detail how the Latin American pawns were to be sacrificed and replaced. *If the Presidents of Mexico, Venezuela, and Columbia knew about this, they'd abandon their plans and cut all ties with China.* As Kate kept reading, she thought, *What if they did know? What if we told them? Would they even listen to us? They might listen to the banker, if we could get our hands on him.* Kate made a mental note to ask her superior at the Agency about the efforts to find and apprehend the banker.

Kate quickly realized that she had too many mental notes in her head. She needed to start writing them down. She went back to her seat and looked for her notebook. She found it, but her pen wasn't attached anymore. She searched her bag, but there was no pen. Then she searched her jacket.

She found the pen in an outside pocket, but there was something else in the pocket. She pulled out a folded piece of paper. Opening it, she saw "Kostya" and a sat-phone number. *Slick bastard! I never even felt him put it in my pocket. Now I can get in touch with him no matter where he is.*

Kate put the number in her shirt pocket and started writing down all the things that she was trying to keep in her mind.

By the time the plane landed at Joint Base Andrews, Kate not only had a substantial to-do list, but she also had the beginnings of a fairly radical idea.

As she stepped onto the tarmac, her senses were assaulted with the high-pitched whine of jet engines and the smell of exhaust and jet fuel. She said good-bye to Adam, who got into a car waiting to take him for his debriefing at the White House. Rosemont was waiting for her himself with his car and an armored truck to take the Chinese papers to the Pentagon.

"Welcome home, Kate," Rosemont said as she approached him.

"Good to be home," Kate responded.

She watched as the boxes were unloaded from the plane. After making certain that all of the boxes were in the truck and that nothing was left behind on the plane, she thanked the pilots and walked to Rosemont's car.

"Do you want to go to the Pentagon or home?" Rosemont asked.

"The Pentagon," Kate said. Then she added, "But can you take the long way? I have a crazy idea that I want to run past you."

"You've had a lot of those lately," Rosemont noted as he steered his car toward the Air Force base's main gates. "Have you run it past Steve yet?"

Kate was confused. "What do you mean?"

Rosemont chuckled. "I'm not blind, Kate. I see what's happening with the two of you. You make a great team and have managed to keep the relationship from affecting your performance, which is why I haven't said anything. I just assumed that you'd run any ideas past him before bringing them to me."

Kate blushed. "I'm not confirming or denying anything. But in answer to your question, no, I haven't run it past Steve yet. It came to me on the flight, and there was no time to discuss it with anyone."

"Not even Adam?"

It was Kate's turn to chuckle. "He was the right person for his part of the mission, but he's not the person to share abstract concepts with. He deals in specifics—facts and figures—and the scope of this idea is really beyond him."

Rosemont nodded. "Okay. Tell me your crazy idea."

As they drove, Kate outlined the plan that had been forming in her mind. Reading the Chinese plans for Latin America had just cemented her thinking.

Rosemont listened to her without interruption. When she finished, they drove in silence for a while. Then Rosemont said, "If anyone else came to me with what you just did, I'd throw them out of the car at full speed as we were going over a bridge. But because it came from you, I'm actually thinking about it."

"You think I'm nuts?"

"Certifiably insane," Rosemont confirmed. "But you might be right, and this might be the most brilliantly insane scheme ever devised. It might just save our butts if it works; but if it fails, the U.S. will never survive."

"If China succeeds in taking down the Caliphate and the Latin American Block, how long do you think we'll survive anyway?" she asked. "Every gun from every other corner of the world will be pointing at us with a Chinese finger on the trigger. We could hold out for one, maybe two years, depending on whether the Chinese decided to use nukes. After that, we'd disappear like the rest of the world. I'm not ready to give up without a fight, and this time it *is* the fight of our lives."

Kate fell silent. Then she added, "I keep thinking about that quote from Teddy Roosevelt: *It is not the critic who counts;*

not the man who points out how the strong man stumbles, or where the doer of deeds could have done them better. The credit belongs to the man who is actually in the arena, whose face is marred by dust and sweat and blood; who strives valiantly; who errs, who comes short again and again, because there is no effort without error and shortcoming; but who does actually strive to do the deeds; who knows great enthusiasms, the great devotions; who spends himself in a worthy cause; who at the best knows in the end the triumph of high achievement, and who at the worst, if he fails, at least fails while daring greatly, so that his place shall never be with those cold and timid souls who neither know victory nor defeat."

"I've always loved that quote," Rosemont said. "But I'm not the one you have to convince. First, you have to convince the team; then you'll have to convince the president. And you're right. There isn't much time. I'd estimate that we have between six and eight weeks to pull off the greatest miracle since the birth of our savior. Maybe even longer than that."

"It's almost Christmas," Kate reminded him. "It's a time for believing in miracles."

188

CHAPTER 13

The armored truck arrived at the Pentagon the same time as Rosemont's car. Several armed security officers met the truck and started loading the contents onto hand trucks.

"Where are they taking my documents?" Kate asked.

"To the last conference room down our hallway next to the break room," Rosemont replied. "It's not being used, so I'm putting the translators in there so you can work with them more easily. Of course, it means that we can't have any more open door meetings or working sessions, but it's a small price to pay for the intel that those documents will provide."

Kate and Rosemont entered the Pentagon and headed for their secure workspace on the third floor, followed by the security officers. "When do you want to reach out to the rest of the team?" Rosemont asked.

"Might as well get it over with," Kate replied.

"Okay. After you meet with the translators and let them know what you need, go round up the team, and I'll meet you in the conference room."

Kate led the security officers to the conference room at the end of the hallway. A group of ten individuals waited for her.

She recognized a few of the faces from the agency. She introduced herself as the security officers unloaded the boxes, and for the first time, Kate noticed the GRU emblem and wide red stripes on each of the boxes. *Russian boxes with Chinese documents inside. What a combination.*

After the security officers left the room, she opened one of the boxes and put the contents on the table. "These boxes contain strategies and detailed plans about what's happening around the world right now. This is the most valuable bit of intel ever acquired, but some of it dates back to the early 1990s, and it's in Mandarin. It has to be translated into English and it needs to be done quickly. I cannot stress enough how critical this is. This won't be a 9-to-5 assignment, so if you have things to do or places you have to be, either cancel your plans or get out now. This is about the future existence of our country and the world, so if you think anything is more important than that, you're on the wrong team."

No one moved. "Very well. Pick a document and get started, and I'll check in with you periodically."

"Do you care where we start?" the translator next to Kate asked.

Kate picked up the folder that had the original strategy created by the Chinese chess grandmaster. "This one needs to get translated first. The rest of the folders span decades of planning and plotting. Any folders related to what China has planned for the western hemisphere—especially North America—is critical for the military, and any folders related to Russia and northern Europe also have a high priority. After that, try to translate folders from the same geographic area so you can spot linkages and common themes. If you find something that seems particularly important, make a note of it and pass it along to me."

Kate walked over to one of the whiteboards and wrote the access information for the secure data storage being used by Rosemont's team. "This is where you are to put all of the electronic copies of your translations, but I want a paper copy placed in the folder with each original Chinese document."

Below the access information, she wrote the key for how to name the translated documents. "This is how I want the documents named, and I want the name of the translated document written on a label on the outside of each paper folder. Are there any question?"

One of the translators from the CIA raised his hand. "Kate, do you mind telling us where this came from?"

"They're from a Chinese agent working with the Russians, but I picked them up from the GRU headquarters at the Severomorsk Naval Base in Murmansk this morning."

The translators just stared at her with their mouths open as she left the room.

After Kate left the translators to their work, she went around to the other workrooms. "We're meeting in the large conference room in five minutes," she said.

Five minutes later, the entire team was assembled in the conference room. Rosemont entered the room, activated the SCIF, and then turned toward Kate and began applauding. The rest of the team joined in, and several members of the team shouted, "Bravo!"

Kate blushed and smiled. It was the first time that the rest of the team—apart from Steve, Clay, and Grant—made her feel like they appreciated her efforts.

Rosemont asked Kate to give the team a quick update on her trip to Norway and Russia. She didn't bother mentioning that the intel she brought back proved Handbasket was right; it was clear that they already knew. But she did add once piece of information that she hadn't shared with Rosemont yet.

"By the way, I now have a high-level contact in the GRU, thanks to MI-6. *Very* high-level. He's someone we can leverage if we need backchannels to get information in and out of Russia.

I promised him that, if we found anything in the documents I brought back that had value to their war effort against China, I'd share it with him. In return, he shared some valuable information regarding China's strategy for the invasion of Europe. It was that intel, along with some of the documents I read on the plane, that gave me an idea. I shared the idea with Rosemont, and he said he'd normally throw anyone making that kind of suggestion out of the car at high speeds on a bridge."

There was laughter around the room. Kate continued, "But he also told me to run it past all of you to see what you think. Is it crazy? Probably. Is it doable? Well, you tell me. Is it practical or necessary? I believe that it is. It may be our best chance to survive what's going on all around us. But before we get started, should I go put on a bullet-proof vest first? I remember the last idea I presented in this room."

Laughter filled the room.

Thirty minutes later, no one in the room was laughing.

Kate presented each of the major components of her plan.

"Based on the Chinese documents I was given by the Russians, the buildup of Latin American troops along the U.S.-Mexico border is part of the Chinese plan, but it's not supposed to benefit the Latin American Block. The U.S. is supposed to destroy the troops, leaving Central and South America defenseless. The Chinese will then sail their soldiers over to take possession of the Latin American Block.

"If there's a way to let the Presidents of Mexico, Venezuela, and Columbia know that they're being used as pawns and that they're supposed to be destroyed for China's benefit, maybe we can prevent the bloodshed and turn the Latin American Block into our allies. But how do we do that? We could let them see the Chinese plan, but there's no guarantee they'd believe it. We could apprehend the banker and force him to admit what's going on, but we haven't found him yet, and we might not be able to find him in time.

"If it becomes necessary to destroy the Latin American troops along our southern border, we should not only use saturation bombing to destroy a twenty- to thirty-mile-wide strip of land on the Mexican side of the border, but we have to make it difficult for the Chinese to use the situation to their advantage. We need to destroy every port and mine every harbor on the Pacific side of Central and South America so the Chinese can't land troops there. And if the Chinese bring their fleet into the Atlantic, we'll need to destroy the Atlantic ports and mine their harbors, too. Then we'll need to extend our naval screen south to prevent the Chinese Navy from approaching any Central or South American country. We must deny them their prize, which in this case is a way to gain a military foothold in the western hemisphere. No Chinese forces can be allowed to gain a presence anywhere in the Americas, and we need to take back the Panama Canal from China's control.

"Now, before you remind me that the U.S. Fleet isn't large enough to protect the entire western hemisphere, I know where we can get more ships."

"Where?" Moira Kirkland asked.

"Russia and the Scandinavian Peninsula," Kate replied.

She put up a map of the northern half of the eastern hemisphere on the screen behind her. She pointed to China and Russia's Pacific naval bases. "Look. Here are the ports where China's combined Pacific fleets are located." Then she pointed to the Arctic passages being created by icebreakers along Russia's northern coastline. "Here is the northern sea passage that the Chinese are creating. According to the Russians, it will be completed in early to mid-January. At that time, according to Russian sources inside the Chinese Navy, the Chinese will send a fleet to blockade the Scandinavian ports as well as the Russian naval bases on the Kola Peninsula. That will trap what's left of the European naval forces while the Chinese Air Force, launching from captured air bases in eastern Russia, bomb all military targets left in northern Europe, destroying the surviving fleets, armies, and strategic weapons, not to mention the governments-in-exile and their rescued treasuries."

Kate then pointed to the Suez Canal. "At the same time that the first Chinese fleet is making its way north through the Arctic, the Chinese will send their carriers, supply ships, and troopships south and around southern Asia to the Suez Canal, the Mediterranean, and then around Europe's Atlantic coast to the Scandinavian Peninsula, where they'll offload their soldiers and flank the Russian forces holding back the Chinese at the Urals. Russia and the Scandinavian countries will fall."

Kate turned to the room. "But if we send our Atlantic fleet to Norway, along with every cruise ship in the North American Atlantic and any other blue-water ship that can make the voyage and hold passengers and equipment, we can rescue the remnants of the European forces and governments and bring them back here. Any of their ships that are blue-water capable will become part of our fleet. Any mid-range ships that can make it to Iceland will be escorted there. Coastal vessels will be scuttled. Our naval air squadrons will destroy the Scandinavian ports when we leave, making it difficult to land troops there. It will deny China their prize.

"We'll send word to the Russian forces to meet us at one of the Norwegian ports. If they need extra ships to evacuate their personnel and equipment, and we have any extras, we'll send them to Murmansk to help with the evacuation, although the civilian ports in the area should have more than enough cargo ships for them to use. Then we'll have the Russians destroy their naval bases on the Kola Peninsula, just like we did with Pearl Harbor. Again, we'll deny the Chinese their prize. All Russian naval and air forces, along with their tactical and strategic weapons systems, will be evacuated, and once they reach the rendezvous point, the combined fleet will return to Norfolk before being redeployed south. The Russian Air Force will provide cover for the fleet as far as Iceland, where they'll land and become part of Iceland's and Greenland's defenses. The Chinese tried to shoot me down as I was leaving Russia, and I was in a clearly marked U.S. Air Force jet, so they've already shown they'll attack American forces without provocation. We'll need the Russian air screen to make it out of there safely.

"I wish there were a way to warn the Caliphate about what China plans to do to them once they reach the Atlantic, but Islamists would never listen to us. And after what I discovered they're doing across Europe, I say good riddance to them. China will take Europe, then the Middle East, and then Africa. At that point, they'll control the eastern hemisphere. But while they're doing that, we'll use the European solders we rescue, along with our own ground forces, and we'll invade the Latin American Block. We'll overthrow their pro-Chinese and anti-American governments, obliterate the cartels and seize their wealth and access to their Chinese bank, and we'll restore freedom to the people. Then we'll raise an army of Latin Americans to protect their part of the hemisphere from Chinese aggression. At the same time, we'll mobilize our own people to increase the size of our army, build new naval ships, and build new airplanes.

"By the time the Chinese own the eastern hemisphere, we'll have the larger naval force, our armies will be evenly matched, our air forces will be evenly matched, and our nuclear arsenal, which will include the European nukes, will be evenly matched. We'll reach a stalemate. China will have to abandon its current strategy and start playing a whole new game—*our* game. And between the Alaskan, Canadian, Venezuelan, and Mexican oil reserves, we can remain self-sufficient from an energy perspective. We're already self-sufficient agriculturally, and we'll rebuild our manufacturing capabilities just like we did in the early days of World War II."

Kate realized she had been getting steadily louder as she

spoke, so she lowered her voice. "There is massive risk in this plan. We have to know what the Chinese fleets are doing while keeping them from realizing what we're doing, we have to get the combined fleet out of Europe without being detected, we have to keep the Chinese Air Force from finding us while keeping them under constant observation, and we have to get everything ready in just a few weeks. The good news is, any attack on the Latin American forces along our southern border must be seen. The Chinese must believe that we're playing into their hands once again. Let them think that, so long as they don't see what we're really doing."

Kate sat down and looked at Rosemont. Rosemont nodded—his way of saying "good job."

Rosemont looked around the room. "Okay, you've heard her crazy plan. Now, don't hold back. What do you think?"

"So this idea is based on Russian intel and not the Chinese documents you brought back with you?" Vandyke asked.

"That's right," Kate confirmed. "The Chinese documents are just now being translated. This plan is based in intel from Russian sailors who are being forced to man the ships captured by the Chinese."

"What about the Chinese submarines and the Russian subs that they captured?" Kirkland asked. "Will they be accompanying the two Chinese fleets?"

"Not according to the Russians," Kate replied. "I know it sounds strange, but the Chinese think that no one knows about their plans. The Russians believe that the subs will be used to protect the Chinese coast and their current captured territories, since virtually their entire blue-water surface fleet is moving into the Atlantic. Besides, the Chinese have some of the finest anti-submarine weapons in existence, so the Russians believe that the Chinese don't think they have anything to worry about."

"Where do you see us using the European naval vessels?" Kirkland asked.

"At first they could be used to help liberate Latin America. After that, we can use them wherever they're needed, including around Iceland and Greenland to keep China out of the North Atlantic."

"Will the Russian and Scandinavian governments and militaries go along with this?" Grant asked.

"They begged us for this kind of help when we were over there," Kate responded. "Adam Chester, who travelled with me, met with their government contacts, and he's at the White House right now presenting their formal requests for assistance, including evacuation. And my contact in the GRU sees this as the only way that a piece of Russia will survive into the future. Yes, they'll not only go along with it, they'll do everything in their power to help it succeed."

"So the Chinese planned to sacrifice the Caliphate and the Latin Americans all along?" Steve asked.

Kate nodded. "It's all there in their strategy and detailed plans. Let Islamists and the cartels each conquer one of the geographic regions. Then when they're victorious, stretched thin, and unable to defend themselves, the Chinese move in and destroy them. The analogy used in the plan was Siamese fighting fish. Two fish fight to the death while a third one watches. Then, when one of the two fish wins, the third fish comes along and eats both of them with ease. That's the Chinese plan for their so-called allies. China is the third fish."

"Do you think that China will use nukes in Europe?" Vandyke asked.

Kate shrugged. "They seem to have gone out of their way to avoid it so far. Why destroy something for a century if you can take it and use it for yourself? But we have to be careful about pushing them into a corner where it seems like a viable option. It's the greatest variable to any response that we make. But if we do nothing, we'll be speaking Mandarin within two years, should any of us survive the invasion. I already speak

Mandarin, but I have no intention of bowing to a Chinese overlord."

"You going out in a blaze of glory?" Liz Sweeny quipped.

"No," Kate corrected her. "Just dying in a pile of spent brass."

The meeting lasted another hour. No one had anything negative to say about Kate's plan, but they all agreed that it would take careful planning and great speed to pull it off in time. Rosemont looked at the clock and saw that it was getting late. He told the team to start fresh in the morning and develop a unified plan to present to the president within forty-eight hours. Then he deactivated the SCIF and sent everyone home for the night.

Kate checked in with the translators and made sure that they had her phone number should they need anything. Then she headed for the workroom she shared with Steve. He was waiting there for her.

"Where did you leave your car before flying out to Norway?" he asked.

Kate had to think about it for a moment. "Rosemont sent a car to take me to Andrews, and he picked me up, so I guess my car is at home."

"You look exhausted," Steve noted as they walked to the security door.

"I feel like I've been on the go for two straight weeks," Kate acknowledged. "I was too keyed up on the flight over to relax. Then there were the meetings in Norway, the flight to Murmansk, going through the documents, the flight home, getting shot at, reading through more documents, and then coming back here and diving into work again... honestly I feel I could sleep for a week!"

Steve looked at her. "Do you realize you're still wearing your tactical gear and you're still armed?"

Kate stopped and looked down at what she was wearing.

"Ha! I never even thought to change clothes on the plane. No wonder Rosemont was shocked that I wanted to come straight here. Do you think that's why everyone was so nice to me in the meeting? Hell, I'm surprised I got past security!"

"It pays to have the golden ticket," Steve quipped, holding up his access badge.

Kate laughed. Then she yawned.

"Come on," Steve said. "I'll drive you home."

Kate didn't argue. "Thanks, Steve."

The next morning, after Kate checked on the translators, she and the rest of the team met in the conference room. For the first time that Kate had observed, the team focused on figuring out how to do something, rather than tearing down ideas and suggestions from the other team members. By lunchtime, a working plan was beginning to take shape.

"How are we going to handle refueling the ships?" Liz Sweeny asked. "It won't be an issue for the nuclear vessels, but the cruise ships and other civilian ships that we commandeer can't carry enough fuel for a round trip. And some of the ships in Norway and Russia might not have enough fuel for the voyage."

"What about taking super tankers with us?" Lieutenant Commander Benson suggested. "They can fuel the ships before we leave Europe, and we can send them on to the bases around Murmansk to be sunk in their channel like we did at Pearl Harbor if necessary."

"The channel at Murmansk is too deep and wide to be blocked like we did at Pearl Harbor," Kirkland said. "Plus there are five separate channels and inlets on the Kola Peninsula where their naval bases are located. There's no way to block them all."

"How long will it take the fleet to get over there and back?" Grant asked.

Kirkland did some quick calculating. "Assuming all of the ships leave from Norfolk, a carrier strike group at full speed taking the most direct route can make it to Oslo in five to seven days depending on the ocean conditions. But cruise ships and super tankers will take closer to thirteen days to get there. On the trip back, if the fleet goes to Iceland and then turns south toward Norfolk, it will take the slower ships six days to get from Norway to Iceland, and another nine days from Iceland to Norfolk. So, calculating based on the slowest ships in the fleet, it'll take thirteen days to get there and fifteen days to get back, not counting any stops along the way. And it will take the Russian fleet two to three days to reach the Norwegian rendezvous, depending on where that is and the speed of the slowest Russian vessels."

"And how long will it take the Chinese fleets to reach Murmansk?" Grant asked.

Kirkland checked the numbers on her tablet. "A cargo ship traveling from Shanghai to Murmansk via the Suez Canal takes thirty-seven days. An aircraft carrier can make it in twenty-one days. A cargo ship traveling from Shanghai to Murmansk via the Arctic route takes twenty-two days. An aircraft carrier can make it in twelve. The Arctic numbers obviously depend on ice and the condition of the route."

"So, two weeks to get there, two weeks back, and however many days to load, fuel, rendezvous, and then leave," Grant summarized. "And the Chinese blockade fleet will make it in twelve days, with the carriers and support ships arriving nine days later, unless the carriers and support ships leave earlier than the blockade fleet. How many days do we think it will take to load and fuel the ships for the trip back?"

"Depends on how much there is to load, how many ships have to be refueled, and on the port or ports," Kirkland said. "It would be better to use as many of the northern ports in Norway as we can to spread out the workload. If we use Oslo or the southern ports, we're open to Stinger fire from Denmark or speed boats operating in the area."

Kate wrote herself a note to mention that to Adam. "We'll need to consult with the European government and military representative about how much we're bringing back here to know how long it will take to load the ships, and we can't have that conversation until the President approves the plan. We'll have to leave the time needed in Norway to load and refuel as a variable for now and come back to it once we have presidential approval and we know how many ships we can commandeer. If we can't find many ships, then the time to load goes down because we won't be loading that much."

"I can find out how many cruise ships and cargo ships are idle at the moment," Benson offered. "The Coast Guard maintains that information on a regular basis. We know every ship in every port, when it got there and from where, when it's scheduled to leave and for where, and if the ship is idle because of the regional conflicts. I can get that by tomorrow."

"Great, thanks!" Kate said.

The next morning, Benson provided the team with a list of blue-water capable ships that could be commandeered for the mission.

"In addition to the naval vessels docked at Norfolk, Mayport, and the New London sub base at Groton, there are twenty-four cruise ships capable of crossing the Atlantic docked between Galveston and New York, including four in the Bahamas, plus thirteen supertankers and twenty cargo ships docked between Jacksonville and Baltimore."

"That's quite a fleet," Grant remarked.

"And a slow one," Kirkland pointed out. "It's going to be hard to keep the Chinese from detecting what we're doing, and if they spot us in the Atlantic, it's possible that they could send their entire fleet through the Arctic and trap us along the Norwegian coast."

"Let's add that to the risks," Kate suggested. "And we should add the food and fuel necessary for the voyage, plus the effort to recall the crews for those ships. They might be scattered across the country by now."

"I hate logistics," Peterson muttered.

"Be glad the military runs on it," Vandyke said with a smirk. "We know what to do."

By the end of the day, there were still gaps and unanswered questions in the plan, but as a proposal for the president to consider, the team felt confident that it was as complete as it could be.

They had just finished making copies of the proposal when Rosemont entered the room. "We're meeting with the president in an hour," he informed them.

"I thought we were meeting with him at 7:00 AM," Kate commented. "What changed?"

"Mexico," Rosemont replied. "The Latin American Block units deployed at the border have started shooting into the United States at our troops."

The team met in the Situation Room an hour later. The president, vice president, and the president's Chief of Staff were there. The other attendees included the Joint Chiefs, the Director of the CIA, the National Security Advisor, the Secretary of Homeland Security, the Secretary of Defense, and the Secretaries of the Army, the Navy, and the Air Force. Adam Chester also attended.

Kate recapped her trip to Norway and Russia, what she learned from the Chinese documents given to her by the GRU, and then she presented the high-level outline of their plan. Other members of the team provided the details about the various aspects of the plan, and Grant provided the list of unanswered questions, incomplete information, and next steps.

"So what's happening along the border is part of the Chinese plan to get rid of the Latin American military forces, and we're supposed to do it for them so they can seize Latin

America unopposed?" The president sounded incredulous.

Kate nodded. "Yes, Mr. President. China has plans to deal with the Caliphate themselves. It probably stems from their historic hatred of Islam. But they're setting us up to do their dirty work for them over here. Pitting one pawn against another. It's brilliant, but it doesn't really help our situation."

"Any luck finding the banker?" the vice president asked.

"Not yet," the Director of the CIA reported. "If he's smart, he's back in China by now."

"I'm told that the Chinese documents being translated have the names of all the key players," Kate added. "We just haven't found those pages yet. Once we do, we'll know his name and can find him more easily."

"And all of the Chinese information came from a typist who turned it all over to the Russians?"

"Yes, Mr. Vice President," Kate replied.

Secretary of Defense Wolfe turned to the president and asked, "What do you think, Mr. President? The European governments-in-exile have requested our help, Russia has requested our help, China's fleets are going to be heading for the Atlantic, and we're almost in a position to retake Latin America, ending the threat to our southern border. It's risky, but it's bold, and maybe bold is what we need to ensure that we survive."

The president looked at the Joint Chiefs. "Gentlemen, what's the opinion of the military?"

"I don't see where we have a choice any longer, Mr. President," the Chief of Naval Operations said. "If we're going to endure, we have to act. We need more ships, planes, and soldiers. This is a way to get them with minimal investment."

"But maximum risk," Chief of Staff Voight interjected. "We could lose the entire fleet."

"It's a calculated risk, Mr. Voight," the naval officer responded. "But this is war, even if it hasn't been officially declared. The Chinese have been manipulating us for over thirty years. If this plan gives us a way to shatter their plans and force them to create a new strategy to react to *our* moves and countermoves, then I'm all for it. I say we should proceed."

The Army and Air Force officers agreed.

The president looked at his cabinet members, and they nodded in agreement. Then he looked at his Chief of Staff. The two men locked eyes, but finally Voight nodded.

"Very well," the President stated. "You have my approval to proceed. Since this is an operational matter now, I'm placing it under the control of the Navy, but I want Rosemont's team, along with Mr. Chester, to be part of the operation all the way. Understood?"

"Yes, sir, Mr. President."

The president stood. "Make it happen."

CHAPTER 14

Murmansk • Washington, DC
November 2027

It was the week of Thanksgiving, and the U.S. armed forces were mobilizing to make Kate's plan a reality. Cruise ship crews had been located, and the ships were being repositioned to ports near Norfolk, as were the supertankers and cargo ships. Adam had been in contact with the European government representatives that he had met with in Oslo and Murmansk, and Kate was given permission to approach Colonel Petrov now that the president had given his approval for the mission.

On the Wednesday afternoon before Thanksgiving, Kate curled up in front of the fireplace at her house and called Petrov on her secure sat-phone. It took a few rings before he answered.

"Kostya? It's Kate."

"Kate! It's good to hear from you. Are you well? I heard that your plane was attacked by the Chinese."

"I'm fine, thank you, Kostya. It's the first time anyone has tried to shoot me out of the sky, though, but your pilots saved us. I'm sorry about the two that you lost."

"They volunteered for the mission. They wanted to make certain that you returned safely to America."

"I have news," Kate said.

Kostya interrupted her. "So I've heard. Your government has already contacted my government."

"I know. I wanted to give you the details myself."

Kate explained the plan. At first, Kate could tell that Kostya thought she was joking, but when she outlined the details of the plan, he seemed convinced of her sincerity. As it turned out, he hadn't heard about Pearl Harbor being scuttled, but he definitely believed that the naval bases on the Kola Peninsula could be destroyed in the same way.

"It's a pity we can't block the channels like you did at Pearl Harbor," he commented. "But there are too many, and they're too wide and deep. Oh, by the way, have you discovered anything in the Chinese documents yet?"

"As a matter of fact, yes," Kate replied. "The Chinese deployment to the Atlantic to crush Russia from the west was part of the plan all along—not just for conquering Russia, but to have a large enough force in Europe to wipe out the Caliphate there before moving south. The original Chinese invasion force was never going to cross the Urals. They'll be deployed south to take the eastern Middle East, with the European forces in support from the west, and then they'll both take Africa."

"So we played into their hands by taking a defensive posture at the Urals to protect western Russia," Kostya commented. "If we had counter attacked, it would have disrupted their strategy. What a waste."

"Kostya, both of our countries have been playing into their hands for over thirty years. Don't beat yourself up for not seeing what nobody else saw. Just focus on what we're going to do to make their grand plan crumble around them."

"By the way, thank you for remembering what I asked of you just before you left," Kostya said. "You did exactly what I was hoping that you'd do, even though I never thought you would or could actually do it."

"You're welcome. It was the intel you gave me that

206

convinced the president to approve the plan. Now we just have to make it happen."

"When will that be?" Kostya asked.

"I'll let you know soon. Are you going to be onboard one of the ships sailing over here?" Kate asked.

"That's still being decided," Kostya replied. "My family is here, and I'm not sure I can just abandon them, even if it's to save something of Russia for the future. I have obligations…"

"I understand," Kate said. "Will no military families be evacuated?"

"We don't have the ships, and you're not bringing enough with you for that many people."

"What about airlifting them to Iceland?" Kate suggested. "Surely there are enough jets sitting at your airports to get thousands of civilians out before the Chinese arrive. The planes could refuel in Iceland and land in Canada or the U.S."

There was a pause on the line. "That's actually a brilliant idea. We have enough fighter jets to escort them, and it will make the military and government personnel who are evacuating feel better about leaving. I'll pass along that suggestion."

"And I'll inform my government so we have housing set aside for them."

They talked for a while longer. Then Petrov commented, "I understand this week is called… Thanksgiving? How will you be celebrating?"

"Normally, I'd spend it with my parents, but there's just too much going on around here. My boss has invited everyone on the team over to his house tomorrow, and then I'll be spending all day Friday going through the documents that have been translated so far. There is the name of a certain banker that I want to find."

"What banker?" Kostya asked.

"The one who got all of the drug cartels around the world to unite into a single syndicate. The one who has been pulling the strings in Latin America for the past several years. My government wants him in custody, and I'm going to find his name if it's the last thing I do."

"If I hear anything, I'll pass it along," Petrov promised. "We know who some of the bankers in China are—especially the ones trying to buy everything in Europe that was for sale. We'll grab any of them that we find and sweat them for the name you're searching for."

"Thank, you, Kostya! *Dasvidaniya*"

"*Quid pro quo. Dasvidaniya*, Kate."

Rosemont had an impressive spread for Thanksgiving dinner, and the aromas coming from the kitchen were intoxicating. Kate arrived at 1:30 PM, a few minutes before the food was ready. The house was decorated for autumn, and hardwood fires blazed in the three fireplaces on the first floor of the huge house. One of Rosemont's daughters gave Kate the quick tour, and Kate was thoroughly impressed by how beautiful everything was and the attention to detail in almost every corner of each room. *Rosemont's wife must love decorating for the holidays.*

The members of the teams with families didn't attend, but all of the single members—most of the team—were there, and they all brought huge appetites. Kate ate more than she planned. She couldn't help herself; it was all so good!

Rosemont's rule for the day was that no one could talk business, politics, or current events. As it turned out, football was the major topic. Kate slipped out of the den as the male team members were getting into a heated debate over the big game that afternoon. She and the other female members of the team ended up in the kitchen with Rosemont's wife and daughters, sampling Rosemont's fine wine selection and enjoying the testosterone-free conversation.

The sound of Rosemont's booming laugh reached every corner of the house, and Kate found it interesting. *He's always so serious at work. It's good to know that he can relax and enjoy life when he's home.*

When the big game started, Steve entered the kitchen, looking for something to snack on. He ended up staying there with Kate and the others. By the evening, Steve and Kate were sitting at the breakfast table by themselves, oblivious to everything else that was going on around them.

When the party started breaking up at 8:00 PM, Kate invited Steve back to her house. It didn't take much convincing. They thanked Rosemont for a wonderful day, and his wife loaded each of the guests with several containers of leftovers.

Steve followed Kate back to her home. The night air was cold enough that he felt comfortable leaving his leftovers in the car. He helped Kate take hers inside, and he got the fire going while she put them away.

"That was a great Thanksgiving," Kate said when she joined Steve on the couch. She placed two glasses and a bottle of wine on the table. Steve glanced at the label and whistled softly.

"You're serving the good stuff today."

"Why not? I feel like celebrating. It might be the last time we do for a long time." She snuggled next to him.

"You have doubts about the mission?" Steve asked, reaching for the corkscrew on the tray in the middle of the coffee table.

"Yes and no," Kate replied. "Things can always go wrong, even with the best planned missions, but I'm worried about the Russians."

"Colonel Petrov? He seems to have gotten under your skin."

Kate smiled. "Not like that. We were just two intelligence officers exchanging information. He had the documents I needed, and I had the skills to translate them for him. I gave him reasons to trust me, and he shared vital intel with me that we could never have obtained in any other way. I still don't know why, but I'm grateful that he did. No, I was actually thinking about the civilians. I spoke with Petrov yesterday, and he told me that no civilians, including the families of the servicemen and women who are redeploying over here, were being evacuated. He said they didn't have the space. I reminded him that his airports are filled with empty jets that could airlift thousands of civilians to safety via Iceland."

"That's a good suggestion." Steve poured the wine and handed Kate a glass.

She took a sip. "I'm glad that Rosemont agreed and passed it along to the president. But what if something happens to one of those planes on the flight out? What if my suggestion causes the deaths of hundreds of innocent civilians? I made a simple suggestion, and suddenly it's part of the mission plan. It's too much. I'm an analyst. I help people make decisions. I don't change the course of world events."

"The hell you don't," Steve said gently. "Everything you've done since I met you is altering world events. Yes, you create analyses to present to decision makers, and they make the decisions based on that information, but it's your analyses that are guiding the decisions being made right now. You're the chess master's principal opponent, and he doesn't even know that you're the one he's playing against. He thinks we're playing *his* game, but really the world is now playing *your* game. And by the time he realizes it, it'll be too late. 'Kate's Handbasket Gambit' will be moving into its endgame, and he'll be playing catch up to you."

Kate giggled softly. Then she admitted, "I'm scared."

"If you weren't, I'd have Rosemont commit you to an asylum. We're caught up in a game for the world itself. No one has ever played for stakes this high or this important. But you're the one who saw through the mist and shadows, you're the one who figured out the chess master's game, and you're the one who devised the strategy that will change the game. You *should* be scared. But remember, you're not alone. You have a team helping you define the plans, you have an entire navy turning your ideas into actions, and you have a nation standing behind you, even though they don't know it's you they're standing behind. They think they're standing behind the president, and they are. But he's standing behind you, as are we all. You've got this. We've got this. And even if we lose a few along the way, we'll gain more than we lose thanks to you."

"And if we don't?"

"Then we don't," Steve replied. "And we'll just have to create a new strategy and try again."

Kate put her wine glass down and grabbed Steve by the shirt, pulling him closer until her lips met his. "Thank you," she whispered.

"My pleasure," Steve replied, putting down his own glass and returning her kiss.

Kate pushed him back on the couch. "It will be…"

Steve woke up at 6:00 AM the next morning. The wine was gone, including the second bottle. The fire in the fireplace had long since gone out, but the embers glowed and smoked, giving off warmth against the chill. Steve and Kate were still on the couch, wrapped in a blanket, skin against skin. The musky smell of sex still lingered in the room. Kate was asleep, and Steve lay next to her, watching her sleep.

The sex the night before had been incredible, but it had been different from the other times. They were no longer exploring each other's bodies; they were familiar enough with each other to focus on giving and taking pleasure. But there was something else: a vulnerability… but more than just that… a desperate need for a deeper connection than mere physical sex could provide.

Kate had always taken charge the other times they had been together, but this time Kate surrendered control to Steve.

He wondered if this was how she was dealing with her uncertainties. *Have we moved from just physical gratification to passion, or are her doubts causing her to try for a different kind of sexual release—an emotional release, rather than a purely physical one?*

I wonder if I'll ever know.

Kate woke up almost thirty minutes later. It took her a moment to realize where she was and who was next to her. She saw that Steve was awake and shifted her position to be on top—looking down at him. Then she kissed him. "Good morning."

"Good morning," he responded. "You must have needed the extra sleep. You're usually up before I am."

"Must have," Kate said, unwilling to get up and get dressed yet. "Are you hungry?"

Steve nodded.

"What do you want?"

Steve looked guilty. "You know what I really want?"

Kate shook her head.

"Some of Mrs. Rosemont's leftovers."

Kate laughed. "Oh, my God, so do I!"

Kate didn't move, and Steve's thoughts began to move elsewhere. He nuzzled her ear with his nose. "But we can wait for breakfast, if you'd like," he whispered.

Kate didn't need to be asked twice.

It was after 8:00 AM when they finally got off the couch. Kate put on only her shirt and draped the blanket over her shoulders. Steve was wearing boxer shorts and an undershirt when he joined her in the kitchen. This time, she let him help her get the meal ready.

As they ate, Steve commented, "I love Thanksgiving leftovers for breakfast."

"Me, too. I also love making turkey sandwiches from the

leftovers."

"How do you make yours?" Steve asked.

"Rye bread, mayo, a touch of deli mustard, salt and pepper, Havarti cheese, lettuce, and the turkey. You?"

"Dark wheat bread, a slice of dressing, cranberry sauce, turkey, and gravy."

Kate made a sour face. "I've known a lot of people who love that, but I can't stand it. Something about cranberry sauce on a sandwich just turns my stomach."

"What's the weirdest sandwich you've ever had?" Steve asked between bites.

"Sliced bananas, mayo and peanut butter, on cinnamon raisin bread," she replied. "It's delicious, but definitely weird."

Steve laughed.

Kate pretended to pout. "What's so funny?"

"My weirdest sandwich is a variation of yours. It has all the same ingredients, but add sliced pickles, lettuce, and cheddar cheese. My dad loved it. Mom and I hated it."

Kate laughed, but Steve saw a distant look in her eyes. "What's wrong? Last night, you seemed... different. I've never seen you cry before."

Kate blushed, something else that Steve hadn't seen. "Have you ever needed an emotional release so bad that you thought you'd burst?"

Steve shook his head.

"Well I needed one last night. I've felt like there was this dam inside me, bottling up my emotions, and if I didn't break through it, I'd lose myself and become a soulless analytical automatron. I needed you to break through whatever was making me hold back, and you did. And it was wonderful! I'm sorry if it caught you off guard. I've been keeping things penned up tight lately to get the job done, but I can only do that for so long. Thanks for being there to help me."

"You're welcome. Any time."

Kate smiled. "I'd love to give you the chance to break through again, but I have to get cleaned up and get to the office."

"On the Friday after Thanksgiving?" What's so important that it can't wait?"

"I'm reviewing the translated documents," Kate replied, standing and clearing the dishes off the table.

"Not without me, you're not." Steve got up to help. "We're partners, and I'm going to help you go through the intel."

Kate just stared at him for a moment. *It would be good to share the work between two people. We can get through it all much faster.* Finally, she said, "Well, thanks. I can use the help."

Steve looked at his watch. "Meet you there at 10:30 AM?"

Kate looked at the clock, did the math, and smiled. "That gives us just enough time." She dropped the blanket on the floor, pulled the shirt off over her head, and pushed Steve into one of the kitchen chairs. "You'd better hang on."

Steve reached Conference Room B ten minutes after Kate. Anyone looking at her would never know what they had done three times the night before and twice that morning.

"Good morning," she said casually, looking up at him.

Steve smiled. "Good morning. Been here long?"

Kate shook her head. She had collected the completed folders from the translators down the hall and had already started reading through the documents. She pointed to the stacks on the table. "The stacks are organized by region," she said. "I'm starting with the documents related to Russia. Pick a stack and get started."

Steve looked at the stacks and found the one regarding Latin American. "I'll start with this one."

"I thought you'd pick the China stack, given that Asia is your area of expertise."

Steve sat down and opened the first file folder. "Yes, but I want that banker."

214

Two hours later, as Kate was reaching for another folder, she noticed Steve sit straight up in his chair. "I found him!" he exclaimed.

Kate perked up. "Found who?"

"The banker. His name is right here. Shusong Han!"

"Let me see," Kate stood and walked around so she could read over Steve's shoulder.

On the page was a list of names of bankers from the Industrial and Commercial Bank of China—the largest bank in the world—that were tied to the Chinese strategy. Some were assigned to purchase companies and move their operations to China. Others were assigned to fund terrorism and other insurgent and subversive activities, including taking control of U.S. politics and media outlets. But the name Shusong Han was listed as the head of the global drug syndicate and the chief banker for the Latin American Block.

Kate sat next to Steve, slid aside the panel in the table, and accessed the tablet underneath. When she entered the name Shusong Han, the search returned no results. Kate walked around the table to her bag. She pulled out her sat-phone and dialed Petrov's number.

"Hello, Kate," he said when he answered the call.

"Hello, Kostya. I have a name for you."

"Straight to business as usual," he said wistfully. "That's why you'll never be a Russian."

"Of course not," she replied. "I'm Norwegian. The name of the banker we're looking for is Shusong Han. I've got the list of the other bankers from the Industrial and Commercial Bank of China that have been assigned to aspects of the Chinese strategy. Do you want the whole list?"

"Certainly. Can you read it to me?"

"Wouldn't it be easier to send it to you?"

"Normally I'd say yes, but things are crazy around here at

the moment."

Kate motioned for Steve to hand her the folder. Then she read the list to Petrov.

"Have you found anything else that might help us?" Petrov asked.

"Not yet," Kate replied. "But I'm still reading through the documents regarding Russia, so maybe something will turn up."

"Thank you, Kate. I'll see what I can find out about these bankers. Call me if you find something. *Dasvidaniya.*"

"*Dasvidaniya*, Kostya."

Kate ended the call and handed the folder back to Steve. "Thanks. Good work finding the name of the banker. Maybe the Russians can tell us where he is. I wouldn't mind sending a drone up to follow him."

Steve laughed. "Or take him out." He looked at his watch. "It's lunch time. Let's go downstairs and grab a bite."

"Can we bring it back up here?" Kate asked, gesturing toward the unread folders. "So much to do…"

"Sure."

Colonel Petrov stared out the window of GRU headquarters at the Severomorsk Naval Base. Even though it was only mid-afternoon, it was already dark. He turned away from the window and called for one of his subordinates.

"Yes, Comrade Colonel?"

"Aren't there drug dealers operating along our southern border, trying to corrupt our brave soldiers defending Mother Russia from the godless Chinese?"

"Yes, sir."

"Send a squad down and capture everyone you can get your hands on. I need to question them."

"Yes, Comrade Colonel."

The subordinate left the office. *If I can find one of them who's willing to talk, I might find someone in or near Russia who's in contact with this syndicate. Then I might find more about this banker for Kate. It's the least that I can do, since she's the one who made the suggestion that will save my family when Murmansk is evacuated.*

Kate finished with the stack on Russia and moved on to the European stack. The plans for the Caliphate to decimate the European infrastructure and destroy all of its cities were spelled out in detail. But when Kate read the plans for Europe after the Chinese had squashed the Caliphate, she was shocked.

"Are you finished with the Latin American stack yet?" She asked Steve.

"Yes. I'm on the Asian stack now. Why?"

"Did you read anything about the Chinese plans for Central and South American *after* we destroyed their military?"

Steve put down the folder he was reading. "Actually, yes. I was going to mention it to you later. The plan was to destroy whatever cities we didn't and leave them in ruins. They want the continent to return to nature—overgrown and uninhabited."

"They have the same plan for Europe," Kate told him. "The Chinese are letting the Caliphate destroy everything, then once the Chinese crush the Caliphate, they're going to leave the continent in ruins and let nature reclaim it all. There's a reference in this folder to a 'Green Policy' of recreating massive green spaces to ensure that the planet's air supply is secure for centuries."

"I saw that same reference," Steve confirmed. "They want the rainforests to grow back. It looks like there are two continents that they want to remain uninhabited once they rule the world."

"Curious, don't you think?" Kate commented. "They have a massive overpopulation problem, and yet they're sectioning off two whole continents to remain uninhabited."

"Well, they've got eastern Russia, Australia, and North

America where they can start shifting their population after they control the world," Steve reminded her.

"Have you come across their plans for their own Islamic population yet?" Kate was curious about China leaving its own Islamic population intact after wiping out the Caliphate forces and conquering the Middle East and Africa.

"No, but it's on my list. My guess is that China will begin exterminating their Islamic communities once the Caliphate has been eliminated, but I need to confirm that."

Kate nodded and went back to reading. Several hours later, she looked at her watch and realized that it was almost 7:00 PM.

"How close are you to being finished?"

Steve looked up. "Another hour or two, and that's not counting the additional folders that the translators have been bringing."

Kate looked at the new stacks that had appeared throughout the day. There were at least as many unread folders left as there were read folders. "It's going to take us the rest of the weekend to get through these, isn't it?"

"At least. Why don't we call it a night and start fresh in the morning?"

Kate liked that suggestion. "Dinner?"

"I've got Rosemont's leftovers at my place," Steve suggested.

Kate hadn't seen Steve's home, and she was curious. "Sounds good. Give me twenty minutes to finish this folder, and I'll be ready to go."

Kate was impressed with Steve's place. It was a brick federal-style three-story house located just south of Mount Vernon, George Washington's home. The neighborhood looked like it had been there for nearly a century, and the brass plaque on the door indicated that the house had been built in 1845.

The inside of the house had clearly been completely rebuilt

within the past thirty years to include all of the modern appliances and conveniences, but it retained the historic charm. The furnishings were traditional and comfortable, and while the artwork on the first level was mostly landscapes, the artwork on the second level, where Steve's study was located, dealt mostly with the revolution and the first Civil War. Portraits of Washington, Lee, Longstreet, Stuart, and Steve's ancestor, General Barksdale, covered the walls of his study, and there were miniature cannons on most of his bookshelves. The master suite took up the entire third floor, and it was beautiful. It had two sitting areas, a massive double walk-in closet, and a master bathroom that rivaled most luxury hotels. All three floors had a fireplace: the master bedroom, Steve's study, and the den.

"Your house is amazing," Kate commented as they returned to the first floor to fix dinner. "It's obvious that you love history—particularly military history—but I'm surprised that I don't see too many things related to your time in Asia."

"I didn't bring back much from my time over there," Steve said as they entered the kitchen. "I regret that now, but at the time I didn't want to be dragging around a bunch of stuff."

Kate helped Steve remove the food and start loading portions into oven- and microwave-safe dishes. "I know what you mean. I had this notion when I first started with the Agency that I'd bring home something from all of my field assignments, but I quickly realized that I needed to just get in and out with my intel, my analysis, and my life. I have my memories but without the clutter of that stuff piled all over my house."

Kate spent the night at Steve's, enjoying his company. She normally didn't like sleeping in someone else's bed, but she willingly made an exception to experience again what they had shared the night before.

The next morning, she drove home to shower and change before meeting Steve back at the Pentagon. The translators completed their work at noon, and Kate thanked and then dismissed them after they stacked all of the original documents in the corner of Conference Room B.

Kate and Steve finished reading through the files just after midnight. Between the two of them, they now understood the entire Chinese strategy.

"I can't believe the list of U.S.-based companies that the Chinese bought," Kate said, putting the last of the North American folders back in its stack.

"And I can't believe the list of politicians, civil servants, professors, entertainers, and journalists that the Chinese bought," Steve responded. "No wonder we elected a socialist so easily three years ago. There's enough evidence in these documents to charge thousands of people with conspiracy and treason. Should we turn that information over to the Justice Department?"

"That's up to Rosemont," Kate replied. "Our primary job is to provide analyses about what China has planned for North America, Latin America, Europe, Russia, and the countries controlled by the Caliphate. The military can't create a defensive strategy without that information. Later, we can circle back and detail what the Chinese already accomplished so the authorities can deal with the witting and unwitting collaborators."

"So what's our next step?"

"We need to create a summary for Rosemont to pass along to the president," Kate said as they straightened up the conference room for the night.

"Between the two of us, we should be able to get that knocked out tomorrow," Steve suggested.

Kate nodded. "Let's get an early start so we can both read through each other's parts."

"Meet here at 7:30 AM?"

Kate nodded, yawned, and stretched.

As they walked toward the parking lot, Steve asked, "Are you heading back to your place?"

Kate took his hand. "As much as I'd like to have a repeat of last night and the night before, I'm just too tired. Rain check?"

"No worries," Steve replied. He walked her to her car, which was parked one row over from his own. He kissed her cheek. "See you in the morning."

She returned the kiss. "See you then. I'll bring breakfast."

Steve was the first to arrive the next morning, and he got started documenting the contents of the folders that he had read. He focused on the information that would have the most meaning to Rosemont, the President, and other senior officials.

Kate was fifteen minutes late arriving, but Steve soon saw why. She had stopped at a bakery to pick up breakfast. She put the box on the table and then pulled out a large bottle of juice from her bag. Steve looked inside the box while Kate got plates, cups, and napkins from the break room.

Sweet pastries filled the box, along with bagels and cream cheese, and croissants filled with meat and cheese. The smell of the food was intoxicating. "This looks terrific!"

Kate handed him a plate and a napkin. "I wasn't sure what you liked, so I got a little of everything."

"Perfect! That's what I like."

They filled their plates and then got to work.

Late that afternoon, Kate read their combined summaries. When she finished, she shook her head and looked at Steve. "I had no idea the scope of their plans. How could anyone have conceived of all this?"

Steve shrugged. "I don't know. I only know that we have to stop them."

"Do you think we can?"

"What choice do we have?"

Kate shrugged. "None."

CHAPTER 15

Beijing • Murmansk • Norfolk • Washington, DC
December 2027

The first week of December arrived, and preparations for the mission were in high gear. Army units, armored divisions, and artillery batteries were positioned all along the U.S.-Mexican border, ready to repel any incursion. The Navy was busy preparing to sail to Norway. The Air Force and the intelligence community were consumed with preparing for the air assault against the Latin American armed forces and figuring out how to keep the Chinese from figuring out what the Navy was doing.

The Navy task force heading for Norway would be comprised of two Gerald R. Ford-class aircraft carrier strike groups: the USS John F. Kennedy strike group, under the command of Rear Admiral Morton Prescott, and the newly commissioned USS Enterprise strike group, under the command of Rear Admiral George Flemming. Each strike group would also include two guided missile cruisers, four anti-submarine and surface warfare destroyers, and four fast-attack submarines. The military cargo and troopships, as well as the civilian cruise ships, cargo ships, and supertankers, would be spread out between the two strike groups.

Vice Admiral William Alexander had overall command

for the mission and the task force, and his mission operations center would be onboard the USS Enterprise. Most of Rosemont's team would either be with him or with the ground and air forces along the U.S.-Mexican border.

Two ports had been chosen for the evacuation of Europe's surviving forces. Bergen in southwestern Norway would load the heaviest equipment. Its cranes and lifts could handle the largest cargos, and it was located next to Norway's main naval base. Bodo, almost in the middle of the northern coast would load mostly smaller cargo. It was the farthest north of the ports, and it was where the Russian Navy would rendezvous with the U.S. and European fleets. One carrier strike group would guard each of the ports until loading was complete and the Bergen ships had repositioned to Bodo.

The Norwegians and the governments-in-exile in Norway had been notified of the plans, and they were carefully relocating their ships, personnel, and equipment to the areas around those ports. This was made more difficult by the Scandes along the northern Norwegian coast, but the Europeans managed to get it done. The few remaining passenger jets on the Scandinavian Peninsula were already flying refuges out of the area, refueling in Iceland before continuing on to Canada.

The Russians were preparing their fleet as quickly as they could. Dozens of cargo ships in the area had been commandeered to transport the weapons and other military equipment being evacuated. Preparations were being made to destroy all remaining military assets in the region as soon as the fleet sailed for Bodo. The Russians had enough fuel to reach the Norwegian port, but they would need to refuel their vessels before leaving for the U.S. The Russians didn't want the American fleet to waste time sending slower vessels all the way to the Kola Peninsula to handle the fueling.

The Russian Army positioned along the Urals was preparing to pull out and redeploy to Moscow and St. Petersburg for the winter. They understood that they were being left behind to harass the enemy as much as possible until defeat became inevitable. They accepted their assignment with a resigned dignity.

The British Army units, who had made it from Scotland to Norway before the Caliphate insurgents cut off all escape, offered to remain behind and help defend their Scandinavian hosts. The other army units from Europe made the same offer, vowing to harass and confound the enemy for as long as possible. They also planned to organize the remaining civilians into local militias to help with the defense of their homeland.

The Norwegian government appreciated the offer, but it informed the soldiers that they'd be evacuated. "Sacrificing your life for us is commendable, but there are battles left to fight where your services are needed," King Haakon of Norway explained to the soldiers and their governments-in-exile before he was evacuated to Canada.

The plan was for the U.S. naval task force to leave Norfolk in the second week of December, arriving in Norway just before Christmas day and leaving on New Year's Eve. It would be tight to get everything loaded and the ships refueled in a week, but the Europeans and Russians committed to make it work.

Admiral Alexander had been given explicit instructions by his superiors: Under no circumstances were the U.S. ships to still be in Russian or Scandinavian waters when either Chinese fleet entered the Atlantic. He intended to carry out those orders.

Colonel Petrov was notified that the prisoners he wanted had arrived. He strode over to the interrogation center to see how many drug dealers and their couriers had been captured.

As he entered the building, his aide snapped to attention. "Thirty seven dealers, four couriers, and three suppliers, Comrade Colonel."

"Excellent work," Petrov complimented him. "I'll start

with the suppliers."

Russian interrogation techniques were effective, but hardly humane. Petrov wanted information about the banker very badly, so he was willing to use more direct methods. He had no time for prolonged torture or psychological approaches designed to break a person's will and resistance.

When he entered the cell of the first supplier, who was sitting on a cot against the wall, Petrov was carrying only a chair and a steel baton. He sat down in front of the prisoner and immediately smashed his baton into the prisoner's kneecap, breaking it.

The prisoner screamed in pain.

"Do I have your attention?" Petrov demanded.

The prisoner nodded, clutching his injured knee while tears poured down his face from the pain.

"What do you know about your Chinese banker?"

"What Chinese banker," the prisoner replied.

Petrov broke the man's other kneecap.

"Do you need me to repeat my question?" he growled.

"No… no… my Chinese banker. What do… you want to know…?"

"His name and where he is, for a start."

The prisoner seemed about to pass out from the pain. Petrov slapped him hard across the face with his backhand.

"Stay awake," he commanded.

The prisoner nodded. "Han. His name is Shusong Han. He's with the… Industrial and Commercial Bank of China. He… runs the… syndicate… behind the scenes."

"And do you know where he is at the moment?"

"Um… China?"

Petrov's hand flew so quickly that the prisoner never saw it. It knocked him back so hard that his head hit the wall behind him.

"Where in China?" Petrov asked coldly.

The prisoner didn't answer.

"I see." Petrov lifted his baton. "What shall I break next?"

His arm moved, and in instant later, the prisoner's left arm was broken just below the elbow.

"Macau! The banker's in Macao. There's a meeting there for all the bankers tied to China's secret initiative."

"And how do you know that if it's secret?"

The prisoner was sobbing by this point. "Because we had to get our deposits to him before he left, and the paperwork had to be made out to the Macao branch of the bank. He said he'd be back in a week."

"Do you know where the meeting is in Macao?"

The prisoner shook his head. "At the bank probably, but I don't know."

Petrov stood. "You've been very helpful." He looked sympathetically at the prisoner writhing in pain. "Here, let me help you." His baton whipped out and hit the prisoner in the neck, crushing the man's windpipe. Petrov watched the man suffocate for a moment, and then he turned and left the cell.

"I'm afraid he died," Petrov told his aide. "Where's the next supplier?"

By the time he was done interrogating the prisoners, he had confirmation of the banker's name, that he was heading for a meeting in Macao, that other bankers tied to the Chinese initiative would be there, and that the meeting was being held in the Industrial and Commercial Bank of China building.

When he returned to his office, he verified the exact coordinates of the bank building, and then he placed a call to the head of the Russian Air Force. "I need a drone strike against a target in Macao. Can you handle that?"

"What's the target?" the general asked.

"The Industrial and Commercial Bank of China building in Macao." He gave the GPS coordinates of the building.

"When do you want it?"

"As soon as possible. Mid-morning would be good. My target is only there for a few days, meeting with a valuable set of collateral targets."

"Do you know where in the building your target will be, or do you want the entire building destroyed."

"Destroy the entire building, General. But it can't look like we did it or the Americans. Do any of the Caliphate countries have drones?"

"Syria and Iran have drones," the general replied. "Pakistan, too."

"Have it look like Iran's behind it."

The general chuckled. "Does tomorrow work for you?"

"Perfect, General. Thank you."

Petrov then called Kate's satellite number. When she answered, he said, "It's Kostya. How are you?"

"I'm well. You?"

"Doing very well. Things are proceeding here rapidly, but we'll be ready. Will I see you for Christmas?"

"There's a good chance," Kate replied.

"Wonderful. I have an early Christmas present for you."

Kate sounded excited. "You found my banker?"

Petrov chuckled. "Found him and set things in motion to end him by this time tomorrow."

"End him?" Kate exclaimed. "I was hoping to capture him."

"He's in Macao," Petrov told her. "We can't extract him from there, and we have no way to follow him if and when he leaves. But we can throw a wrench in the Chinese plans by removing him from the game."

"That makes sense," she conceded. "So how did you find him?"

Petrov told her about the arrests he had made and the subsequence interrogations—leaving out the methods used to extract the information. "I'm told there are other bankers on your list who are supposed to be there.

"I wonder why they're meeting in Macao instead of Beijing." Kate was thinking aloud.

"Perhaps they're maintaining the illusion that China isn't actually behind their activities," Petrov suggested.

"Good point. How are you going to end him for me?"

"A drone strike made to look like Iran was behind it."

Kate started laughing. "Iran? You're setting up the Caliphate for the assassination?"

"Well, I can't very well make it look like you did it or we did it. And it's not just assassination. The strike will bring down the entire building."

Kate roared with laughter.

Petrov smiled. "Now you sound like a Russian!"

"But I'm still Norwegian," Kate reminded him.

"I'll call you tomorrow and let you know if the strike was successful. I don't know how long it will take for us to learn the identities of the dead, but I can at least tell you if the building is still standing or not."

"Thank you, Kostya. Merry Christmas.

"Merry Christmas to you, Kate. *Dasvidaniya.*"

"*Dasvidaniya.*"

Liang Hao met with his team of bankers via video conference. They were at the Macao headquarters of the Industrial and Commercial Bank of China, and he was in his office at the Central Military Commission headquarters in Beijing. He would have preferred to meet with the bankers in person, but he was forbidden to travel until his strategy had run its course and China was the master of the world. Still, video conferencing meant that his pawns didn't have to travel to Beijing all the time, which would help avoid suspicion.

He was just about to tell them that they were done for the day and could reconvene in the morning, when the picture went black.

He turned to one of his ever-present military aides. "I lost connection with Macao."

"I'll check on it for you, Chief Strategist."

The aide was gone for a long time, but when he finally returned, his face was ashen.

"What is it?" Linh Hao demanded.

"There was an explosion in Macao," the aide reported. "The Industrial and Commercial Bank of China building... isn't there any longer."

"What happened?"

"No one knows, Chief Strategist. There was a massive explosion, but no one knows how."

Liang Hao was concerned that so many of his most valuable pawns were in the building at the time. "Find out. I must know if this was an accident or deliberate, and I need to know who is responsible."

"Yes, Chief Strategist."

If this is an accident, then it is just one of those unanticipated variables that I knew might affect the plan. I warned the Party and the military that things like this could happen. I'll need to replace the bankers immediately so there will be no disruption to their duties.

But what if this is not an accident but a deliberate act? That means someone wanted that building destroyed. Is it related to the plan? Were my bankers the target, or is there another reason someone wanted that building destroyed. And if it's related to the plan, who knew that the bankers would be there? Who could have known that the bankers were part of the plan? Someone here in Beijing trying to make the plan fail? Or one of our enemies trying to disrupt the next phase of the plan?

But who could it be? The Latin Americans? They would be lost without Shusong Han. Lost and broke. The Islamists? They would be just as broke, but not so lost. As long as they have infidels to kill, they have enough to keep them busy. Maybe they feel they no longer need our support in their holy cause. If only they knew that their holy cause was just them carrying out our strategy, a strategy that will lead to their own destruction. Could they have figured out our endgame? I will have to look into that.

What about the Americans? No, they would have no way to know about the bankers and no way to trace them to Macao. The Russians? They are hanging on to life by a thread. There is no link between the bankers and Russia, so even if they knew, why would they care? No, not the Russians.

Then who did this?

Petrov called Kate the next day as promised, but apart from confirming that the building was completely destroyed, he had no additional news to report. "It will take days... even weeks to sort through the rubble and identify the bodies," he told her. "But we'll continue to monitor the situation as much as we can. If I hear the name of your banker mentioned, I'll let you know."

Rosemont met with his team two days before the fleet was scheduled to sail from Norfolk. Adam Chester was there as well. Rosemont wanted one last chance to review the assignments and wish everyone well.

Benson was returning to his Coast Guard command, and Clay was returning to his duties with the FBI. Sweeny, Petersen, Michaels, and Vandyke were deploying with the forces along the Mexican border. Kate, Steve, Grant, Adam, and Moira Kirkland were deploying with the fleet sailing for Norway. Shortly before reaching Norway, Kate and Steve would be flown by Osprey to the Severomorsk Naval Base, where they would sail with the Russian fleet to the rendezvous.

"Are there any questions about your roles?" Rosemont asked.

No one had a question.

"Then good luck to you all. And keep in touch. I'll be at the Situation Room here in this building until the naval mission's over and you're back in U.S. waters."

Liang Hao met with the senior military leaders to discuss a change in plans.

"I understand that weather could be a factor in the schedule for taking the blockade fleet through the Arctic as planned," he said when the meeting began.

"That's correct," the commanding admiral replied. "All indications are that the Arctic will be covered by a blizzard that will last most of January."

"Will it reach the Scandinavian Peninsula?"

"The indications are that it will not reach that far west."

Liang Hao thought about this development. He had never liked the idea of a winter campaign in Russia—it had never been successfully attempted—but he deferred to the wishes of the military on that point.

"Does the Arctic sea-lane have to be completed before we send the blockade fleet through?" he asked.

"No, the fleet can follow a couple of days behind the ice breakers. It would even save time, because the icebreakers wouldn't have to retrace their steps to keep the lane free of ice."

Liang Hao nodded. "Then what if we move the timetable forward a couple of weeks. We will send the blockade fleet into the Arctic before the end of December, and we will have the fleet going through the Suez Canal reach the Scandinavian Peninsula ten days after the blockade fleet arrives."

He looked at the calendar on the wall. "If the blockade fleet can reach the Peninsula no later than the last day of December, we can begin the air attack on New Year's Day, and invade the Peninsula by mid-January. And, instead of the bombers returning to their bases in eastern Russia, we will keep them and their fighter escorts in Europe so they will be available should the western Russians or the Caliphate do something unexpected."

Laing Hao looked at his calendar again. "Can the blockade fleet be ready to sail by December 19th?"

"Yes, Chief Strategist."

"And can the Main fleet taking the Suez Canal be ready to leave by December 19th?"

"It will be close, but we'll make every effort to have the fleet underway by the 19th. The 20th at the latest."

Liang Hao. "Good. Then our blockade fleet will deploy around the Scandinavian Peninsula no later than December 31st, and the air attack will begin on January 1st."

On the eve of the fleet departing for Norway, Steve brought dinner over to Kate's house. Kate had a gas grill, but Steve brought a portable charcoal grill for the steaks. "Sometimes I just prefer the flavor of the natural coals," he explained.

Kate was more than happy to let Steve cook the meal. She delighted in watching him do things he enjoyed doing. And evidently, Steve not only loved cooking, he excelled at it.

As it turned out, the meal was fantastic. Everything was cooked to perfection. Steve also handled the cleanup, which surprised Kate, but it secretly pleased her. She was learning to let go of her need for control where Steve was concerned.

After everything had been put away, they sat on the couch, watching the fire in the fireplace.

"This will be our last time alone for the next several weeks," Steve noted as Kate poured them a glass of wine.

Kate nodded, putting the bottle on the tray in front of them. "The carrier will be crowded, there's no telling what will happen when we reach Russia, and the voyage home will be nerve-wracking until we're out of range of the Chinese fighters and bombers."

"Well then, we probably shouldn't waste a single

moment." Steve took her glass and put it next to his on the table.

He kissed her and they held the embrace for quite a while. Then Kate reached for her wine, drained it, and stood as she put the glass back on the table. She held out her hand. Steve took it and stood, following her upstairs.

The intensity of their lovemaking was greater than any they had shared so far. Kate didn't need a physical or emotional release as much as she needed a connection that went much deeper and lasted longer than the intimacy of the moment. Steve sensed it and found his own pleasure intensified by the change of focus.

They made love several times that night, not wanting to let go of each other for even a moment. When they had finally reached the point of exhaustion, they held each other close, enjoying the feel of their bodies touching each other as they lay side by side.

After a while, Steve whispered, "Are you awake?"

"How could I sleep after *that*?"

Do you mind if I break a rule?"

Kate looked at him suspiciously. "Exactly which rule are you talking about, because if it's one of the things I told you I don't do, the answer is still 'no.'"

Steve laughed softly. "No, it's not that. I need to ask you a work question. It has been bothering me for days."

"Okay. But just this once." She gave his arm a gentle squeeze.

"I'm worried about the timeline once the fleet reaches Norway. Admiral Alexander wants everything loaded and ready to sail home in under a week, but based on the intel I saw from Adam, I don't see how that's long enough to get it all done. The Europeans have a huge list of items they wanted loaded, and I just don't see the two ports we've selected being able to handle it all."

"Technically three ports," Kate corrected him. "We're

using the naval base at Bergen along with the commercial port next door."

"I still don't think that even three ports will be able to get it all done in time. There needs to be a way to prioritize the cargo being loaded so the critical items are loaded first. That way, if we have to leave quickly, whatever's left behind won't be as important as what's already loaded."

"Moira's working on that," Kate told him. "And if we have to stay in Norway for a few extra days into the New Year to get the cargo loaded, it won't be a problem. The Chinese blockade fleet won't arrive until at least the second week of January at the earliest. We'll be long gone by then."

CHAPTER 16

———— • ————

**Mexico City • Norfolk • North Atlantic •
U.S.-Mexican Border • Washington, DC
December 2027**

The next morning, Kate made a quick breakfast for the two of them. A car was scheduled to pick them up in less than an hour and drive them to the Pentagon, where a helicopter would fly them to Norfolk. Grant and Adam were meeting them at the Pentagon for the flight down. Moira Kirkland was already at Norfolk, working with Admiral Alexander on the planning and scheduling of the Norwegian part of the mission.

Steve's bags for the trip were in Kate's front hallway. He had come by car service the night before so he could leave his car at home while he was away. He had already showered and dressed when he came downstairs.

They ate quickly, and then Steve cleaned up while Kate went to take a shower. Steve also cleaned the portable grill, disposed of the charcoal, and placed the grill in Kate's garage. *I'll pick it up when we get back. Or maybe I'll just leave it here for the next time we want to grill.*

"What time does the fleet sail?" Steve asked when Kate came downstairs with her bags.

"At four this afternoon," she replied. Then she said, "The seas are calmer than usual for this time of year, but they'll get rougher as we go further north. Did you bring Dramamine with you?"

"I've never used it," Steve informed her. "I don't get seasick."

Kate smiled. "Well, I'm bringing some just in case. I don't like throwing up in front of a bunch of men. Besides, there's no privacy onboard a ship at sea."

Steve kissed her neck. "Do you think we'll have any *alone-time* onboard the ship?"

Kate pulled away and shook her finger at him playfully. "You know the Navy's rules about sex onboard their ships. If we get caught, it'll embarrass Rosemont and the rest of the team. We just can't chance it. And don't even think about doing anything around the Russians. They're going to be watching us like hawks. I don't need them snickering at us every time one of us walks by."

Steve was about to make a comment when they heard a horn honk in Kate's driveway.

"Car's here," Kate said.

Steve grabbed both of their bags and took them out to the car. Kate activated her house alarm system, locked the front door, and joined Steve.

"I need to check one last thing." Kate reached into her backpack and found her sat-phone, right next to her pistols. "Good, it's here. I'm ready to go."

They got into the car and headed for the Pentagon.

The winds were light and the sky overcast as the helicopter lifted off and headed for Norfolk. The route took them over miles of barren trees, rolling hills, and yellow-tan grasslands. No one spoke much during the flight—their minds too focused on the mission about to begin. Kate noticed Steve periodically glancing across the cabin at her—smiling when he got caught—and she smiled back at him.

Liz Sweeny sat in the command center located just outside El Paso, Texas. El Paso had been chosen because it was almost the center point of the U.S.-Mexican border, and it was the home of the DEA's El Paso Intelligence Center, which had all the facilities needed to oversee the operation. None of the other members of the team assigned to the border were at the command center with her at that time. Petersen was with his Border Patrol unit near McAllen, Texas, on the eastern end of the border. Michaels was meeting with the army units near Douglas, Arizona. Vandyke was helping coordinate intel with the air wing command at Laughlin Air Force Base, in Del Rio, Texas, which was a training base that had been repurposed due to its proximity to the border.

The monitors along the far wall of the command center were filled with images from satellites and drones patrolling the border region. The Latin American troops continued to arrive and deploy along the border, but there was no indication that they were preparing to move north. In fact, there were no supply lines or supply depots set up, making Liz wonder how they could remain on the border for much longer, let alone invade the United States. She mentioned her concerns to the general commanding the joint border forces.

"This *is* strange," the general conceded. "It lends evidence to the theory that the Latin American soldiers are being set up for us to destroy them."

"I wonder how long they'll just wait there before finally turning around and going home."

"I guess that depends on who's giving the orders down there," the general replied. "The Mexicans or the Chinese."

The presidents of Mexico, Venezuela, and Columbia met with the two cartel leaders at the Presidential Palace in Mexico City.

"Why did we send all of our troops north if they're just going to sit there along the U.S. border?" the President of

Mexico asked. "More troops arrive daily, but they're not doing anything. Why haven't we received instructions from the Chinese about what the soldiers are supposed to be doing up there? Do the Chinese fear an invasion? If so, why do they think that it would have to come through our northern border?"

"Come to think of it," the President of Venezuela commented, "Why haven't we heard from our banker lately? No deposits have been recorded, no payments made... is he on holiday or what?"

"We haven't heard anything from him in more than a week," the head of the eastern cartel said. "We've tried to reach him several times, but there's no answer. We've started putting *all* of our money into the Cayman banks just so all that cash isn't lying around creating a fire hazard."

The two cartel leaders laughed.

"Us, too," the head of the western cartel confirmed. "It's like he's disappeared, which has me worried. He's the only access we have to our money in the Chinese banks."

"We have the same problem," the President of Columbia admitted. "If we don't hear from him soon, our treasury will be depleted, and we won't be able to pay our soldiers or anyone else. We'll be broke."

"What about our supply shipments from the Chinese?" the President of Mexico asked. "Have any arrived lately?"

The President of Venezuela spoke up. "Yes, but they were shipments that had left China before the banker disappeared. No new ships have left China since then."

"Do we have any other ways to reach the banker or the people he works with?" the head of the eastern cartel asked.

No one responded.

"Then what are we supposed to do now?" he asked.

Kate, Steve, Kirkland, Grant, and Adam stood on the flight deck of the USS Enterprise as the task force pulled out of Norfolk. It was an incredible sight to see all of the ships sailing through the channel.

When they reached the Atlantic, the escort ships deployed into formation alongside the carrier and around the civilian vessels that were accompanying them to Norway. Kate chuckled at the sight of cruise ships sailing behind an aircraft carrier, but she also knew that this mission was deadly serious.

Once the submarines had disappeared below the surface to begin their patrols, Kirkland suggested that they return to the mission operations center. There was a lot of work to do.

The seas grew rougher as the task force moved northeast, but not enough to put any of the civilian ships at risk. The mission operations center was a hive of activity as the task force made its way across the Atlantic. Kate, as the liaison with the Russians, spent most of her time communicating with the Russian admiralty and with Petrov to ensure that everything was proceeding according to plan.

As the days progressed, Kirkland began to have the same nagging feeling that Steve had before they left. There was too much cargo and too little time to get it all loaded. By her estimates, the fleet would not be ready to leave Norway until January 3rd, placing their departure four days behind schedule.

Admiral Alexander was not happy about the new schedule, and he continued to pressure Kirkland and the others to find ways to make the loading and refueling happen faster. Grant relayed the Admiral's concerns to the governments-in-exile and their militaries in Norway, but he was getting strong push-back from them.

"They won't budge, Admiral," he explained at one of their daily staff meetings. "They say they've stripped down what they're evacuating to only the most essential items. They're not willing to give up even one more pallet."

"And you relayed my instructions?" Admiral Alexander

asked.

"Yes, sir, but I don't think you want to hear what their responses were."

"Military or civilian responses?"

"Either," Grant replied.

"Tell me," the admiral demanded.

Grant complied.

Alexander's face turned beet red, but he said nothing. Finally, he said, "Fine. We'll do what we can. But if the Chinese show up, whatever isn't loaded already is being left behind. Make certain that they understand *that!*"

"I've made that clear to them," Grant confirmed, "but I'll reiterate it on my next calls."

Turning to Kate, he asked, "Are the Russians ready?"

"They seem to be, Admiral," Kate replied. "They'll leave for the rendezvous just after we arrive, so they'll be ready to sail when the rest of the task force is."

"Good." The admiral turned to Kirkland. "Do we have a final tally on the number of ships the Europeans are adding to the task force?"

Kirkland told him.

"I'd feel better if we had a third carrier," the admiral commented.

"We *will* have another carrier," Kate reminded him, "and we'll have the protection of the Russian Atlantic, Baltic, and Black Sea fleets. In addition to support and logistics ships, they're bringing at least thirty-five warships, including their one carrier, and almost forty submarines."

"But that carrier is several years past its expected decommissioning date," the admiral reminded her.

Kate nodded. "Yes, but its last refit extended its life for another ten to fifteen years. She's still seaworthy, fully armed, and has over thirty aircraft aboard."

The admiral nodded. The Russian fleet would be a

valuable addition to the task force—especially the submarines—since the remnants of the European fleets would be vulnerable due to being overloaded with cargo and personnel.

As the task force approached the north coast of Scotland, the carrier strike groups went on high alert. Caliphate forces wouldn't be able to see the ships sailing past, but if the British radar systems were still operational, the Caliphate might still be able to detect them and use captured British weapon systems to launch an attack.

The electronic warfare departments watched closely for any evidence that they had been spotted by radar, but there was no indication that they had been. The fleet sailed past Scotland unobserved.

Once past Britain, they reached the point where the two carrier strike groups would separate and lead their support ships to the two Norwegian ports. Kate and Steve said goodbye to Adam, Grant, and Kirkland before transferring over to the USS John F. Kennedy, which would be guarding the port of Bodo during the Norwegian portion of the mission.

On Christmas Eve, as the carrier strike group and its support ships approached the Norwegian coast and the port of Bodo, Kate and Steve boarded their U.S. Marine Corps V-22 Osprey for the 500-mile flight to Murmansk.

"Are you excited to be going back to Russia?" Steve asked.

Kate shook her head. "I'm excited for this mission to be over so we can see what impact it had on the Chinese strategy."

Steve laughed.

Neither Steve nor Kate had ever been on board an Osprey before, but they had seen them many times flying around Washington. The Navy chose an Osprey so they wouldn't have to set down and refuel without escort gunships to protect them, and there seemed little harm in letting the Russians see inside one since their military was about to merge with the U.S. military.

The aircraft took off vertically, thanks to the Osprey's ability to take off and land like a helicopter. Once airborne, Kate heard the wings pivot, and the aircraft began moving forward away from the fleet.

The flight took less than two hours. The Russians gave them permission to land at the naval base, rather than the nearby air base, so it would be easier to load the Osprey onboard the Russian's carrier. The aircraft slowed to a hover and then landed like a helicopter. When Kate and Steve stepped out of the aircraft onto Russian soil, Petrov and the Russian Admiralty were waiting for them, along with the Russian President, who insisted on evacuating with the military instead of with the civilian air flights.

Petrov stepped forward to greet Kate, and she introduced him to Steve. Petrov then introduced them to the gathered admirals and to the Russian President.

"I am very pleased to meet you, Ms. Davidsen," the president said. "And you, too, Mr. Barksdale. We had just about given up all hope when your Mr. Chester informed us of your plan to help."

"We're honored to work with you and your military, Mr. President," Kate replied. "We have a common enemy. Once our combined forces are gathered, we'll change the game on them."

The president smiled warmly. Then he looked around. "I don't know if I'll ever be able to return to my beloved Russia, but someday, the children or the grandchildren of those evacuating *will* return and *will* reclaim our homeland."

"Absolutely, Mr. President."

The activity at the Severomorsk Naval Base was impressive. Petrov showed them the plans for destroying all of the ships being left behind and the bases and shipyards on the Kola

Peninsula, including Severomorsk, Polyarny, Skalisty, Olenya Bay, Nerpa, Roslyakovo, Ura Bay, Ara Bay, Nerpichya Bay, Bolshaya Lopatka, and Malaya Lopatka. Kate saw dozens of cargo and logistics ships moving through the channel to the staging area in the Barents Sea west of the Murmansk fjord. Ships sailed past all day and all night.

The next day, the final preparations for departure were made. The Osprey—its wings and rotors folded in the compact storage configuration—was loaded onto the Russian carrier, and Kate, Steve, Petrov, the commanding admiral, and the Russian President boarded the Russian flagship. The other admirals were spread out across the fleet. Late in the afternoon, the carrier followed the last of the smaller ships into the channel, past the Polyarny and Skalisty naval bases, and on toward the open sea.

Kate stood on the carrier's flight deck, watching the lights along the fjord glide by. Once they cleared the fjord, the salt air was quite cold, and in the moonlight, Kate saw ice floes forming to the north. *I hope the ice won't slow us down getting to Norway.*

All of the Russian ships were assembled at the staging area four hours before dawn the next morning. Their submarines were already patrolling the route to Bodo.

Kate, Steve, and Petrov were invited to join the president and the commanding admiral on the bridge to watch the destruction of the Russian naval bases and shipyards. As soon as the order was given, Kate saw a white-orange fireball appear on the horizon. The detonations grew brighter as more of the buildings and facilities were destroyed, including all of the docks, dry-docks, lifts, and cranes. The light from the explosions grew as bright as the sun, and Kate had to shield her eyes.

The commanding admiral gave the order, and the fleet got underway. Their next stop was the port of Bodo.

Kirkland and Grant were frustrated, as was Admiral Alexander.

Grant was the acting liaison with European government officials, and Kirkland served as the liaison with the European militaries and the ports. They were doing their best to keep everything on schedule, but the Europeans seemed determined to restructure the schedule at every turn.

Everything seemed fine when the U.S. ships arrived. Work began immediately to load and refuel the U.S. and European ships. However, Kirkland discovered quickly that the cargo being loaded was not what was agreed to in advance. Civilian possessions were being loaded ahead of the military assets. Even the government officials, who understood the need to move quickly, were having their own possessions loaded first, taking up space and time that the Navy didn't have.

"How are we going to stop this?" Alexander demanded. He had spent the last ten minutes shouting at Kirkland and Grant, and this was the first time he was actually giving them time to respond.

"They won't listen," Grant insisted. "Nothing I've said to them makes any difference."

"Then how do we handle this?" Alexander asked Kirkland.

"We stop the cranes and threaten to dump the non-military cargo overboard," she replied. "We'll actually have to dump some to show we're serious. I'd suggest starting with the cars. They'll sink. Furniture might float and interfere with the ships."

Alexander turned to an aide. "Throw every civilian vehicle overboard. Then find every civilian vehicle in the staging area, move them out of the staging area, and blow them up."

Alexander turned to Grant. "You go tell the European leaders that we'll refuse to load any civilians if they don't start working with us instead of against us."

"Yes, Admiral."

Kate, Kirkland, Grant, and Steve talked via sat-phone that evening.

"How is everything going?" Kate asked.

"Slowly," Kirkland replied. "We had to get tough with the European civilians. They were trying to load their personal items ahead of the military assets, and we had to start dumping some of it overboard and setting the rest on fire until they realized just how serious we were. I think we destroyed over thirty cars so far. But now things are running smoothly."

"How long will it take to get everything loaded?" Steve asked."

"We should be done loading the military assets by late on New Year's Day. The civilian assets that were agreed to will take another day and a half after that."

"So January 3rd?"Kate asked.

"I believe so."

"The carrier air groups are flying patrol missions day and night," Grant reported. "So far, there's no sign that the Chinese know we're here. I have no idea what the Caliphate forces know."

"Are you ready to destroy the ports when you leave?" Steve asked.

"Yes," Grant replied. "Most of the ports are for fishing vessels and other coastal vessels. They'll be left alone. Only the ports with cargo terminals will be destroyed, and there are only a handful of them."

"How are things with the Russians?" Kirkland asked.

Kate responded. "We're en route and on schedule. The Russian bases on the Kola Peninsula have been destroyed. The Chinese won't be able to claim any of them as a prize. The Russian Army is redeploying to Moscow and St. Petersburg as we speak. Oh, and the Russian president cannot stop thanking us for our help."

They talked for a while longer and then ended the call after agreeing on a time for their conversation the next day.

Petrov stared at the report in disbelief as he stood in the intelligence command center, where all satellite, drone, and human intelligence information was being sent now that the fleet was evacuating. "Are you certain? Are you *absolutely* certain?"

'Yes, Comrade Colonel. It's been triple checked. There is no mistake."

God in heaven! "Get Ms. Davidsen and Mr. Barksdale down here. Now!"

"At once, Comrade Colonel."

Petrov stared at the report again. *God damned Chinese!*

Kate and Steve arrived ten minutes later. Kate took one look at Petrov and knew that something was terribly wrong. "What happened?"

Petrov handed her the report that he had been clutching. Kate had to smooth the pages flat to read them. She scanned the information and then looked at Petrov—eyes wide.

"This is accurate?"

Petrov nodded.

Kate turned to Steve. "The Chinese blockade fleet has been sighted in the Artic sea-lane. They're not waiting until the lane is completed. They're staying about a day behind the icebreakers."

"When will they reach the Norwegian coast?"

"New Year's Eve."

CHAPTER 17

Artic Sea-Lane • Beijing • North Atlantic •
Norwegian Coast
December 2027 & January 2028

Kate immediately pulled out her sat-phone and called Moira Kirkland.

"What's up?" Kirkland asked when she answered her phone. "We're not supposed to talk for another two hours."

"The Chinese blockade fleet left ahead of schedule and is already inside the Arctic sea-lane. They're following the icebreakers. They'll reach Norway by New Year's Eve."

"Shit! What about the fleet coming through the Suez Canal?"

Kate relayed the question to Petrov. He shrugged.

"They don't know, but they're looking into it."

Kirkland muttered a few choice expletives. "Well, one thing's for goddamned sure. If one fleet's on its way, the other can't be more than a week or two behind. The other fleet has the supplies for the first fleet. Shit!"

"Is there any way to speed up loading the cargo and fueling the ships?" Kate's mind raced, looking for alternatives.

"No. We're barely going to be finished by the 3rd. There's no way we can finish before the 31st."

Petrov waved at Kate to get her attention.

"Moira, hold on for a moment." Kate put the sat-phone on mute. "What's up?"

"I have an idea, but I need a little time. Tell her you'll call her back in two hours."

"But—"

"Trust me. Two hours. Tell her."

Kate unmuted the phone and told Kirkland that the Russians were working on something. Then she said she'd call back in two hours.

"I'll inform Admiral Alexander. I'm sure he'll want to be on that call."

"Okay. Talk to you then." Kate ended the call.

"What are you up to?" She asked Petrov.

The Russian just smiled. "Something that you Americans cannot do."

Petrov walked to the communications center and asked the lieutenant on duty to place a call to the admiral commanding the submarine fleet. It took several minutes, but finally the admiral was reached.

"Yes, Petrov?"

"Sir, the Chinese blockade fleet has moved sooner than expected. They'll be here by the 31st."

"Will the Americans be ready to leave before then?"

"No, sir," Petrov replied. "Loading the cargo and refueling the ships, including ours, will take until the 3rd."

"Then we're lost," the admiral said. "The Chinese will either pen us in, and their aircraft will blow us all to hell, or the U.S. will be forced into a shooting match that will trigger a war, making the U.S. just as unsafe for us as remaining here."

"You see the problem perfectly."

"Are you telling all of the admiralty this, Petrov, or are you wanting something from me?"

Petrov chuckled. "What if we could slow down the

Chinese, sir? Give the Americans time to finish loading and fueling, and then get out of here before the Chinese arrive? If their fleet hasn't arrived to blockade our ports, their bombers won't come, and we could still manage to slip out unobserved."

"You mean my subs?"

"Yes, Admiral. I mean your subs. Do you have two attack subs you could send to the Artic and two more you could send to the Suez Canal?"

"Why the Suez Canal?"

"Because the other Chinese fleet is taking the southern route to get here," Petrov explained. "It includes their carriers, troopships, and support ships. Now, if the carriers were sunk in the canal, blocking the canal for months while they clear the wreckage, every ship behind the carriers would have to back out and take the route around Africa to get here. It would take another month before they arrived at least, and you know what *wonderful* weather we'll be having in another month."

"I thought we wanted to avoid sinking Chinese ships because we feared Chinese reprisals."

Petrov laughed. "We're evacuating Russia. What can they do to us once we're gone?"

"And our comrades that we've left behind?" the admiral asked.

"Once the Chinese know that we're gone, why launch nukes? What purpose would it solve, other than making the land uninhabitable for a century?"

"All right, Petrov. I think I can accommodate you. What are the rules of engagement?"

"We're at war with China, sir. Stop the icebreakers, sink the blockade ships, sink their carriers, and block the Suez Canal from being used by the rest of their fleet while we run for safety in the West."

"Understood."

"Good hunting, Admiral."

Petrov left the communications center to inform the commanding admiral that four submarines were breaking off to delay the Chinese arrival.

When Kate called Kirkland back at the prearranged time, Kirkland immediately gave Kate a video conference link because of the number of people who would be involved in the call.

Petrov was happy with this, since the commanding admiral and others wanted to be part of the call as well.

When everyone was finally linked into the call, the attendees from the U.S. included Kate, Steve, Grant, Kirkland, Adam, and Admirals Alexander, Prescott, and Flemming. The Russian participants included Petrov, the commanding admiral, the captain of the carrier, and the Russian president.

After quick introductions, Kate translated the Russian intelligence report about the Chinese blockade fleet for the Americans on the call. She then relayed Petrov's plan to use submarines to slow down the Chinese and buy the Americans time to finish loading and refueling before the Chinese arrived.

"Are you prepared to sink Chinese ships?" Alexander asked.

"Admiral Alexander," the Russian commanding admiral began, "We're already at war with China. A war that we're about to lose. This is the one thing that absolutely separates you from us. You're trying to avoid shooting or being shot at by the Chinese. We have no such restrictions. In fact, shooting at the Chinese right now is something that we're very much looking forward to. And if it helps you and the other European nations participating in the evacuation... well... everybody wins."

The Russian president interjected. "My admirals believe that we can buy your fleet at least three if not four days before the Chinese decide to send in their bombers anyway. If you can squeeze every second out of the time it takes to load and refuel the ships, we'll all be long gone before they arrive. And I'm committing our Air Force to intercept their jets should we still be here when they come to bomb the ports and military assets, so no matter what, you'll still be able to get away safely."

Alexander nodded. "Thank you, Mr. President. Thank you all. We'll double our efforts to finish on time. Will you arrive at Bodo as scheduled?"

"Slightly ahead of schedule actually," the commanding admiral said proudly.

"Very well. We look forward to your arrival."

When the call ended, the president thanked Petrov for his quick thinking. "You may have just saved us all."

Four Yasen-Class Russian Attack Submarines broke away from the fleet. Two headed for the Arctic, and two headed for the Mediterranean. Their orders were to prevent the Chinese from reaching the Atlantic at all costs.

The two submarines heading south had at least a six-day journey to reach the mouth of the Suez Canal. While they were prepared to sink the Chinese vessels in the Mediterranean, the strategic value of blocking the canal was too great to be ignored. With luck, they'd reach the mouth of the canal and wait, submerged, until the Chinese fleet was sighted.

The two submarines heading for the Arctic reached the expected western point of the sea-lane being opened up by the icebreakers. Their orders were to sink the icebreakers before the sea-lane could be completed, and to then sink as many of the blockade ships as possible before making their way to Iceland.

The two northern submarines deployed and began patrolling the sea-lane for the Chinese ships and any submarines that the Chinese might have deployed into the Arctic.

The Russian fleet reached Bodo, and the tankers immediately began refueling the fleet. In spite of being on the largest ship in the Russian Navy, the carrier was a small one, and the northern seas made the voyage a rough one. Kate was grateful that she had packed plenty of Dramamine. The last thing she wanted was to be seen by Russian sailors throwing up onboard their flagship.

As soon as the carrier dropped anchor, Kate smelled that all-too-familiar scent that she equated with the Norwegian coast—fish. The smell was everywhere, given that fishing was the life's blood of the coastal nation. There was also the smell of the salt air mixed with a hint of diesel fumes from the fishing fleets operating all along the coastline.

Kate, Steve, and Petrov watched in fascination at the activity going on around the Norwegian port. In the midwinter darkness, they saw the running lights of the ships that were loaded and fueled anchored south of the port, and ships waiting to be loaded and fueled anchored to the north.

Kate looked at how the northern lights illuminated the Scandes in the distance, giving the snow-capped peaks a greenish tint. She remembered the times her parents had taken her skiing in those mountains, and she longed for such simple times. *Will I ever be able to ski there again? Will anyone?*

The wind picked up, and the sting of the salt air forced her to turn her back and face Petrov. "Just out of curiosity, Kostya, how many nukes made it out of Russia?"

Petrov chuckled. "Normally, Kate, I would lie to you, but since you're providing the new home for our nukes, I can tell you that every nuke west of the Urals has made it out, along with about thirty to forty percent of the mobile nukes from east of the Urals. The rest were captured when the Chinese overran our naval and air bases."

"And how many is that exactly?"

Petrov told her.

Kate flashed him a dark look. "That's more than you're supposed to have, Kostya. You signed treaties to dismantle more than that."

"We dismantled most of the ones aimed at you, but we

kept the ones aimed at China. And when Chinese aggression began to escalate, we... decided to keep a few extra just in case."

"But you reported them as deactivated," Kate accused.

"We had to keep China from finding out what we were doing," Petrov said innocently. "After all, in my experience, the American inspectors that your government sends over are notorious... what's the word that you Americans use... blabbermouths."

On the morning of December 29th, the five Chinese icebreakers reached a point less than ten miles from the western edge of the sea-lane. After confirming that there were no Chinese submarines in the area, the two Russian submarines moved into attack position.

In less than thirty minutes, all five icebreakers had been hit with two torpedoes each below the waterline and were sinking rapidly. The crews had no time to abandon ship, and the ships sank below the frigid water without a trace.

The next morning, the lead ships of the blockade fleet reached the end of the completed sea-lane and stopped. The way forward was not clear, and the icebreakers were nowhere to be seen. In fact, there wasn't even enough room to turn around because the fleet was following too closely behind the icebreakers to give them time to widen the sea-lane.

As the day progressed, more of the blockade ships arrived and were forced to stop. The two Russian submarines took advantage of the situation and began their attack. From their firing positions beneath the icepack, the Chinese ships couldn't use their anti-submarine weapons effectively. One by one, the Chinese ships were hit with torpedoes and sank beneath the Arctic. Some of the trailing ships tried to back out of the kill-zone, but the submarines followed them and sank them, too.

Once the bulk of the Chinese fleet had been destroyed with torpedoes, the submarines surfaced and began firing their cruise missiles at the blockade ships farther away to keep from having to chase them down across the north coast of Russia and to preserve their remaining torpedoes. Within an hour, all of the blockade ships had been hit, damaged, or destroyed. The submarines submerged and proceeded southwest toward Iceland.

"Happy New Year, Steve," Kate said shortly after midnight. She and Steve were in the intelligence command center, reading the reports on the destruction of the blockade fleet and the progress refueling the Russian fleet.

"Happy New Year to you, too. May 2028 be a better year than 2027 started out to be." Steve motioned for Kate to follow him. They went up on the flight deck of the carrier and looked around the Bodo harbor. "Just look at how well the year ended. Could you have imagined three months ago that all this would be happening? That you'd figure out who the enemy was and then devise a way to change the game on him? Look at what you've done! All this," Steve swept his hand across the view of the Norwegian harbor and coastline, "is because of you! It was your idea. Yes, lots of folks made it happen, but it was your idea to begin with. And I got to be part of it. That's what makes 2027 a great year for me, and it's why 2028 will be even better."

Kate looked around quickly, and seeing no one, gave Steve a quick kiss. "Thanks. It means a lot."

"Any time."

The refueling was completed on the morning of January 2nd, and the supertankers at all of the ports moved out of the way so the cargo ships could finish loading.

Admiral Alexander met with Kirkland to review the remaining cargo. All of the military cargo had been loaded, and all that was left was civilian items.

"Is everyone on board their ships?" he asked.

Kirkland nodded, "Yes, sir. All that remains is cargo."

"If we left now and sailed for the rendezvous at Bodo, would we be leaving anything of value behind?"

"Of value, sir? Not to us, but perhaps to their owners."

"Then notify the docks to stop the loading and prepare the strike group to get underway. We're leaving."

Kirkland hid a smile. "Yes, sir."

Kirkland relayed the orders, and then she called Kate. "We're preparing to get underway and rendezvous with you."

"You finished loading all the cargo already?"

"No. Admiral Alexander decided not to finish loading the civilian cargo."

"Civilian cargo?" Kate asked. "We didn't have any of that here at Bodo."

"Well we had it here," Kirkland responded.

"I thought you destroyed it all."

Kirkland laughed. "No just some of the automobiles. The politicians were trying to load the civilian cargo first. We had to explain to them why that wasn't going happen. But we told them that we'd take whatever we could after the military assets were loaded. Now that the refueling is done, we're leaving, and whatever cargo wasn't loaded will be destroyed when we bomb the harbors."

"We'll be ready for you," Kate promised. "See you tomorrow."

Shortly after the carrier strike group and the civilian ships got underway, bombers took off from the USS Enterprise. They destroyed the naval base and the cargo terminal at Bergen before returning to the carrier. The unloaded cargo was also destroyed. Another wave of bombers took off to destroy the cargo terminals along the Swedish coast.

Liang Hao was in the command conference room, listening to frantic reports from the Chinese Navy officers. All communications with the blockade fleet had been lost. All communications with the icebreakers had been lost. No one knew where the ships were or what had happened.

"A fleet does not simply disappear," Laing Hao reminded them. "Either they are there, or they were destroyed. There is not another option."

And if destroyed, that means they were discovered.

Liang Hao was so busy trying to deal with the problem of how to blockade the Scandinavian Peninsula that he didn't give the southern fleet a second thought. He needed to salvage his original plan, and he was obsessed with that.

Turning to the Air Force officers, he asked, "Can we go ahead and launch the bombers to destroy the military assets on the Russian Kola Peninsula and in Norway, Sweden, and Finland?"

"Yes, sir. It will take a day to load and fuel the planes, but they can take off for the Kola Peninsula as soon as that's done." Destroying the Russian bases on the Kola Peninsula first had always been the plan. There was plenty of time to destroy the other military assets on the Scandinavia Peninsula.

"Proceed, then. If those military assets are destroyed, it will not matter as much if our blockade fleet is there or not."

The John F. Kennedy carrier strike group, along with its civilian ships and the Russian fleet, were ready to sail when the Enterprise carrier strike group and its civilian ships arrived at Bodo. The Russian and U.S. Navy ships deployed around the civilian ships. Then the task force set sail for the United States. Jets from the Kennedy took off and destroyed Bodo's cargo terminal and port before returning to the ship. Fighter squadrons took off from all three carriers—along with jets from the Russian Air Force that would remain in Iceland—and began patrolling around the combined fleets, looking for Chinese or Caliphate ships that might try to attack. Only the Russian fighters had authorization to engage preemptively any Chinese jets they encountered.

The first wave of Chinese bomber squadrons reached the Kola Peninsula several hours after the combined fleets left Norway. Even in the low winter light, the squadron commander could see that there were no military ships docked in the harbors around Murmansk and that the docks and shipyards had already been destroyed. Flying west, he saw that the same was true for the other Russian bases. The commander contacted his superiors and reported his observations.

"Return to base." He acknowledged the order, turned around, and led his bombers back to their base east of the Urals.

The second wave of Chinese bomber squadrons reached the northern coast of the Scandinavian Peninsula shortly after the first wave had returned to base, and they found that none of the European military assets were visible anywhere. They crossed over to the southern coast, but the assets weren't there either.

Liang Hao heard the report and made the Air Force officer repeat it. "The Russian fleet is gone, the naval bases and other military facilities have already been destroyed, and the remnants of the European militaries have disappeared *before* our bombers arrived? How is that possible? Where could they have gone?"

"I don't know, Chief Strategist. The squadron commanders simply reported that there were no military assets remaining in the target zones. The commander of the second wave noticed that ports and naval bases in Norway and Sweden had been destroyed, too, but that was the only unusual thing he observed, apart from the military assets being missing."

"So there is no way that the military assets were deployed to Sweden along the southern coast?"

"No, Chief Strategist. The commander of the second wave

checked before reporting in."

Laing Hao was dumfounded. *There is no way they would attempt an invasion of the mainland and attempt to drive off the Caliphate. We have no intelligence that there are underground bunkers large enough to hide those assets, not to mention the ships. They would never scuttle their only means of defense and just surrender. That means that they either escaped or they are planning an attack.*

Liang Hao was so preoccupied with what was happening in northern Europe that he didn't hear the Navy officer standing in front of him.

"I'm sorry, what was that?"

The Navy officer repeated himself. "The commander of the fleet heading for the Suez Canal wants to know if he should proceed or return to base."

"Has he reached the Canal yet?"

"Yes, Chief Strategist. Most of the fleet is already in the Canal, heading for the Mediterranean."

"It makes no sense to have them back out of the Canal or enter the Mediterranean and just turn around. There is still the Caliphate and the Russian Army west of the Urals to deal with. Have them proceed."

"Do you think the missing Russian and European ships are trying to intercept our fleet? It does contain our invasion forces, so it would be a tempting target."

"If they knew about it," Liang Hao point out. "But they do not. They cannot. So no, I do not believe that the Russians and Europeans are deploying to intercept our fleet.

"Yes, Chief Strategist."

The two Russian submarines waited below the surface of the Mediterranean less than three miles from the mouth of the Suez Canal. Every hour, the lead submarine rose to periscope depth to see what traffic was coming through the Canal before submerging again.

Finally, their patience paid off. The lead submarine saw two Chinese aircraft carriers and dozens of troopships and support ships approaching the mouth of the canal. The captain of the lead submarine notified the other submarine's captain, and both redeployed into attack position.

The Yasen-Class Russian Attack Submarines had one of the most sophisticated torpedo targeting systems ever created, allowing them to target ships that were not in their direct line of sight or line of fire. From their positions on each side of the Canal, they could hit any ship in range of their torpedoes.

The lead Chinese carrier was a quarter of a mile from the mouth of the Canal. With all torpedo tubes loaded, the submarines prepared to fire.

The lead submarine fired six torpedoes into the hull of the lead carrier. While it reloaded, the second submarine did the same to the second carrier. Then they both fired a barrage of torpedoes into the following ships.

The lead carrier detected the torpedoes and had the chance to radio a warning before the torpedoes hit and the hull of the carrier was ripped open in six places. The second carrier activated its anti-submarine weapons system and fired anti-submarine missiles in the direction of the approaching torpedoes, but it only managed to fire a single barrage before being hit. Several of the support vessels behind the carriers fired their missiles, too, but they couldn't launch countermeasures in time to save them from the torpedoes.

Missiles fired from the second carrier struck the lead Russian submarine. The hull ruptured, and the submarine rapidly took on water. It hit bottom, cracking the hull open wider. Water rushed in faster, killing the entire crew.

The second submarine was able to reposition itself and fire countermeasures in time to avoid the Chinese missiles. It reached a safe distance and rose to periscope depth to observe the damage. What it saw made the crew cheer.

The Chinese carriers had listed to one side and sunk in the canal, blocking any possibility of a ship making it into the Mediterranean from the canal for months while the wreckage was removed. Several support ships and three troopships were also sunk. The rest of the Chinese fleet would have to back out of the Canal a hundred and twenty miles to the Red Sea's Gulf of Suez, since the Canal wasn't wide enough for the ships to turn around.

The submarine submerged deeper and headed west toward the Atlantic.

Liang Hao's face was ashen as he read the report from the Mediterranean. Two carriers, three troopships, one destroyer, and four cruisers destroyed inside the Suez Canal, blocking the mouth of the Canal and forcing the rest of the fleet to back out all the way to the Red Sea. The attack had been by at least one submarine of unknown origin.

The weather was turning worse, and the window of opportunity for the first successful winter offensive against Russia had closed. It would be well into the spring before troops could be sent to western Russia and the Scandinavian Peninsula to begin the conquest of Europe.

Liang Hao could only think about how to salvage the overall strategy in light of recent events.

At least the strategy for the Latin American Block is moving forward. Latin America is broke and near starving— despite the death of Shusong Han. When the Americans destroy their military, we'll be free to sweep in and conquer. If I move the timetable forward on that part of the strategy, I'll be able to redirect the gambits and achieve victory.

THE
ENDGAME

"To secure ourselves against defeat lies in our own hands, but the opportunity of defeating the enemy is provided by the enemy himself."

— Sun Tzu, "The Art of War"

CHAPTER 18

———— ● ————

Beijing ● Norfolk ● Southern Pennsylvania ●
U.S.-Mexican Border ● Washington, DC
January-June 2028

It took seventeen days for the task force to return to Norfolk, including one stop in Iceland to deliver the ships that couldn't make it all the way across the Atlantic and to deliver cargo and personnel that were remaining in Iceland to bolster its defenses.

The two Russian submarines that destroyed the Chinese blockade fleet in the Arctic met up with the task force at Iceland and began their patrols around Iceland and Greenland. The Russian Air Force squadrons landed in Iceland, refueled, and began their patrol of the airspace around Iceland and Greenland as well.

Chinese jets, searching for the missing Russian and European naval ships, appeared on radar several times, but they never approached the task force.

The other carrier strike groups of the U.S. Atlantic fleets were ready to deploy along the Central and South American coasts as part of the U.S. blockade of the western hemisphere. There was concern among the Joint Chiefs that the Chinese might take advantage of having a fleet in the Red Sea—remnants of the fleet that had been deployed through the Suez Canal—and redeploy those ships around the southern tip of Africa to land troops meant for Europe on the east coast of Latin America. The new mission of the U.S. Atlantic carrier strike groups was to prevent that from happening.

The British fleet, with its two carrier strike groups, remained in the Caribbean, but it was also being used to transport the Royal Marines and the U.S. and Caribbean troops that would land along the northern coast of South America once the liberation of Latin America began.

Those strike groups left Norfolk just as the task force was approaching. The two carrier strike groups with the task force were to be resupplied and refueled before redeploying to protect the North American coast. The Russian ships were to deploy to Iceland and Greenland to protect those two nations once the liberation of Latin America was completed.

President MacKendrick and Vice President Morey were waiting at Norfolk when the task force arrived. They greeted their fellow heads of state and escorted them to Washington to discuss plans and refugee resettlement. When Kate and Steve disembarked from the Russian carrier with Petrov, they saw Rosemont waiting for them, grinning like a proud father. Kate introduced Petrov to Rosemont.

"This is Colonel Kostya Petrov of the GRU," she said to Rosemont. "Kostya, this is my boss, Gregory Rosemont, Presidential Special Advisor for Global Intelligence, and Chairman of the Global Intelligence Council. You two should get to know each other."

"I look forward to it." Rosemont shook Petrov's hand. "But for now I need to get my team back to Washington to prepare for the next phase of the plan."

Rosemont gestured for Kate and Steve to follow him to the car waiting to take them to the helicopter. Adam and Grant were already inside. Steve joined them, but Kate hung back for a moment.

"I have to go, Kostya. Once you've been processed and

assigned a billet, contact me and let me know where you are."

"I will, Kate. Hopefully I'll find where my family is being housed so I can see them again before my next assignment comes in. Take care of yourself, and good luck with the next phase. You did good, Norwegian. You did good. But you really should have been a Russian."

Kate laughed. "*Dasvidaniya*, Kostya."

"Until we meet again, Kate."

On the helicopter ride back to Washington, Kate, Steve, Grant, and Adam updated Rosemont on their mission. Rosemont informed them about what had happened at the Suez Canal. Kate relayed Petrov's report that, while Macao had released no victims' names from the destruction of the Industrial and Commercial Bank of China headquarters, there had been no sightings of Shusong Han since the drone attack. In fact, based on a sharp increase in cash deposits in the Cayman Island banks, it appeared that no one had seen the banker in some time.

"Colonel Petrov is definitely someone you'll want to tap into," Kate said. "He's brilliant, resourceful, a bit ruthless, but he knows his business. It would be good to have him working for our intelligence community in some capacity."

"I'll keep an eye on him," Rosemont promised.

"So what's happening on the Mexican border?" Steve asked.

"Almost all of the Latin American troops are massed along the border, but they haven't moved. Evidently they've received no orders to invade, but they haven't been ordered to return home either. Liz informed me that they still have no supply lines or supply depots, so they can't last much longer."

"Is it still the plan to destroy them?" Grant asked.

Rosemont nodded. "As soon as all of the carrier strike groups are in position, the Air Force will begin saturation bombing a twenty-mile-wide path along the northern Mexican border while the Navy destroys most of the South American ports. We've decided to keep a few of the ports operational for the Navy's use, but not for Chinese transport ships."

"There are a lot of border towns in the target zone," Kate mentioned. "Tijuana, Tecate, Mexicali, Mariposa, Guadalupe, Matamoros… Will they all be destroyed?"

"Yes," Rosemont replied. "But the President is going to issue warnings for all of the border towns to evacuate before the bombings commence. He doesn't want to massacre civilians."

"What if they don't leave?" Steve asked.

Rosemont shrugged. "They had their chance. President MacKendrick tried several times to reach out to the presidents of Mexico, Columbia, and Venezuela, but they refused to take his calls. He wanted to tell them that they were being played and that their banker was setting them up to be destroyed. If they had only listened, then all of this could have been avoided."

A week later, all of the carrier strike groups were in position, except for the two American and one Russian that had been part of the task force. But since these three groups were not going to be involved in the Latin American operation, the president decided that the mission could proceed anyway.

For days, U.S.-based signal jammers broadcasted warnings to evacuate the border area on every television channel and radio frequency. Satellites and drones observed the civilian evacuations in most of the cities and towns, but the military units remained along the border.

At dawn a week after the broadcasts began, sorties of bombers took off from airfields all along the border. The saturation bombings began. At the same time, the carrier strike groups launched their bombers to destroy most of the Central and South American ports, cutting off the Latin American Block from being assisted by Chinese supply ships or troopships.

The leaders of the Latin American Block, with no way to

contact their banker or the Chinese who were aiding them, found themselves cut off and out of options. Each of the leaders felt that the Chinese had betrayed them, but they never spoke it aloud. In the end, they decided to fight instead of surrendering and facing the consequence of their actions.

Once the bombings were over, the combined U.S.-Canadian-Caribbean-European forces began the invasion and liberation of the Latin American nations. Fighting was heaviest in Mexico, Venezuela, and Columbia, but with the bulk of their armies gone, and the cartel forces spread thin, resistance was light.

The Panama Canal was liberated quickly, which prevented any damage being done to the locks, railways, docks, and industrial facilities. That was the only fighting that involved Chinese soldiers, who had been deployed along the Canal for years. They fought well, but they couldn't hold out against the combined liberation forces.

Liang Hao was ushered into the meeting room where Xi Jinping and the senior military leaders were waiting for him. He was concerned, but he did his best to hide his emotions.

Do they think that I have failed? Do they consider a few unexpected situations to be failure? They are wrong. The game is not over. Western Russia has not yet fallen into our hands, but it will. The European military assets have escaped our grasp and are now in the United States, but they will not help the Americans for long. The Latin American Block has been lost to us, but they will keep the United States so occupied that we can move unobserved into position to crush them. The Caliphate is still in possession of Europe, the Middle East, and Africa, but we can still conquer the Caliphate and the rest of Europe once winter is over. All we need is a new strategy that addresses what has happened in the western hemisphere. They must give me the time I need to create it!

Xi Jinping's face was like a mask. Liang Hao couldn't see a trace of emotion, but when the Principal Leader of China spoke, his voice conveyed all the rage that his face failed to show.

"Thirty-seven years, Liang Hao." The contempt in the voice of the Principal leader was evident. "For thirty-seven years we've planned, plotted, spent—oh, how we've spent—on your plan to make China the master of the world. This entire nation has been consumed by a single purpose, and you were the architect of that purpose. My predecessors bought into your chess games, pledging every resource that this nation had to offer in support of this one goal.

"As I understand it, chess is about moves and countermoves. So tell me: when the United States began making countermoves different from what you expected—specifically its recent Civil War—and when Canada began making countermoves different from what you expected—specifically breaking apart and joining the United States—and when the United States decided to make a move to send its fleet to help evacuate the Russian and European military assets not yet in our or the Caliphate's control," Xi Jinping's voice grew louder as he spoke. "And when an unknown enemy made a move by sending a drone to destroy the headquarters of one of our banks in Macao and kill several of your bankers, and when an unknown navy made a move and sank our blockade fleet in the Arctic and our flagship carriers in the Suez Canal, how is it that you failed to make any countermoves of your own to regain the upper hand in this chess game? Your plan began to fall apart, and you did nothing! The entire western hemisphere appears to be lost to us, and you did nothing! Can you explain this to me, *Chief Strategist*?"

When Xi Jinping stopped speaking, the silence was deafening.

Liang Hao stood in silence with his head bowed. *How can*

he ask me that? Look at what I have accomplished. Yes, there have been setbacks, but China is poised to be the master of two thirds of the world! And once we have the eastern hemisphere firmly in our grasp, crushing the western hemisphere will be a simple matter. This is a chess game—a battle of intellect and will. He is upset that I did not react to a few minor issues that occurred as the Middlegame was being played? He's in no position to judge whether I've succeeded or failed when the game isn't over yet.

"I'm waiting, Chief Strategist."

Liang Hao heard the edge in the Principal Leader's voice. Finally, he said, "It is true that the Brilliancy against the United States did not end favorably, and the contingency strategy also did not end favorably when Canada revolted against the capitulation decree, just as the Americans did. And it is true that one third of the Trinity Gambit is not going as expected— specifically the Latin American Block. But the other two Trinity Gambits have succeeded. The western Pacific is ours, and we are still in excellent position to finish the Russian campaign this spring and then crush the Caliphate, taking complete control of this hemisphere. Yes, a new strategy must be developed for the western hemisphere, but there is time to do that while we complete our work in this hemisphere. The Americas cannot stand alone. We will conquer them; we just need to rethink our approach."

Xi Jinping glared at his Chief Strategist. "Trillions spent, thousands of lives lost, ships lost, planes lost, and victory after victory snatched from our grasp, and all you can think about is how to salvage this utter disaster you call your 'Gambits?' You are not here to tell me how to fix this catastrophe. I've already decided how to do that. We will finish what we started in Russia, and we will grind the Caliphate under our boots, eliminating Islam once and for all. And yes, we will someday have to face the Americas for control of the world, but that is not my immediate concern. My immediate concern is to recover from these intolerable losses that occurred during your tenure as this nation's Chief Strategist. And if you think for one minute that you'll have anything to do with crafting any new strategies for China, you are sadly mistaken. Your services are at an end, Liang Hao. You are dismissed."

Xi Jinping gestured with his hand, and six soldiers approached his former Chief Strategist. Liang Hao looked at them and looked back at Xi Jinping with shock in eyes. The soldiers grabbed him and started to remove him from the presence of the Principal Leader.

"You are not allowing me to finish the game?" Liang Hao shouted, unconcerned about the consequences of his words. "I have never failed to finish a game that I have started. How dare you? Do you know what I have done for China? Do you appreciate what I have done for *you*? Setbacks happen. Opponents make unexpected moves and countermoves. This can happen in any game. But you do not change players in the middle of the game simply because you do not like how the game is going! The game is not over until the king falls, and our king is still in play. I still have moves to make!"

The soldiers led him out of the room, down to the first floor, and out to the courtyard of the Central Military Commission's headquarters. Standing in the center of the courtyard was a squad of ten soldiers holding rifles. "Execution?" he roared. "I'm being executed because of a few setbacks? No! I must be allowed to finish the game! I have not failed yet. Stop! Do you people know who I am? I am the Chess Grandmaster of China!"

Liang Hao's knees felt weak as he approached the center of the courtyard, but he forced himself to keep walking. *If I'm to be shot, I will not be shot on the ground like a dog.*

When Liang Hao reached the center of the courtyard, he was roughly turned to face the ten soldiers. He heard the orders being given, but his mind could not fully comprehend what they were shouting. He closed his eyes and, in his mind, began working on a strategy that would solve the western hemisphere problem and salvage his gambits. The sound of ten rifles firing was the last thing he ever heard.

The Presidents of Mexico, Venezuela, and Columbia were killed when the Presidential Palace in Mexico City was stormed. The leaders of the cartel and most of their operatives were killed in the following weeks, as the criminal powerbase that had dominated Latin America's politics and economy was broken.

It took six months to liberate the Latin American Block, and once that was completed, relief groups and supplies— including food and medicine and other staples—began pouring into the region to help the people get back on their feet. The Latin Americans, tasting freedom again for the first time in years, hailed the combined liberation forces as heroes.

While the invasion force was liberating Latin America, Kate and Steve spent nearly two months going back through the translated Chinese documents in detail. They summarized all of the ways that the Chinese had infiltrated North American businesses, politics, educational institutions, bureaucracies, and media outlets. The names of every person who knowingly and unknowingly accepted Chinese money or placed themselves under Chinese influence were listed in the reports that were turned over to the Justice Department. These reports became the basis for one of the largest investigations ever conducted by North American law enforcement. At the end of the investigation, several thousand indictments were obtained and arrests made on charges ranging from domestic terrorism, dereliction of duty, bribery, extortion, conspiracy, and treason.

By the time the dust settled from the arrests, trials, and convictions, most news outlets had been shut down for their complicity in the Chinese strategy, the executive ranks and boards of directors of a number of large corporations had been gutted, active and retired politicians had been arrested and were serving life sentences in federal prison, hundreds of government employees and political appointees had been arrested and were also serving lengthy sentences in state and federal prisons, and a large number of the most prestigious institutions of higher learning—including every Ivy League university in the country—were permanently closed.

Similar information related to Central and South America was also documented and turned over to the liberated Latin American countries, so their governments could seek justice against any surviving conspirators.

Justice was served.

The president, Secretary of State Chandler, and Secretary of Defense Wolfe flew Marine One out to the British compound in southern Pennsylvania to brief Prime Minister Halstead and other members of the British government-in-exile about the results of the Latin American campaign and the future role of the British fleet in the defense of the Caribbean island nations. King William also attended the meeting, along with the British ambassador, Sir Harold Dumbarton.

"I understand that the British Army units evacuated from Norway played a key role in the liberation of Mexico," Prime Minister Halstead said once Secretary Wolfe provided his report.

"Yes, sir," Wolfe replied. "They volunteered to lead the assault on Mexico City, and they performed superbly."

The king nodded with a hint of a smile on his face.

"I understand that the losses of the combined forces were relatively light," Halstead noted.

"That's correct," Wolfe confirmed. "By placing their armies along our southern border, the Latin American Block lost their ability to fight back once their armies had been destroyed.

Most of the fighting was with cartel members, local militias, and the few countries down there that have been at odds with the U.S. for years and would resist anything we did to help them. Fortunately, that was the policy of their governments. The people felt quite differently once we removed those governments and gave the people back their freedoms."

"So what are the plans for the Royal Navy?" the British Defence Minister asked.

"Your two carrier strike groups and the rest of the British fleet are a critical component in the defense of Caribbean island nations, the southeastern United States, the northern coast of South America, and the Panama Canal," Wolfe replied. "We'd like to keep them deployed where they are. The Caribbean governments have expressed their gratitude for the fleet's presence, and the fleet's performance was instrumental during the early stages of the liberation of Latin America. With the number of British subjects residing in the Caribbean, the fleet's presence helps them with a sense of continuity in the changing reality of what has happened to our world."

Prime Minister Halstead looked over at the king, who nodded.

"And what about the liberation of Britain from the Caliphate?" Halstead asked.

President MacKendrick responded. "All indications are that the Chinese are still planning to invade Europe and wipe out the Caliphate there before moving south to do the same in the Middle-East and Africa. If we were to attempt any liberation of the British Isles at this time, it would put you and us in direct conflict with China once their invasion begins. For now, we believe the best course of action is to wait and watch. We will continue looking for ways to affect the eventual liberation of Europe, but at this time, it would be too costly and would potentially bring us into direct conflict with China, which is something we need more time to prepare for. Our manufacturing industries are just now beginning to recover from decades of outsourcing to China, and it will take a while before military production is sufficient to make any conflict with China evenly matched."

Halstead and the king nodded sadly. For the present, the British government would have to remain in exile while the Caliphate continued destroying what had been left behind.

On a beautiful Friday afternoon in the early summer, Rosemont convened one last meeting of the team to recap all that they accomplished during the nine months since they first met. Each member of the team would be returning to their regular duties, although most were receiving promotions and medals for their service to the nation.

"The European and Russian forces have been successfully integrated into the North American and North Atlantic militaries," Rosemont reported, referring to the combined United States, Canadian, Caribbean, Greenland, and Iceland armed forces. The United States ended up annexing the remaining Canadian provinces and territories—at their request—and integrated all military units into a single armed services branch of the government. This had not been the president's first choice of action, but in the end, it seemed the only way to get the remnants of Canada to all work together. Years of pent-up mistrust and co-existing under an unresponsive government had made them too antagonistic toward one another to reach any consensus.

"Negotiations are almost completed to make Iceland and Greenland protectorates of the United States, and the Russian forces are on loan to them until the treaties are signed. Negotiations are also underway with the Caribbean nations to either formalize the same agreement or allow them to go their separate ways, now that the Latin American threat has been neutralized."

Rosemont looked around the room. "You have all done an outstanding job, and I'm proud to have served with each of you. You saved the country, and you saved this hemisphere from enslavement. As Churchill once said, *'Never in the field of human conflict was so much owed by so many to so few.'* He could easily have been talking about you. I hope we have the opportunity to work together in the future."

After the meeting was over, Kate and Steve returned to their workroom. All of the intel folders, the boxes of Chinese papers provided by the GRU, the translations of those papers, and their analyses and reports, had already been taken to CIA headquarters for permanent storage. The room was empty, except for the whiteboard markers all over the panels around the room.

"Want to come back to my place for dinner?" Steve asked.

"Sure." Kate smiled at the thought.

"Want to stay for the weekend?"

"I thought you'd never ask."

They walked out of the conference room, turned off the lights, and walked past Rosemont's office. It was dark, but Kate could tell that everything of Rosemont's had already been removed.

As they exited their secure area, a guard was waiting outside to collect their security credentials. Kate and Steve handed over their access cards and then headed for the parking lot.

As they exited the building, Steve breathed the summer air deeply. "We changed the world, didn't we?"

"At least our part of it," Kate agreed as they walked toward their cars.

"No, I think we changed all of it in at least some way. What we did for this hemisphere is easy to see. But there are other parts of the world still enslaved. If they ever find out about what we've done, it'll give them hope. And the Chinese will have to rethink their plans for the world. We forced them to do that. We forced them to play *our* game for a change. I don't know who will win in the end, but I know that we at least won this round—our moment of peace in the eye of the storm."

Kate looked at Steve and smiled. "And we got to do it together."

Steve put his arm around her shoulder. "And who will ever know if that one thing made the difference in the end."

"You make it sound like destiny," Kate said.

"Isn't it?" Steve asked. "I like to think it is."

"Maybe it is. And maybe in the middle of the tempest, two strangers managed to find a bit of joy amidst the chaos, and that joy sustained them until they found a way to defeat the chaos and change the world."

"I like that."

Kate giggled. "I knew you would."

EPILOGUE

History would later rename "Handbasket" and the "Trinity Gambit" to something more descriptive and accurate: *World War III*. Fought on multiple fronts—driven by plans within plans stretching out over decades, and involving witting and unwitting players who were kings on one day and pawns for sacrifice the next—China came within a hair's breadth of conquering the world. But the indomitable spirit and determination of a diverse group of people who refused to surrender and who came together in opposition to their common enemy, changed the game out from underneath the Chinese and won for themselves a brief respite from the fighting, the intrigue, and the endless manipulation of their political institutions and economic systems.

The world never looked the same again, but never again did it come so close to falling into the abyss of totalitarian darkness.

In the debrief with the president and his key advisors after the liberation of Latin America, Rosemont summed up the contribution of his team and all that the United States accomplished as a result of "Handbasket:"

"Tho' much is taken, much abides; and tho' we are not now that strength which in old days mov'd earth and heaven, that which we are, we are: one equal temper of heroic hearts, made weak by time and fate, but strong in will to strive, to seek, to find, and not to yield."

—Alfred, Lord Tennyson, "Ulysses"

The End

ABOUT THE AUTHOR

Award-winning author William Speir was born in Birmingham, Alabama in 1962, attended the University of Alabama, and graduated from the University of Alabama at Birmingham in 1984. He spent over 25 years in corporate America, serving as a management consultant, consulting practice leader, IT executive, and HR/Payroll executive for top tier consulting firms and Fortune 100 companies.

During William's corporate career, he published several articles on leadership and the human impact of organizational/technology change. His first experience with book publishing was with a series of ten textbooks he authored about field artillery in the 19th century. These textbooks were later consolidated into a single volume and re-published in 2015 as

Muzzle-Loading Artillery for Reenactors.

In addition to his artillery manual, William has published 17 novels, including a 9-book action-adventure series (*The Knights of the Saltire Series*), five historical novels (*King's Ransom, The Saga of Asbjorn Thorleikson, Nicaea - The Rise of the Imperial Church, Arthur, King,* and *The Besieged Pharaoh*), one fantasy novel (*The Kingstone of Airmid*), and one science fiction novel (*The Olympium of Bacchus 12*).

William is a 5-time Royal Palm Literary Award winner: 2014 Second Place Unpublished Historical Fiction for *King's Ransom,* 2015 Second Place Unpublished Historical Fiction for *The Saga of Asbjorn Thorleikson,* 2017 Second Place Published Historical Fiction for *Arthur, King,* 2017 First Place Published Historical Fiction for *Nicaea - The Rise of the Imperial Church,* and 2017 First Place Published Science Fiction for *The Olympium of Bacchus 12.*

For more information about William Speir, please visit his website at WilliamSpeir.com.

Progressive Rising Phoenix Press is an independent publisher. We offer wholesale pricing and multiple binding options with no minimum purchases for schools, libraries, book clubs, and retail vendors. We offer substantial discounts on bulk orders and discounts on individual sales through our online store. Please visit our website at:

www.ProgressiveRisingPhoenix.com

If you enjoyed reading this book, please review it on Amazon, B & N, or Goodreads.
Thank you in advance!